ACTAEON 9

Abduction

Jeromy Peterson

ISBN: 978-1-952360-01-5

ACKNOWLEDGEMENTS

I have a lot of people to thank for helping me bring this book to publication. As far as books go, at roughly 72K words, it is a relatively short read. Nonetheless, it is my first publishable work of fiction, and so it means a lot to me. The first half of this book was dictated into a Google document from a smart phone, during moments snatched throughout the day. Ultimately, this meant that a lot of editing and reformatting was required; an effort for which I owe thanks to a number of people. Here is the list:

Thank you to my wife Lissa, who is the only person who may have read through this book more times than I have. She is my Alpha reader, my first and last line of editing, and the love of my life.

Thank you to my kids for thinking that their dad is the best writer ever, even though he has only ever written a single, self-published story.

Thank you to Josh and Natali Pearce, for content editing and for liking this story even when it still needed a bit more polishing.

Thank you to Cinnamon Fuller, for helping me fix the things that I didn't know were broken.

Thank you to Shane Motsumoto and SER Soundworks, for your voice and for helping me to make this book just a little bit better.

CONTENTS

1 MILLENNIUM

Hunter Smith looked down at the metallic, oval plaque that marked the center of Millennium Park in downtown Chicago. The plaque stated that the park had been dedicated on July 16th of 2004 as a gift from the Mayor to the people of Chicago. He smiled to himself and thought, "Thanks, Mayor." It really was a nice park. He wasn't from Chicago, and he hadn't lived here long, but the park had become one of his favorite hangouts. "If I ever meet that mayor," his thoughts continued. "I'll have to give him a big pat on the back."

These were the types of idle thoughts that meandered through Hunter's head as he waited for his friends to arrive. It was early Saturday evening. The sun had disappeared behind the skyline, and it was getting cold enough for Hunter to see his own breath frosting in the crisp October air. The first snowfall of the year had come the night before. It had been a heavy snowfall for October and much of it had melted off beneath the warm sun of the following day. The ground, however, was still marked by sparse patches of white. He had planned this excursion with his friends a few days earlier. They would come to the park first and then walk down to Giordano's for some of their amazing deep-dish Chicago-style pizza. When Hunter had first moved to Chicago with his family two years ago, he hadn't been all that impressed with 'Chicago's famous pizza.' He had thought that BJ's back in Mesa, Arizona made much better pizza and they served incredible cream soda as well. After more than a year in Chicago though, the pizza had grown on him, and he fancied himself as something of a connoisseur of deep-dish style pizzas. Giordano's, in Hunter's estimation, made the best, hands down. However, he had still not found any place in Chicago that served an amazing cream soda, which was a total bummer.

His family didn't actually live in Chicago. They lived in Northbrook, which was kind of like a suburb of Chicago. Nobody knew where Northbrook was unless you came from Illinois or lived in Illinois. So, whenever he called or texted his friends from Arizona, he just told them that he lived in Chicago. It was easier that way.

Hunter had hoped to ride the train in from Northbrook with his friends, but his dad stepped in at the last moment and offered him a ride. He said that he needed to spend some time at the office and that he wanted to have a good 'father to son' talk with Hunter while they traveled. In turn, he would let Hunter ride the train home with his friends. Hunter had been disappointed at first but in truth, he had really enjoyed the trip. His dad was pretty good at asking pointed 'life' questions and then listening while Hunter answered. These talks had really become a great way for Hunter to get problems off his chest. By the time he got to the park, he was actually pretty sorry that the time with his dad was coming to an end.

Hunter turned from the mayor's plaque to face the gigantic silver-colored structure that loomed up from behind. He and his friends had come to refer to the gargantuan example of postmodern artwork as, 'The Gigantic Silver Bean' or as Hunter preferred, just 'The Bean.' There was really no better description that you could conjure up to describe The Bean. It was gigantic, probably bigger than most people's houses; the whole thing was made of silvery chrome metal and it was shaped like a bean. He wasn't sure what cryptic symbolism the artist had in mind when crafting The Bean, but he did enjoy the way that it reflected the city lights after the sun went down.

He began to walk idly toward The Bean with his hands in his pockets, his thoughts turning to the delicious pizza that he would soon be devouring, when he heard someone call from behind.

"Hey, Hunter!" He turned to see April coming up the main walkway into the park. April was fourteen, just a few months younger than Hunter. Her face was round with small pretty features. She had brunette hair cropped to shoulder length and at five feet two inches, she was more than a head shorter than Hunter. Just seeing April made him feel happier. When he had first come to Chicago, he had needed a major attitude adjustment. He had quite nearly hated everything about the city. Had it not been for April befriending him, he was pretty sure that he would have gone on hating Chicago forever. He probably would have grown up to become a grumpy old man that hobbled about mumbling to himself that he never should have left Mesa, Arizona. April had saved Hunter's life. Well, maybe that was a slight exaggeration. At the very least, she had saved his social life. In fact, he was pretty sure that she was the reason Chicago-style pizza had started tasting better. She smiled and waved. Hunter smiled back and started walking her way.

April was originally from Salt Lake City, Utah. She had moved to Chicago with her family just four years earlier. Her dad was a lawyer and had taken a job with a relatively prestigious law firm that worked out of Arlington Heights, another suburb of Chicago. Her family, like Hunter's, lived in Northbrook and she attended school with him at Wood Oaks Junior High. She was something of a science nerd and she competed on the school's track team. Hunter really liked her a lot but there was no way that he was going to admit that she was anything more than a friend.

Following April up the walkway came Cade, Jared and Summer. Cade was tall for his age, almost six feet with sandy brown hair, dark eyes and skin tanner than anyone in Chicago should have been allowed to have. Jared was Cade's polar opposite with creamy white skin, freckled cheeks and a mangy mop of red hair that seemed to be protesting its destiny to sit atop Jared's head. It reached out in all directions as if trying to grab at people and things that passed by. Summer was blonde, pretty and bubbly. She dressed in expensive clothing. Her hair was styled fashionably. Her makeup was perfect and her smile infectious. Hunter was very grateful for his friends. He had spent his first year in Chicago thinking that he would never find a place to fit in and then he met April and she had introduced him to Summer, Cade and Jared.

He met his friends about halfway between The Bean and

the park entrance and April gave him a hug. She was the most naturally friendly person that Hunter had ever known. She was the type of girl that felt at ease giving everyone she saw a hug. It was her standard way of saying hello. Hunter wasn't exactly the shy type but compared to April he might as well have been an introvert. Physical contact had been way off limits. Though he was still not the most talkative person in the world, she had really helped him to open up and he felt comfortable hugging her back. Actually, he liked it a whole lot.

"Hey, Lumphead!" April used her standard opening. Hunter earned the nickname a few months earlier when he had become distracted during soccer practice and had taken a hard-kicked ball to the cranium. He wondered if she knew that he had been distracted looking at her.

"Hey . . . Science Girl." He tried new nicknames every time he saw her. None of them had stuck yet. April just didn't do things that were embarrassing enough to earn her an enduring nickname.

"Really? That's the best you can do?"

Hunter gave her a sideways grin. "You know, it would help if you could do something monumentally embarrassing, like pee your pants in public. Then I could call you Princess Tinkles."

She punched his arm. "First of all, yuck! Secondly, I will never make it so easy for you."

Suddenly, Cade shot by with Jared riding on his back, red locks flying in the wind, heading for The Bean. He waved one hand in the air like a cowboy on a bull and yelled, "Yee hah! Git along little doggie!"

Jared and Cade were always a little bit wilder than Hunter. It was good to have friends that spiced up life a little. Ever since they had convinced Hunter to join the school soccer team, they had been hanging out a lot more. April often referred to them as The Three Musketeers.

Summer walked up behind April setting her chin on April's right shoulder. Rolling her eyes, she said, "You know what they say. Boys will be boys and men will be . . . well . . . boys. Hi, Hunter."

"Hey, Summer."

"Hope you haven't been waiting too long."

"Nah, I probably only beat you guys by five minutes."

Summer walked out from behind April and started in the direction of The Bean also. As she passed Hunter, she said, "Cade and Jared wanted to hang out at the park for a little while before we go for pizza. Hope you don't mind."

"Sounds good."

Hanging out at the park would be nice. It might even give him a chance for some one-on-one time with April.

She started toward The Bean, nudging him in the shoulder as she passed. "Come on. Let's go see what they're up to."

The evening continued on and Hunter was really enjoying the time with his friends. They played a few rounds of zombie freeze tag. Jared and Hunter raced while carrying April and Summer on their backs. Cade refereed the affair declaring Jared the winner by a very small margin. Hunter and April took a walk around the park together while Jared, Cade and Summer used their phones to take funny pictures of their reflections off the chrome surface of The Bean. They all tried to make a standing human pyramid, which nearly ended in disaster because of the icy ground. By the time they were done playing, there was no remaining glow on the horizon and the city lights were shining in full force. You couldn't see the stars very well, but you didn't go to Millennium Park to see the stars. You went to see the lights. They played off the silvery surface of The Bean and lit up the area around it in multicolored hues. The park wasn't overly crowded. There might have been a few hundred people meandering about in the large plaza, but the nearby streets were bustling with men and women going about their business.

They stood in a loose circle talking idly, and Hunter could feel the unspoken consensus that this portion of their fun evening was coming to an end, and that it was time to move on to the next phase of their evening.

April grabbed Hunter's arm and turned him to leave the park. "Let's go get some pizza. I'm starving!"

She leaned her head against his shoulder and he let her lead him away from The Bean and toward a relaxing evening of pizza with his friends. As they neared the walkway that exited the park, Hunter heard a high-pitched whistle coming from behind, and it seemed that a flickering light source had sparked to life from the same direction. A sudden commotion of voices picked up and they turned to see what was causing the excitement.

A pulsing beam of light came from the top of The Bean shooting into the sky. It seemed that the City of Chicago had prepared a laser show for the park.

"Funny," said Hunter, "I don't remember hearing anything about a laser show tonight."

"Me neither," April responded, "Let's watch."

Bulges of light pulsed rhythmically down the beam seemingly absorbed by the giant silvery piece of artwork. As the show continued The Bean seemed to grow bright and its chrome surface swirled with light and energy. They all stared in amazement as the show progressed. The bulges of light that pulsed down the beam increased in frequency and the high-pitched whistle grew louder and higher. It reached an uncomfortably loud level where the onlookers began to cover their ears. Plugging his own, Hunter looked at April with a grimace and gave her a 'let's go' nod toward the park exit. She was covering her own ears and bobbed her head in agreement. They turned to leave.

At that moment, The Bean exploded in a deafening roar and time slowed down. As in, time truly slowed down. Motion slowed. Sound slowed. Only the explosion itself moved with any noticeable velocity. Fragments of molten metal flew from the explosion toward the onlookers and it seemed to Hunter that he could see each glowing fragment as it hurled lethargically through space. In an instant of terror that seemed much longer than the actual microsecond that passed, he realized that everybody was about to die.

Then the explosion reversed. The expanding concussion imploded. Time sped up and the molten missiles hurled inward. The mass of material that made up The Bean collapsed into a white, glowing, silver globe no bigger than a soccer ball. For a moment, there was calm. Hunter's ears rang, and he felt dazed. He looked around. Each of his friends seemed to be experiencing the same disorientation. Suddenly a blue translucent shock wave exploded out from the silver soccer ball knocking everybody to the ground as it washed over them. When the shock wave was about a hundred yards from its epicenter, it froze, forming into a semi-transparent blue dome that encompassed much of the park and nearby street.

As Hunter hit the ground, he felt a strange sensation of weightlessness. The back of his head thumped hard against the concrete and he rebounded sluggishly into the air, floating above the ground. He struggled to see through blurry vision and confused thoughts. He floated face up, and he was rising slowly. He began to twist frantically side to side. He could see that hundreds of people around the park and in the street floated in the air. He looked for his friends and found Cade drifting above him and to the left. He was limp and floated slowly away from Hunter towards the edge of the dome. He could hear shouts and cries from others around the park.

Cade!" Hunter called. No response came and Cade didn't move. "Cade!" again, no response. Hunter grew frantic. He began to look about in a frenzy! "April! April! Summer! Jared!"

"Hunter?" a voice replied from somewhere behind him. It was April. She sounded dazed and confused. "What's going on?"

"I don't know. Are you okay?"

"I think so. I hit my head pretty hard," she replied.

Hunter twisted to try to see her, "Can you see Jared or Summer?"

Before she could reply, gravity took hold again and they were slammed back down into the concrete. Though he had not been very high off the ground, the wind was knocked out of Hunter and his head hit the ground hard a second time. He struggled to stay conscious. Something was wrong. He was pinned to the ground. No, he wasn't pinned exactly. He was just way too heavy. He was so heavy that he couldn't lift his own weight, and even breathing was difficult. It was as if gravity had increased. He lay motionless for a few moments and then with considerable effort, he tried to lift his right arm. It raised slowly from the concrete, but he found that if he stopped straining even for a moment, his arm fell quickly back to the ground. He tried to sit up, but with an enormous effort he found that lifting his head to look around was all that he could accomplish, and this caused him to feel dizzy, nauseous and breathless as if it strained his heart to pump against the mild incline created by lifting his head.

He lowered his head slowly and lay motionless for a time trying to catch his breath and take control of his frenzied thoughts. A low thrumming noise came from the blue dome that encompassed the park. He could hear one of the girls whimpering from behind him. It sounded like Summer. He could hear moans and cries from other people around the park. He stared up at the dome. There seemed to be an oscillating pattern of ripples in the blue energy field that moved in synchronization with the thrumming. He rolled his head to the left and looked toward the perimeter of the dome. He could see the distorted forms of people moving around on the outside. However, no sound that he could hear came from beyond the dome. He looked to the right and found a foot in his face. It looked like April's foot. It lay still and was pigeoned outwards as the increased gravity tried to pull her toes toward the ground.

"April?" he called but there was no answer. "April!" more frantically.

She didn't respond and she didn't move. Hunter was scared and on the verge of panic. The problem was though, that a person in a state of panic should be allowed to run around screaming, maybe even throw some things. In the current situation, he really only had two options. He could try to remain calm and lie still or he could freak out and lie still. The added gravity robbed him of breath, and he doubted that he could scream even if he wanted. He rolled his head back and stared skyward. As he did so, the shadowy and distorted outline of an aircraft came into view overhead. The dark figure of the craft grew larger. It seemed to be descending and as it broke the blue translucent surface of the dome a deafening roar filled the plaza.

The aircraft looked like something from a made-for-TV science fiction movie. It was knobby and more or less ovular in shape with four large, downward facing thrusters that roared and let off waves of heat that warped the air. Hunter could imagine it as a troop transport loaded with futuristically equipped alien soldiers. 'This can't be real,' he thought.

It continued to descend until it was about halfway between the ceiling of the dome and the ground. It then slid sideways toward the street where the largest number of people were pinned down. Hatches along the side of the craft opened and Hunter could see the silhouetted forms of heavily armored men. The figures he saw could have come straight out of a space age first-person shooter video game. Though the ship still hovered high above the ground, they began to jump from the hatches. The increased gravity pulled them toward the Earth with startling acceleration. Each of them landed in a crouch, hitting the ground hard enough to shatter concrete beneath the force of their impact. This couldn't possibly be real. He suddenly felt his solid world dissolve into confusion.

They moved quickly toward the incapacitated park goers. Hunter watched as the first soldier drew a complex looking pistol and pointed it at a lady sprawled out on the concrete. He heard a light pop, followed by a scream and then the soldier bent over, grabbed the lady and hoisted her over his shoulder. She seemed to have gone completely limp. He ran back toward the ship, paused to crouch and leapt into the air. The jump to the ship should have been impossible but the soldier's trajectory carried him on a perfect arc into one of the open hatches on the aircraft. Hunter turned his attention back to the ground. The next few soldiers were preparing to leap. Dozens more were shouldering limp bodies. In moments, the soldiers had cleared a large area near the street. They moved in a very efficient pattern, leaping from the ship, grabbing bodies, and returning. They worked their way around the most heavily populated sections of the park, the craft sliding along to stay in close proximity. It appeared to Hunter that they would take everyone in the park in a matter of minutes.

His mind whirled. They were stealing people. If somebody didn't do something, they were going to steal everybody in the park. He looked around frantically for an idea. He felt helpless. He was helpless.

2 NEAR MISS

"Hunter!" It was Jared. His breathing was labored, and his voice strained, "are you seeing this?"

"Yeah. This is crazy," Hunter replied strenuously.

"We gotta get out of here or they're going to take us."

Hunter twisted around trying to see where Jared's voice was coming from. "Where are you?"

"I'm about ten feet behind you."

"Can you see the others?"

"Yeah. They aren't moving."

Hunter was trying to take it all in. Were his friends okay? They could have been hurt really badly. What was going on? Who were these people? What could he do?

"I think I can crawl to the edge!" Jared interrupted his

thoughts. "I am going to try. You should try too. Maybe we can make it before they get to us."

Hunter could hear Jared begin to strain and pant as he worked to slide himself toward the edge of the dome. Could Hunter just leave his friends? April, Summer, and Cade were helpless. Jared was much closer to the edge of the dome, and might be able to escape, but Hunter doubted that there was any hope for him to reach the edge in time. He lifted his head again and realized that the soldiers had almost reached them.

"Go, Jared! They're almost here!" Hunter gasped.

He could hear Jared as he increased his efforts to reach the edge of the dome. At that moment, a soldier noticed them. He looked directly at Hunter and then he looked beyond Hunter to where Jared was struggling to make his escape. The soldier took two quick leaps soaring past Hunter. He heard the discharge of the soldier's weapon that silenced Jared's grunting and straining. He heard the soldier hefting and shouldering Jared's limp body and a moment later he ran past carrying Jared toward the main body of soldiers and the craft. As he watched, the soldier paused to speak with one of his comrades pointing at Hunter. The second soldier moved away from the main body walking up to Hunter aiming his high-tech pistol directly at Hunter's chest. Hunter was terrified beyond description. His mind raced with panic and he wondered if the strange weapons brought death or just temporary paralysis. He lay on his back and watched as the soldier's grip tightened on the pistol. He braced himself for its imminent discharge, and then the soldier's head exploded.

The bursting head was accompanied by a blinding flash of light and a deafening explosion. For a few moments, he could see nothing but white and he could hear nothing but the ringing in his ears. The whole world disappeared as he was robbed of sight and sound. As his vision returned, and as the ringing in his ears subsided, he became aware of total chaos. Another group of soldiers had entered the dome. They wore sleek black body armor and they discharged blasts of energy from various weapons that were built into their suits. Some fell from the sky slamming into the ground and immediately fired on the first group of soldiers. Others ran in from the edge of the dome. The first group of soldiers did not use their pistols to return fire. Instead they drew energy rifles that had been strapped to their backs.

Soldiers on both sides moved with inhuman speed and dexterity. Explosions caused by the energy weapons propelled dust, smoke, and concrete shrapnel through the air. Two soldiers collided in front of Hunter and he watched as they engaged in hand to hand combat. For lack of any better means of identification, he began to think of them as good guys and bad guys. The bad guys were the first group of soldiers that were here to steal people and they wore tarnished, rugged-looking armor. The good guys were here to stop the bad guys and wore metallic black suits of armor. Hunter watched the two combatants exchange a series of rapid kicks and punches at incredible speed, when the 'bad guy' scored a solid strike to the 'good guy's' midsection which seemed to stun him and cause him to bend forward. The bad guy drew back an arm in preparation to deliver a powerful punch to the head, but the good guy suddenly stepped in close, seizing the bad guy's other arm and spinning. The bad guy was hoisted off his feet and they both spun forward. In mid-rotation, the good guy changed direction swinging his leg around so that by the time the bad guy slammed into the ground, the good guy landed on top of him already holding him in what looked like an MMA style arm bar. The good guy pulled hard, arching his back and torqueing against the bad guy's arm and shoulder. Hunter could hear bones cracking and metal grinding. The shoulder section of the bad guy's armor tore open and a muffled scream broke loose from behind his helmet. The good guy let go of his opponent with one hand and reaching behind his leg, produced a long and jagged knife with a leading edge that glowed green as if traced by energy. Sitting forward and still holding the man's broken arm, he raised the knife high with his free hand and drove it down into his enemy's chest. Hunter was horrified and scared beyond reason. He couldn't believe what he was watching.

The soldier didn't pause for even a moment but tore the knife from the corpse of the bad guy, rolled away in a backwards summersault and rose to his feet. He turned and paused to survey the battle scene. He nodded to himself as if he understood and approved of how things were going. Next, he surveyed the scene of immobilized humans strewn about the park. He rotated slowly and paused when he noticed Hunter, who lay almost at his feet. The soldier took a single step towards Hunter and stood towering over him. Hunter could see now that the man was very tall. He must have stood close to seven feet, though he appeared shorter because of his thick muscular build. He touched the side of his helmet and the visor that covered his face separated into two pieces that slid outwards.

Hunter found himself staring into cold, impassive eyes

that surveyed him with disapproval and disgust. The man, if he was a man, had chiseled features, a long thin nose and dark hair. His face was young, but he carried himself with an air of command and authority. He mumbled something to himself, shook his head and turned away from Hunter closing his visor. In moments, he had leapt back into the battle and Hunter lost him in the chaos.

It was hard to tell what was going on from Hunter's vantage point. He lay sprawled on his back and could only lift his head with considerable effort. He scanned the battle scene trying to see what had become of Jared and hoping that he hadn't been loaded onto the ship but all he could see was dust, rubble, and total confusion. He noticed however, that the two groups of alien combatants were pretty much ignoring the people pinned to the ground around the park. He imagined that some of the humans would be hurt or killed just because they got in the way, but at least nobody was actively targeting them or trying to kidnap them anymore. He laid his head back, closed his eyes, and covered his ears to muffle the continuous sound of explosions. He would have to wait this out and hope that nobody stepped on him or blew him up.

After what felt like a lifetime, but in fact was only a few minutes, the explosions began to subside. Hunter opened his eyes and lifted his head. The bad guys were making a retreat and the good guys were harassing them with laser fire. Hunter began again to scan the park for signs of Jared. Within a few moments he saw what might have been Jared lying face down underneath the body of a fallen bad guy. He tried to see if Jared was breathing or showing any signs of life, but he lay too far away to make out any details. He turned his attention back to the fleeing bad guys. The last of their soldiers were leaping into the craft as it rose toward the domed ceiling. After the last of the bad guys were inside the craft, the good guys ceased firing and held their positions. When the craft was about to break through the upper inside surface of the dome, the energy field flickered and then deteriorated in a jagged expanding circle that spread from the apex of the dome toward the ground. In less than a few seconds the dome was gone, and the dark night sky shone overhead.

It felt to Hunter as if a car that had been parked on his chest was suddenly lifted. He hadn't realized how shallow his breathing had become. In an instant, he could take full, deep, delicious breaths of air, and all of his limbs felt incredibly light. He sat bolt upright and began to stand, but then his head started to swim. He felt like he was suffering from a head rush, but it was so intense that he was sure he was going to lose consciousness. He paused in a sitting position and remembered watching his soccer coach help one of his teammates that had hit his head hard against a metal goal post. Hunter brought his legs to his chest and then ducked his head between his knees taking slow, even breaths. He began to count up slowly. By the time he reached seven, the dizziness was beginning to subside. By the time he reached twenty, he was feeling completely normal again.

He stood up, this time with much more care. He turned to inspect his friends that lay sprawled out on the ground behind him. They were beginning to stir and moan. He knelt down next to April and put his hand to her cheek. Her eyes fluttered open and she looked up at him.

"Hunter?"

"April, are you all right?"

"I don't know. I . . . think so. What happened?"

"I'm not sure. Lay here for a minute."

He took his coat off, rolled it up and tucked it underneath her head. He inspected each of his friends in turn. He worried for them, but they seemed like they would live.

He turned to look where he had last seen Jared and found that the good guy soldiers had begun tending to their injured and were taking up guard posts around the plaza. Medical personnel had also begun pouring into the area to help the dazed and injured civilians. The plaza had become very busy again, but at least this time it didn't involve explosions and fighting aliens. Police and firemen were moving in. The streets around the park were lit up with flashing red and blue lights. He looked across the park for Jared but so many people now moved about that it was hard to see through the bustling crowd of emergency workers. He thought for a moment that he caught a brief glimpse of his friend now lying face up with a medical attendant at his side, but then the view was lost in the busy crowd.

He began to try to cross the plaza when somebody grabbed him by the arm. He turned and found himself staring into the eyes of a police officer.

"Come with me, young man."

"But my friends . . ."

"Don't worry. Somebody will help your friends. How do you feel?"

"I feel okay." That was mostly true.

"Then come with me. We need to clear everybody out of this area as quickly as possible."

"But . . ."

"Please don't argue." The officer cut him off and began to pull him out of the park. "If your friends weren't taken, then they will be okay. You will see them again soon."

The officer was stern and commanding. There would be no argument. He led Hunter by the arm out of the park and to the back of an ambulance. The officer released him to the custody of a pair of emergency workers. He was helped into the ambulance where two other people already sat wrapped in blankets. He waited impatiently and with a jittery, unmasked irritation. He pulled his phone from his pocket intending to call his parents only to find that the screen was black and that it was non-responsive.

"Everybody's phones are broken."

A ruddy teenage boy sat across from Hunter. He was wide-eyed and nervous. He had brown eyes and brown hair that was dirty and disheveled. He rubbed his hands together absentmindedly.

"They must have done something to our phones. They

don't want information about this to get out, man . . . We are so dead!"

He looked away from Hunter, mumbling something under his breath and running a hand through his hair. One of the emergency workers offered Hunter a blanket but he refused. April had his coat and he felt cold, but he didn't want to be comfortable. He wanted – no, he needed to know if his friends were okay and if Jared had escaped. More people were brought to the back of the ambulance and it was nearly full when he decided that he just couldn't wait any longer. The ambulance was going to be ready to leave soon and then they would drive away. He glanced around. The emergency workers were distracted. The rear doors were cracked open. This might be his last chance to make a break for it. He braced himself, took a deep breath and then the doors opened wide. Hunter found himself staring face to face with April. Her face was streaked with tears and an officer stood behind her.

"This is the last one for you guys. She has some bruises, but she will be okay. We've set up operations at Mercy Hospital and Medical Center. Go directly to the east wing."

His tone was almost militant, and the emergency workers responded almost like soldiers. Hunter might have been curious had he not been so relieved to see April. The officer helped her into the ambulance and the emergency worker offered her a blanket, which she accepted timidly. She crossed and sat next to Hunter laying her head on his shoulder. He wrapped his arm around her and let go of a small sigh. At least April was here. At least she was okay.

3 INTERVIEWS

April and Hunter were among the first to arrive at the east wing of the Mercy Medical Center, but within a half hour the whole area was bustling with people. At the hospital, all pretense of being a non-military operation was dropped. Their ambulance was directed into a guarded area where they were given into the custody of soldiers, and no matter how courteous the soldiers acted, April and Hunter couldn't help but be intimidated by the fully automatic M-16 rifles they held at ready.

At the hospital, they were led with the others from their ambulance through a series of hallways to a large cafeteria-sized room where their names were taken, and they were told to wait. Soldiers stood at all the entrances and exits. Whenever Hunter tried to approach the soldiers with questions, he was told to wait patiently. If he asked about alien invaders, they went stone cold and he was given the same answer. So they waited. And waited. And waited.

They sat together while Hunter told April about everything he had seen at the park. They checked April's phone and discovered that it also was not working. April had been knocked out by one of the explosions and couldn't remember anything after turning around to watch the light show. As he recounted his view of the battle and how Jared was taken, she listened wide-eyed and horrified. By the time Hunter finished, he wished he hadn't been so descriptive in his storytelling. April was obviously very shaken.

"I'm sorry. Maybe I shouldn't have told you."

"No, it's okay. I needed to know. It's just . . . This seems crazy and I'm really worried about Jared. What if they took him? Part of me doesn't even believe this is real. I could have woken up as a prisoner of alien kidnappers. I mean, that is so unbelievable that I don't even know whether I should laugh or cry."

They sat in silence for a time.

"You know," Hunter began with a grin. "We might have just missed the biggest adventure of our lives."

April looked aghast. "Are you crazy?"

"Seriously, think about it. We could have been like heroes in a sci-fi movie. That would have been awesome! We might have been some of the first Earthlings to ever visit an alien planet! We probably just missed our one opportunity for adventure and glory!"

She hit him on the shoulder and then she laid her head on that same shoulder.

"Thanks."

"For what?"

"For making me feel better. Hearing you make jokes almost makes me feel normal."

"No problem. That's me. I laugh in the face of danger."

She chuckled and slid her arm through his. April was always a pretty touchy-feely person but distress was making her even more so. Hunter was beginning to think that this whole alien invasion thing might not be so bad.

Suddenly she looked Hunter up and down and pulled away in disgust, "Is that what I think it is?"

Hunter surveyed himself for the first time since the park. The front of his pants were crusted with brown stains, and some spots of gore had made it past his coat and onto his shirt. He remembered suddenly about the soldier's head exploding. Now his expression mirrored hers, and as he looked down at himself, he mouthed the words,

"Alien brains."

He had been splattered with alien brains. April made a muffled gagging noise as she covered her mouth, "Oh Hunter, that is disgusting! You have to find a place to clean that off!"

"Uhh, I'll be back," he said sheepishly, and he went to speak with a guard.

After generating some degree of discussion and

confusion, he was rewarded with a clean set of green nurses' scrubs that were two sizes too big and a trip to the restroom to wash and change. April looked utterly relieved when he returned. He flopped down next to her and they strained themselves to make casual conversation while they waited.

As they chatted, the cafeteria steadily filled with people from the park, and after about four hours, Summer and Cade entered the cafeteria together with a large group of park goers. Both of them looked dazed and nursed head injuries with ice packs. April nearly exploded with enthusiasm when she spotted them. A very energetic reunion between Summer and April ensued. Once the excitement and hugs had subsided, Hunter recounted his story about the battle and how Jared had been carried off. Summer's response to the story was even worse than April's. She looked like she was going to throw up. Cade alternated between amazement and disbelief.

Once Hunter had finished his story, they sat down at a cafeteria table together and a gloomy silence settled over the four of them. Each of them could feel the other's fear. Where was Jared? Hunter thought he had seen Jared lying on the ground. But had it really been Jared? Everything at the park was so confusing. He just didn't feel sure anymore.

As they waited together Hunter suppressed a number of impulses to try to say something funny. He just couldn't bring himself to make a joke. The reality that Jared may have been taken was steadily growing in each of their minds. So, they sat mostly in silence. Each time a new group of people was brought in from the park, they looked up hoping to find Jared in the mix. Each time, they were disappointed. The groups became steadily less frequent and Hunter truly began to feel sick.

People had begun to leave the cafeteria now. Every few minutes a well-dressed man or woman entered with a clipboard and called out a name. Hunter assumed that they were being taken to meet with their families. He yawned and rubbed his eyes with the palms of his hands. He was growing very tired. What time was it? He felt like he must have been awake all night.

"Hunter Smith!"

Hunter looked up, caught off guard. A behemoth of a man stood in the cafeteria entrance scanning the room. He was dressed in a dark stylish suit. He had short dark hair that was cut in a flat top, a five-o'clock shadow and a grimace on his face that looked like it was specifically intended to make babies cry. He couldn't have stood less than 6 foot 5 and he had shoulders so broad that he probably had to turn sideways to fit through most doors. Where had this man found a suit that could fit him? Hunter stared dumbly for a moment.

"Hunter Smith!" he repeated more loudly in a voice like gravel.

Hunter started, "Uhh . . . here!"

He began to stand. As he did, April grabbed his hand. He paused for a moment to look at her. Lines creased her brow. She looked genuinely concerned, maybe even scared. Her hand was clammy, and he could see that she still looked very shaken.

"Clammy Hands," he said with a twisted grin.

"What?"

"You know . . . your new nickname."

She pulled her hand away and wiped it self-consciously on her jeans. "Ha ha," she said sarcastically, "this is serious."

"Don't worry, we've already managed to avoid abduction by crazed aliens. What could be more serious than that? The worst is behind us. I'm sure that Jared will get here soon. He's probably in a hospital bed still unconscious from the alien abduction thing. I'll see you in a few minutes. Okay?"

She seemed to relax a little. "Okay, Lumphead. I'll see you in a few."

He gave her a goodbye wink, stuffed his hands into his pockets and then turned to go. Truthfully, he was pretty nervous, but acting calm for April made him feel calmer as well. He approached the mountain of a man who had called out his name.

"Hi, I'm Hunter Smith."

"Follow me this way, Mr. Smith."

Hunter began to make a half-witted remark about how Mr. Smith was his father and how everyone called him "The Huntmeister," but the man had already turned from the doorway and was headed down the bustling hallway. Hunter started with a jerk and had to take a few quick steps dodging people to catch up. As Hunter pulled up beside the beast of a man he asked, "Are you taking me to see my family?"

"I am not authorized to answer that question."

"Well, can you tell me where we are going?"

"I'm not authorized to answer that question either."

"What's your name?"

"I'm also not authorized to answer that question."

"Are you authorized to answer any questions?"

"I am not authorized to tell you what I am not authorized to tell you." The man managed to hold the conversation in the same flat tone and low, gravelly voice with which he seemed to say everything. They took a few more steps without conversation.

"What color is your underwear?"

Hunter thought he saw the man crack the faintest smile. He grunted and then walked on in silence. Despite his size, the man walked with a self-assured grace. He exuded confidence, control, and something else that Hunter couldn't recognize. Was that dangerousness? Was dangerousness even a word?

They passed through a long series of hallways that met at

right angles. Individuals, like Hunter, who had been at the park, were being led into offices that lined the halls. Some of them had windows and he could see that interviews were being held. He imagined that the offices were normally used by doctors and nurses. For now, they seemed to have been commandeered by government officials for interrogating survivors of the park incident. Some of those having interviews looked scared. Some looked angry, even hostile. Some looked almost frantic. Hunter couldn't understand the myriad of responses apparent in the faces of those being interviewed. It seemed to him that all the real danger had passed and that, in general, people should be relieved.

Suddenly, his massive escort came to a halt beside a door. "Wait here."

The behemoth tapped lightly on the door and very faintly Hunter heard somebody call out, "Come in!" The man entered and closed the door behind him. Like so many other rooms, a large window allowed him to see inside. A table sat out of place in the center of the room with two chairs facing each other from opposite sides. A short balding man in a dark gray suit sat in the seat furthest from the door. A desk was pushed up against the far corner. A large bookshelf dominated the wall opposite the window and various pieces of modern artwork and inspirational pictures decorated the remaining wall space.

The giant approached, standing opposite the little man, and they began speaking. Hunter couldn't tell what was being said but he saw the big man give a folder to the little man as he nodded in the direction of the window. The little man looked out at Hunter and then he opened the folder leafing quickly through its contents. He spoke to the bigger man again, this time with hand motions that seemed to indicate he should go get Hunter.

The larger man returned and opened the door, "You may come in."

As Hunter started past the man, he felt a massive hand rest firmly on his shoulder. He stopped to look up at the giant. He stood very close to the hulking figure and for the first time he got a good look at the man's face. He had dark brown eyes with deep smile lines. His features looked like they had been carved from solid rock. He must have been in his early forties and had flecks of gray that speckled his otherwise dark head of hair. Hunter was close enough that he could feel the man's breath on his face. Despite his hard features and gravelly voice, something about the man's demeanor had changed. What was that he saw in his eyes? Sympathy? Worry?

"My name is Ken. It is short for Kenneth. I am wearing blue boxers with orange polka dots." He gave Hunter's shoulder a gentle squeeze, "Good luck, son."

He released Hunter's shoulder, stepped outside and closed the door taking up a guard position. Hunter watched him leave, feeling a little confused. He turned to face the man at the table who promptly stood up and walked over to shake his hand.

"Hunter Smith?" he said in a rich baritone. He looked at Hunter with a kindly smile and again Hunter could see something behind the man's eyes that looked like sympathy. He could also see now that even though the man was relatively short, he had sharp, lean features, a muscular neck and he offered a handshake that was as firm as grabbing onto a brick.

"Yes."

"Please. Have a seat." He gestured at the nearest chair. Hunter sat and the man walked around the table to take the opposite seat, dropping the file folder onto the table.

"Hunter, I am about to tell you some things that are going to be very difficult to understand. If you choose to believe the things that I tell you, then you may panic. I beg you to stay calm. We only have 10 minutes together and these may prove to be the most important 10 minutes of your life. If you panic and come unglued, then I have to end this interview and you will never get another chance to talk to me. Hunter, do you understand?"

He was stunned by the man's sobriety and by the urgency in his tone. "Yes, sir."

"Can you remain calm?"

"Yes, sir."

"Are you sure?"

"Yes, sir."

The man stared hard at Hunter for a moment and began. "My name is James Lund. You may call me Mr. Lund. I work for the United States government. I am a relocation counselor for the Leeber Slave Treaty Administration.

Today will be one of your last days on Earth. You saw something that unfortunately makes it necessary for us to turn you over to the custody of a different race of beings that live on a planet that is located millions of light years away. This is your exit interview. I am authorized to answer any and all questions that you may wish to ask, though you might choose to just sit and listen."

A sense of dread began to grow inside of Hunter. What did the man say his name was? Lund? Did he just say that Hunter would have to leave Earth and never return? Hunter fought to control himself. He gripped his pant legs underneath the table and tried to focus. Mr. Lund continued his explanation.

"Eight years ago, our planet was discovered by two different extraterrestrial races. Each of them came here looking for slaves. The first of the two races to discover Earth are called the Cravos. Initially, they attacked cities in South America, stealing hundreds of thousands of people. Today you witnessed first-hand just how quickly and effectively they work. The unfortunate reality is that they possess technology which is far superior to our own and without assistance from the Leeber we are quite nearly helpless. The Leeber were second to discover Earth. Shortly after the attacks in South America, the UN called an emergency meeting and without invitation the Leeber showed up. To make a long story short, they offered us protection against the Cravos in exchange for slaves. A treaty was put into place and now each country is responsible for providing a certain number of slaves to the Leeber every year. Roughly, the United States is responsible for sending 10,000. Some countries have put systems into place such as military selective service where citizens are told that they are going off to fight in wars and then they simply never return. In the United States, we have no such system. However, we have reached an agreement with the Leeber that they can take any whom they save from Cravos raids. This agreement helps us to keep our situation secret from the general populace, and Cravos raids have become so frequent in the United States that they fill more than half our yearly obligations to the treaty. Because of this agreement, you will be turned over."

Hunter should have been terrified out of his wits. Based upon what he had seen in the park, he believed everything that Mr. Lund told him. Perhaps it was Mr. Lund's disarming and genuinely concerned manner that calmed Hunter. Perhaps it was just that the entire situation was far too surreal to internalize deeply. He was definitely shocked and scared but he was also in control of his emotions.

"Hunter, do you have any questions?"

He considered for a moment, "Who came up with the ridiculous names?"

"What?"

"You know, 'Leebers.' It sounds like Lemurs. I've seen them up close. They aren't covered in fur and they don't have pointy noses."

"You're not taking this seriously."

"No, honestly, I am taking this very seriously. I'm trying to lighten the mood. You just told me not to panic and then told me that I am losing everything that is important to me and that I will live my days out as a slave on a faraway world. I'm trying very, very hard not to panic."

Mr. Lund grimaced. "I see what you mean. Fair enough," he sighed. "Both names come from attempts to abbreviate and Anglicize titles that were provided by the Leeber. I don't know if they have special meanings. Sometimes the Leeber refer to themselves as the people of Actaeon or Actaeon 9, which is how they refer to their planet when they are speaking English. Do you have any other questions?" He emphasized the word 'other'.

Hunter considered, "There must have been hundreds of people who saw what happened today. How are you going to cover that up?"

"Actually," Lund corrected, "there were about three thousand five hundred. We don't know exactly because we have to estimate how many were actually taken by the Cravos." He paused for a moment, "That is a very interesting question. We monitor continuously for raids. We worked with the Leeber to track the enemy craft as it entered our atmosphere and we had our own team in the air over Chicago even before the gravity beam engaged. The moment we identified their target we dispatched local police to block all pedestrian traffic within seeing distance of Millennium Park. Those on the wrong side of the barricades were taken into custody for questioning. They will all be sent off world. Once the park was cleared, we detonated charges destroying the area. The whole event will be portrayed as a terrorist attack. There will be a lot of questions and conspiracy theories, but in the end, it will be forgotten."

"You can get away with that?"

"We have covered up for three other similar raids this year."

"You said that these raids account for about half of our yearly slave obligation. Where do the rest come from?"

"We get them from a lot of places. We take homeless people. We use prisoners who have little or no family. Every year, more than two and a half million people die here in the United States. Approximately 45,000 are killed in transport accidents and about the same amount die from drunk driving fatalities, homicides, poisonings, et cetera. People die all the time and it isn't hard at all for us to slip in an additional 10,000 disappearances, especially when you realize that we are the ones who control the statistics and reporting. Like I said, we get people from a lot of different places."

"You are being very free with information."

"As I stated earlier, I am authorized to answer any question you want. You will be leaving our world soon and though you have not chosen to do so, you are performing a great service for your country and for humanity. The least we can do is to tell you why all of this is happening."

"How very kind of you," he replied flatly. Mr. Lund just stared back, ignoring Hunter's sarcasm. "How long are you going to keep giving them slaves?"

"The treaty will remain in effect for thirty years. In the meantime, we are developing means by which to defend ourselves against both of the races and we hope that by that point the Leeber will have been given sufficient slaves to maintain a human population on their own world and the Cravos will have stolen enough of us to do the same."

Hunter was stunned beyond words. Could this really have been the only choice? What did he mean by maintain a human population of their own? He closed his eyes and tried to focus. He steadied his breathing. He had to keep asking questions.

"What is it like? Has anyone ever been there and come back?"

"As part of the treaty, an embassy is sent from Earth every year to inspect the living conditions of those we send off planet. I myself have been twice. Each time we visited, we met people who were well treated and seemed happy. The living conditions seemed very agreeable." Mr.   Lund paused and seemed to think about his answer for a moment and then he sighed. "Honestly, when I visited, I felt like they were showing us only what they wanted us to see. Our visits were very controlled. We weren't allowed to go anywhere that we were not directed. Truthfully, we don't know what life is like. I wish I could tell you more."

"I think I saw one up close today. He looked human. Do they all look human?"

"All those that we have dealt with look just like humans. However, in general, they are about 6 inches taller than the average American man. They have faster reflexes than us. They are much stronger. Some of them seem to be able to communicate telepathically. Their negotiators at the UN could possibly read minds or sense emotions. That is honestly about all that we know. We have never had one in custody, so we know very little about their actual physiology."

"Why do they need slaves?"

"Your questions are quite unusual for someone in your predicament." Mr. Lund considered for a moment, "We don't know why they need slaves. They aren't very forthcoming with information."

"You said that each year an embassy travels to their planet. How do you travel? How will we travel?"

"The Leeber provide an escort. As members of the embassy, we are given luxurious accommodations. In all honesty, your traveling arrangements will not be so nice. It is similar to the difference between flying coach on a commercial airplane or flying in your own private jet."

"What will happen to my family?"

Lund sighed and the sympathetic look and tone returned to his voice. "Hunter, that question brings us to a very important part of this interview. Once you leave us, we won't be able to do anything to help you ever again. The last thing that we can do is to offer you a choice regarding your family. We can either tell them that you died in the terrorist bombing of Millennium Park or we can send them with you. We need more people to help us fill our yearly obligation and we have no better method of selecting candidates. If you choose to have them come, we will call them in for exit interviews. They will think that they are coming to discuss the condition of their son. You will be reunited and then we will send all of you away together. You would all be doing your country a great service."

The offer caught him off guard and it filled him with a nervous sickness. He sat, silently considering and trying to think clearly. If he accepted, he would condemn his family to the same uncertain future that he faced, but he wouldn't have to be alone. If he refused, then his family would think him to be dead and he would be sent off alone. Images of his dad, his mom and his little brothers and sisters flashed through his head. For what felt like a lifetime he sat silently and warred with his feelings. Mr. Lund began to eye his wrist-watch.

Hunter closed his eyes. He loved his family. How could he live without them? He loved them. That thought seemed to brighten his mind. He loved them. How could he do to them what was being done to him? He could never drag his family into something so dangerous and unknown. His feelings suddenly came together, and though he was terrified and sick, he knew what his answer was. He opened his eyes and he stared directly across the table at Mr. Lund.

"No."

"Are you sure, because…"

"No," he interrupted fervently. "No," a third time more quietly. "Leave them out of this," he said with finality. "What about my friends?"

"What friends?"

"I was at the park with four of my friends. What will happen to them?"

"I presume that they were taken into custody as well. They will receive the same exit interview as you and the same choice."

"Can I see them?"

"It is likely that you will see them again shortly. Everyone from the park will leave the Earth from the same spaceport. You will be shipped from here to Florida. If your friends choose to have family sent off world with them, then they will arrive in Florida a few days later."

Mr. Lund looked at his watch again and stood up. Ken, the mountain with the polka-dotted underwear, walked back into the room.

"I am afraid that we have run out of time, Hunter. Do you have any final questions?"

Hunter shrugged, "Do you have any advice for a fourteen-year-old boy who is terrified?"

Mr. Lund walked around the table. He put his hands on Hunter's shoulders and turned him so that they faced each other eye to eye.

"Whatever you do, don't fight them. We do not have any proof, but I believe that they can be cruel and unforgiving. I wish that we could tell you more about what to expect, but there is so much that we don't know. You are the calmest young man that I have ever interviewed. I doubt that your friends fared so well. When you see them, pass along what you have learned."

He gave Hunter's shoulder a final squeeze and then he turned him to face the door. "You'll need to go with Ken now. Good luck."

4 SHIPPED

Hunter left the room in a daze. Now that the interview was over, polka-dot-underwear Ken returned to his stoic, non-responsive self. He led Hunter by the arm through more hallways. Images, people, and conversations seemed to spin around him, and yet somehow, he saw and heard nothing. All he could think about was that he would never see his family again. He was losing everything that mattered to him. The last moments that he spent with his dad comforted him, but they also filled him with a desperate longing. It had been less than twenty-four hours since he saw his mom or his brothers and sisters, but somehow it felt like a lifetime. It seemed as if all connections to his former life had been severed in the matter of a few minutes.

They approached a set of wide double doors guarded by two soldiers. Even as Hunter and Ken stopped, the soldier on the left reached into a box and pulled out a tangled set of manacles. Before he could think clearly enough to protest, the soldier knelt, quickly shackling Hunter's ankles and then his wrists. He looked down dumbly at his restrained limbs and then he raised his head to stare at Ken. Hunter's eyes were filled with pleading and tears. Ken looked back at Hunter at first without expression or pity and then suddenly he stood at attention and brought his right hand up into a full salute. They stood staring at each other for a long moment. The gesture confused Hunter, but as he looked into Ken's eyes, he realized that he was being offered the only form of respect or honor that this man had to give, and he took strength from it. His hands were shackled, and he could not offer a salute in return, but he knew what to do. He stood straighter. He lifted his chin and set his jaw in defiance. He could swear that he saw the faintest smile touch the corner of Ken's mouth who then dropped his salute, turned and walked away.

The double doors opened into a wide, outdoor loading dock. People were being herded into the loading area from various entrances and directed by soldiers in green military fatigues. Everyone that wasn't wearing green fatigues was shackled at the wrists and ankles. There were dozens of people crowded together and more were coming in at a steady pace. Hunter was ushered down a long ramp into the main body of captives. The shackles on his ankles restricted his movement to short shuffling motions. He nearly tripped as he stepped off the ramp and was barely able to catch himself by stumbling into a short, middle-aged man in a wrinkled suit.

"Excuse me," Hunter said, but his apology was lost in the shuffle of people and the noise of the frantic crowd. The expressions on faces ranged from dumb fear to angry shouting. Hunter saw teenagers, old women, middle-aged business professionals, and mothers clinging to children. Despite the growing size of the crowd and the tumult of voices, the soldiers seemed to have no problem containing the frantic people inside the loading bay. He could see that they were well practiced in controlling this type of crowd. They didn't seem to mind that people were shouting. Hunter thought he even heard threats being yelled out against the soldiers. The placid and unperturbed responses offered in return might as well have been reserved for unruly animals. They were focused on restraining the crowd but there was nothing personal in their work. The uncontrolled disorder caused by frantic individuals actually seemed to help the soldiers maintain control. The crowd of people jerked and moved spasmodically like a fishing net filled with minnows. Together they might have been able to push in a single direction and overwhelm their captors but chaotic as they were, escape was hopeless.

The deep throaty rumble of a diesel engine could be heard growing louder over the noise of the crowd. Hunter looked in the direction of the rumbling engine and stood on his toes to gaze above the crowd where he could see the top half of a semi-truck backing into the loading dock. The truck pulled a long, double door box trailer that Hunter realized was going to be used to transport human cargo. The truck came to a halt with the hissing release of air brakes, and soldiers quickly threw open the trailer doors and let down a long cargo ramp. No sooner did the ramp touch the ground than the soldiers unsheathed short batons with two prongs on the end that crackled to life with electrical arcs. 'Cattle prods?' Hunter thought. He had seen these before on his uncle's farm in Arizona. However, these batons looked much more menacing. They were longer and the electric arcs seemed more intense. People nearest the soldiers began to back away and the soldiers closed in, forcing the entire crowd to shuffle toward the ramp. Some nearest the truck recognized instantly what was happening, and they proceeded compliantly up the ramp and into the trailer. Others pushed futilely against the crowd, not wanting to be herded into the truck.

"Move, kid!"

Hunter turned to face a soldier staring him down with a crackling cattle prod and he realized that he had been on the edge of the crowd. Others had moved away from him in response to the threat, but he had been overly preoccupied and now stood alone facing down this man. The soldier jabbed the cattle prod at Hunter, and he stepped back.

"Keep going, boy. You don't want any trouble. Just get in the truck with the others."

It had not been his intent to challenge this man. Hunter knew logically that fighting back was pointless. He was a scared fourteen-year-old boy, and his hands and feet were chained. He was facing a trained soldier who was armed. He should just back into the crowd and move along with the others, but something inside of him gave way. Ken had shown him respect and had honored his loss. In contrast, this man was treating him like a cow. Hunter did not know that he would be treated much more poorly in the coming months. He just knew that this man represented the betrayal of his humanity. Somewhere, this man had a mother and a father. He may have had brothers and sisters. He should understand! He should not be participating in this atrocity! He should take a stand for what is right! Somebody should take a stand! Hunter decided that he was going to take a stand. He stood up tall. He raised his chin in defiance and then he launched himself at the soldier in a spastic and entirely pathetic assault.

Hunter managed to reach the soldier and as he fell forward tripping over his chains, the man rammed the baton into his gut. He heard the crackling electrical arc that engaged as the soldier activated the baton and then his whole body spasmed as he fell on his face. It seemed to Hunter that the soldier was holding the baton on him for way too long. Maybe he was trying to make a point. If so, it was probably working. Hunter heard somebody screaming. He thought he heard the words, "Leave him alone. You're killing him." He hoped that wasn't true. The soldier disengaged the baton and then kicked him hard in the side of the head and again in the ribs. He blacked out for a split second when the boot made contact with his temple. He lay unmoving for a moment then he moaned painfully, rolling onto his side and throwing up on the soldier's boots. Hunter had been ready to lose. He just hadn't been ready for it to hurt so much. Had there been any dignity in his charge it was entirely lost in the line of drool and vomit that began to leak from the corner of his mouth.

He felt hands on his arm and a familiar voice.

"Hunter? Are you okay?" He didn't respond. He was still dizzy and sick and in a lot of pain. "Oh, please be okay. Please say something."

"April?" He opened his eyes and rolled onto his back moaning again. She was kneeling next to him. Tears ran down her face. He might have appreciated that those tears were for him, but he suspected that she had been crying even before she saw him get beaten to a pulp. The mere sight of her face washed away some of the sense of loss that he had been feeling. He was not alone. He had not lost everything. He still had a friend.

"Never better," he croaked, and smiling he reached to gingerly touch the black and blue lump that was beginning to form on the side of his head. "I think that your nickname for me is going to be truer than ever."

She looked up abruptly in the direction of the guard and her face became a sudden mask of desperation and fear. Hunter heard the crackle of a cattle prod being activated. "Come on, Hunter. We have to go."

She was pulling on his arm. He sat up despite the sharp pain in his ribs. He hoped they were only bruised. He stood and April pulled him toward the crowd of shuffling people. More than half the group had already been loaded into the truck. Apparently, the thorough beating that he had taken served very effectively to motivate other onlookers into hurrying themselves along. It bothered him to know that his pathetic act of rebellion had only helped his captors. As they joined the crowd moving toward the ramp, he noticed for the first time that April wore shackles also and he stopped moving. April pulled against him.

"Come on, Hunter."

He hated the sight of his friend in chains. It bothered him more than anything else that had happened on this horrific day. She did not deserve this. He looked at her shackles and he felt the same deep indignation that had caused him to pick the fight with the soldier. He was angry. This was wrong. He had to vent his anger at somebody.

April must have seen it in his eyes, because she began pleading.

"Please, Hunter. Let's just go. It will be okay. Please, let's just get in the truck."

Instead, he turned to face the soldier again. The man stared back at him without expression. Hunter realized that nothing this man had done was personal. Whoever these people were, they had done this a lot. This was all part of a prescribed routine and Hunter's beating had just presented an opportunity to create an example that could be used to inspire fear in the rest of his fellow captives. As he held the man's gaze, his anger subsided a little. The crowd began to move away from Hunter again as they filled the truck, and the soldier's indifferent expression was beginning to reshape itself into a grimace. April was still tugging on his arm and whispering pleas for him to come.

The soldier seemed to sigh ever so slightly. The cattle prod in his hand came to life and he began to walk toward Hunter. The bustle of feet and voices grew as people heard the electrical sizzling and increased their pace in an effort to avoid being caught up in a second conflict. They shot backward glances at Hunter that reflected both fear and annoyance. April pulled harder on Hunter's arm and he had to step backwards to avoid losing his balance.

"I win!" Hunter yelled out for everyone to hear. His declaration was confusing enough to cause the soldier and everyone else to pause for a moment. "You have to clean up my puke and it serves you right! My whole plan was to make you beat me hard enough to throw up. I win!"

He got the last word in. It sounded like the type of childish banter that a six-year-old might have used but it would have to do. He let April pull him into the crowd holding eye contact with the soldier for as long as he could.

April and Hunter were among the last to enter the box trailer. As the doors were closing, he looked out across the loading bay to see a very large man in a fine suit looking right at him. He was smiling broadly and openly. It was Ken. The sight confused him utterly. Hunter couldn't help but wonder why he was smiling and how much of the exchange he had witnessed.

Once the doors closed, they found themselves enveloped in total darkness. The truck rumbled to life and everyone stumbled toward the rear of the trailer as they were jerked into motion. Hunter was squashed against the double doors by the press of bodies. Then just as suddenly, they were thrown to the left and then back to the right. For the first ten minutes of travel, they were pulled in various directions as the semi navigated its way through side streets. The space was overly crammed with bodies, but everybody managed to eventually arrange themselves on the floor to avoid being thrown around by the jerky movements of the vehicle.

Hunter and April claimed a spot in the back corner. They sat next to each other with their knees pressed against their chests. April buried her face in Hunter's shoulder and began to sob. Hunter buried his face in her hair and cried with her.

5 DETAINMENT CENTER

Nineteen and a half hours later, light streamed into the trailer as the double doors were opened. Hunter and April were still crammed together in the corner, and Hunter nearly tumbled out onto the ground when the door swung away from him. His limbs were stiff from the cramped sitting position that he had been forced to hold for nearly twenty hours. His eyes squinted and he tried to shade them against the sudden glare of floodlights that filled his vision. Through the blinding display Hunter could see the silhouettes of soldiers letting down the cargo ramp. He stretched his limbs and stood, helping April to her feet also.

They were ushered quickly down the ramp and into a wide asphalt parking lot. From there, soldiers led the group across the lot and into the reception area of a large steel building. Here, they separated single men from single women and they led parents with children away down a separate hallway. April looked at Hunter with worry and apprehension as she was pulled away. He mouthed, "It is going to be okay," and he tried to give her an encouraging smile.

Hunter was led to a line of about thirty other men and boys who were waiting near a door leaving the reception area. He had been almost completely unable to sleep in the semi-trailer and doubted that anybody else had either. He had been awake for almost forty-eight hours and he felt like a zombie. He looked around at the other men standing in line. They all looked about as good as he felt. As he scanned the group of bedraggled, shackled prisoners, he made and held eye contact with an older man. He was probably in his late sixties and he was the only one in the group who seemed to have any spark of life in his eyes.

"Hello, sonny boy," the old man said with too much energy. The salutation caught Hunter off guard. He hadn't realized it but neither he nor any of the other captives had spoken more than a few quiet whispers since they had been loaded into the truck. The darkness, noise and discomfort of their transportation had reduced them all to an exhausted state of quiet submission. In contrast, this man's energetic greeting sounded like he was shouting.

"Uh . . . Hi," he managed in reply.

"You're that young rapscallion that caused so much trouble back on the docks, aren't ye? I can tell by that goose egg what's formin' on ye head."

Hunter returned his attempt at conversation with a confused look. He reached up and touched his bruised temple. Had this man just said he had a goose egg on his head? Who talked like that? "That's me. I'm the troublemaker."

The man's face took on a keen edge. There was intelligence and wisdom in his eyes. "Now son, why'd you go and do a thing like that? All you did was to git ye'self all beat up."

The tone that the old man used said he was asking a serious question and it moved Hunter to want to give a serious answer. "I don't know . . ." He began. "Everything felt so wrong. It seemed that nobody was standing up for what was right. I had to do something. Somebody had to do something . . ." He paused and reflected for a moment. "If I hadn't done something, then maybe nobody else would have and that would have been the same thing as saying that it was okay for them to do what they were doing. What I did was stupid, but it was the only thing that I could come up with."

The old man looked thoughtful. "I think, my boy, that you are right," he chuckled, and Hunter noticed that other men in the line were looking at them, "and I think it's your turn."

The old man nodded toward the head of the line. They had been moving forward slowly during their conversation and Hunter now turned to face a beefy pair of soldiers who were searching each man and relieving him of all his belongings before corralling him through a secured door. Hunter gave up his wallet, house keys, broken cell phone and a pocketknife. The soldier swiped a security badge across a scanner on the doorframe. A small green LED lit up and Hunter heard the latch as it slid open.

A second pair of not-quite-so-beefy soldiers waited on the other side. Hunter shuffled through and they led him down a long hallway to an elevator where the other men from the line waited. The men were being watched by four armed guards. Hunter was instructed to wait with the other men. One of his escorts approached a member of the guards giving orders.

"Take this group down. We will hold the line until you get back."

The guard gave a salute and then activated the elevator with his identification badge. The elevator doors opened and their group, consisting of about ten men and three of the guards, entered. The elevator only had two buttons, one labeled Ground Floor and the other Detainment Center. One of the guards pressed the Detainment Center button. The doors closed and the elevator descended.

The Detainment Center turned out to be not so bad. At least it was better than being hauled around in a box trailer like cattle. It was buried four floors underground and had been built by the federal government to hold the, 'OB' or Out Bound, which is what they called people like Hunter and April that were being sent off world. Similar Detainment Centers had been built at all of the major space shuttle launch ports in the United States. In the news, increased activity at all of these ports had been attributed to government programs that were putting more satellites in orbit to improve GPS communications and to build space stations between Earth and Mars.

In the Detainment Center, they were checked in and fitted with tracking bracelets. An orientation was given by a portly older gentleman with a full head of gray hair, pink round cheeks and a bulbous nose. He seemed friendly and he introduced himself as the facility's warden. He informed them that their bracelets were magnetically encoded and that they would provide access to meals and showers. They were told that they would shower exactly two times per week on a schedule and they would be compelled to take their first shower shortly after arrival. They were provided with clean clothes, which consisted of plain gray pants without pockets, matching t-shirts, underwear and a pair of flimsy slippers. The clothing was made of a light but durable material that had a slight metallic sheen. Their shackles were removed, and they were told that they would be allowed to move about the center freely except during curfew, which was between 10pm and 6am.

By the time the orientation was completed, and he had taken his first shower, Hunter guessed that it must have been early morning. The facility was still under curfew, so they were all sent to retire to their rooms. They were escorted by a group of workers dressed in clothing similar to medical scrubs. The only soldiers that Hunter saw guarded the elevator station, which was, by all appearances, the only means of coming in and out of the facility. He did notice however, that the center's workers contained a very high ratio of large, lean men that seemed to have very militant demeanors. 'Soldiers dressed as workers,' he thought.

Their rooms were very basic. Each was about the size of a large pantry and had just enough room for five sets of bunk beds that would sleep ten men. Hunter's group filed into the room. A member of their escort stood at the door and addressed them.

"Your lighting has been programmed to remain on for

five more minutes. When I leave, the door will lock automatically and not open again until 6 AM. It is currently 4 AM. If you wish, you may leave your room after the door unlocks. You may also choose to sleep longer. However, if you're not in the cafeteria before 10AM, you will miss breakfast. The next meal will be served at noon. The facility is currently at less than half capacity so meals are not controlled by a rigid schedule. You may come and eat anytime while food is being served. Good night."

He stepped back and the door to their room slid closed with a hiss. Hunter could hear the locking mechanism engage. He was exhausted. They were all exhausted. Nobody waited for the lights to turn off. In less than two minutes everyone was in bed and asleep.

Hunter slept until 1 PM the next day. He woke in a disoriented haze unable to remember where he was or how he had gotten there. As his memory came back slowly, he groaned inwardly. He wished that it could all be a bad dream, but he knew that it was not. The lights in their room were on but nobody seemed to be having a problem sleeping through it. By the time Hunter crawled out of bed, seven of the ten men in their room were still out cold.

Hunter woke up starving. He hadn't eaten in two days and he went straight for the dining hall. Finding his way around the Detainment Center was relatively easy. The structure was circular. Housing for the Center's occupants was built around the outside of the circle and was divided into four sections for single men, single women, families and workers. The middle section consisted of a large dining hall, auditorium, lounges, a library and various other rooms. Showers and restrooms were built into the respective housing wings. Lunch was served from noon until 2 PM. He arrived in the dining hall at 1:15 PM. Their captors were kind enough to place clocks on the wall at regularly spaced intervals so that they always knew the time of day.

The first thing Hunter noticed when he entered the dining hall was that it was occupied by men, women, and children. He grew excited at the prospect of finding April and began to scan the tables as he walked toward the serving line. He was disappointed but not surprised that he couldn't find her. Hopefully she was still asleep. There was no line for food. The cafeteria was probably less than one quarter full. They were serving pizza, salad and chocolate milk. Hunter took his tray, found an empty table and sat to eat his food. It wasn't half bad, but it wasn't great either. The pizza was especially mediocre and made him long for the night at Giordano's that had never happened. It tasted pretty similar to the type of food that you might expect to get at a junior high cafeteria. He wasn't eating like someone who had just gone without food for two days. He was preoccupied with thoughts about the park. He couldn't help but wish they hadn't stayed to play even though he knew that he shouldn't think that way. Had they left just a few minutes earlier, this would all be different. He and his family would have read about the terrorist attacks on Millennium Park and they would all be talking about how lucky it was that he and his friends hadn't been there when it happened.

"Hi, Lumphead!"

He jerked his gaze up quickly, forgetting all thoughts of the park, and found himself staring face to face with April. He smiled broadly and she smiled back.

"Ouch!" she said, looking at him with a wince. "You were right. 'Lumphead' fits you better than ever. He must have kicked you really hard. Are you okay?"

Hunter's bruised head was really beginning to look bad. It was actually feeling better, but his bruises had become deep, dark blues and blacks. When he took a shower, he had noticed that his ribs and side were looking pretty bad also. "Ah, it's barely a scratch."

April sat down across from Hunter placing her tray of food on the table. He felt a wave of relief wash over him. Knowing that she was safe truly made him feel better. Again, he was grateful to not be alone. They conversed and ate together for about half an hour. They talked about the park and their exit interviews. Hunter shared everything that he had learned from Mr. Lund. April listened and didn't have much to add except she had also learned that they might spend as long as six months in the Detainment Center. In an attempt to conceal alien activity on Earth, slaves had to be delivered to a Leeber base that was hidden behind the moon. Human space shuttles had been fitted to transport people in groups of one hundred. The launch port in Cape Canaveral, Florida had become one of the most active in the whole country but could still only send up a few shuttles each month during their most busy periods. Ports were also being run out of California, Texas, and Alaska.

They spoke casually. She told him about the women's dormitory. He told her about the strange old man that he met in line when they arrived at the Detainment Center. Hunter was really enjoying their conversation. They even managed to make a joke or two. For a few moments, it felt like they might have been just a couple of ordinary kids eating lunch in a school cafeteria. Inevitably, though, their conversations turned to more serious matters. They talked about Jared, Cade and Summer. It seemed more and more likely that Jared had been taken in the park. Cade and Summer, they determined would probably arrive at the Detainment Center soon. They worried together about what the rest of their lives would be like. They wondered how long they would get to remain on Earth. They both agreed that, if given the choice, they would stay in the Center for as long as possible.

After lunch, they took a walk together. They found recreational rooms where they could play board games. They found public drinking fountains. The Center had a well-stocked library and various lounges. All together, they felt like they were being treated much better than they had feared. After the episode at the hospital loading docks and the disconcerting ride to Florida, Hunter had been sure that they would never see another easy day for the rest of their lives. They found out that an evening assembly was held every night in the main auditorium. Information was shared during these assemblies regarding launch schedules, modifications to the Center's policies or rules, changes in meals schedules, etc. These meetings were not mandatory unless it was announced otherwise, though attendance was highly encouraged.

At their first meeting, they learned that the next launch was scheduled to happen in two weeks. Launches were announced fourteen days in advance and volunteers were requested. Sign-up sheets were placed in the lounges. Each launch could transport one hundred people. They learned from others at the Detainment Center that it was common for as many as 50 people to volunteer for a launch. Most of the people in the Detainment Center wanted to stay as long as possible; however, the only way to ensure that you could travel with family and/or friends was to volunteer for a launch together. All of the additional slots were filled by lottery. Sign-up sheets were left in the lobbies for ten days. Once they were removed, no more volunteers were accepted and everybody was at the mercy of the lottery, which was held on the morning of the 11th day. If a member or members of a family were chosen for transport in the lottery, they would have to travel without the other members of their family. This could cause problems if a young child was drawn without a parent to travel with them, but they never made exceptions to this rule. If a family wanted to travel together, then they had to volunteer during the time when the Center was seeking volunteers. Nobody knew why it had to be this way. The Center didn't offer explanations to the OB. As a result of the fear caused by the lottery, it happened occasionally that, when the Center was filled with OB families, entire shuttles were filled with volunteers. Only single men or women could safely play the odds that came from not volunteering. However, if anybody managed to avoid 'winning' the lottery for 6 months, then they were 'volunteered' for the next available launch by default. Most single people could successfully avoid launches for 2 to 4 months. April and Hunter decided that they wanted to leave together but that they would try their luck with the lottery once or twice in order to prolong their departure.

Over the next few days Hunter and April waited, and they even relaxed a little. They spent a lot of time playing board games and talking. They met a few people who had been in the Detainment Center for as long as five months and they picked up on several rumors about the Center. The workers in the Center provided them with very little information beyond when to eat and where to go to the restroom. Therefore, rumors and gossip were the principal means of obtaining information and/or misinformation. They heard rumors about uprisings in other centers. One young man, who called himself Spits, told them that once their shuttle is outside the Earth's atmosphere, they will be fired at the moon in torpedoes. The aliens try to intercept the torpedoes before they smash into the moon and sometimes, they are even successful.

They heard rumors about failed escape attempts and successful ones. As well, they heard more disturbing rumors that the aliens were actually using humans for food. That particular rumor made shivers run up, down, and back up Hunter's spine. It didn't take them very long to figure out that most of the rumors that circulated around the Center were guesswork, speculation and tall tales. In the end, they decided not to believe any of the gossip.

Steadily, the number of OB staying in the Center increased. People that Hunter recognized as park goers began to show up. By day 5, they were being issued more strict eating schedules. Hunter and April were beginning to really worry about their friends, and then, on day 6, Cade and Summer arrived with their families. They entered the cafeteria late on the 5th evening looking disoriented and nervous. April spotted them first and practically screamed. She leapt to her feet and dashed across the dining hall throwing her arms around Summer. The reunion that proceeded was warm and full of tears. Hunter approached and Summer gave him a hug. Cade gave him a handshake-bro-hug and he received a mix of different greetings from the brothers, sisters and parents of both Cade and Summer. When Summer's mom moved in to give Hunter a hug, she stopped him, grabbing him by both shoulders and looked at his head. She placed a hand gently on his temple.

"Oh, my . . . Hunter, what happened to you?"

He smirked nervously, "It's nothing, Mrs. Dees. I just fell and hit my head really hard against a soldier's boot."

"Not funny!" she retorted and launched into a tirade about abuse and kidnapping and how she was going to teach these dirtbags a lesson. "Look what they did to Hunter's face! He's just a boy!"

She loudly let loose a handful of colorful expletives, half of which must have been antiquated idiomatic expressions from before Hunter's time, because he had no idea what they meant. People in the cafeteria were beginning to stare, and Summer was starting to look embarrassed by the attention that was growing in her mother's direction. Suddenly, Mr. Dees appeared at her side placing a hand on her shoulder.

"Sweetheart," he said calmly. She paused as his quiet words and touch broke her anger. "Now is not the time," he whispered. "Let's go get some food."

"But . . ." she began.

"Not now. Not here," he interrupted and gestured around the room with his eyes.

"Yes, of course." She looked flushed. "Come on, kids." She finished giving Hunter a hug and then led the way for her family to stand in line and get food.

Summer's last name was Dees. She had an older sister that was sixteen named Leila, and two younger brothers, Caleb, age ten, and Sam, age seven. Her mom, Susan was a stout expressive woman with sandy brown hair and a slightly frantic sense of energy. Her dad was rail thin with intense eyes. His face bore all the marks of a man in his early forties. He was slightly balding and possessed a very quiet dignity. He did not often tell his wife what to do but he had a very gentle and powerful way of commanding anybody when it was needed. He gave Hunter's shoulder a firm squeeze as he walked by and said, "It's good to see that you and April are okay."

Hunter watched them get in line for food and he longed for his own family. Maybe he should have had them brought along. Maybe it wouldn't be so bad. Was it too late? His heart and mind longed to rush off and find somebody who could go get his family and tell them that he was alive and bring them to the Center, but his conscience whispered persistently that he had done the right thing. Did that mean that Summer and Cade had done the wrong thing? He wondered if this would ever be a subject that they could talk about.

Cade interrupted his thoughts, nudging him in the shoulder as he walked by. "Wake up, dude. We'll get some grub and see you at the table."

Cade was the living example of what happened when a frizzy redhead married another frizzy redhead. Cade's dad,

Jim Taylor, was mostly bald and he had shaved all of his remaining hair down to the skin. However, Hunter had seen pictures of Mr. Taylor from his youth sporting a mangy mop of curly red hair. He imagined that if Mr. Taylor ever grew his hair out, he would make an excellent circus clown with a squeaky-clean bald head surrounded by a frenzy of crazy red frizz. Cade's mom, Susan, had hair just like Cade's, only somehow, she managed to tame it into presentable-looking hairstyles. Right now, she wore it back in a stylish braid. He also had a younger sister named Aria, who was cursed with the same wild hair. Everyone in their family had lightly freckled cheeks, green eyes and medium builds. They filed into line behind the Dees family.

Hunter and April returned to their table and sat down. They were quiet and Hunter could see that April was wrestling with the same thoughts that bothered him.

"You made the right choice," he said. She looked up from her plate. "We made the right choice," he emphasized.

"I . . ." she began, "don't know." Her eyes began to fill with tears. He reached out and took her hand.

"It will be okay. Let's talk about it later."

She nodded, wiping her eyes. "You're right."

They sat in silence until Cade, Summer, and their families filled the table around them. They settled themselves and exchanged niceties for a few minutes until an awkward silence arose. Cade's dad, Jim, waited for only a few moments before filling the silence with a question.

"Hunter, April, what can you tell us about this place? Have you learned anything about what is going to happen to all of us?"

The table went silent and all eyes turned to Hunter and April. They looked at each other and Hunter could feel her unspoken hope that he would answer the question so that she didn't have to.

"Well," he began, "we haven't learned a whole lot. They don't tell us much and there are a lot of conflicting rumors."

Hunter told them about the nightly meetings. He told them about the facilities and the game rooms. They asked about his bruises and April interjected to explain what happened at the loading docks. Her version of the story made him sound a lot braver and a lot less stupid. He was grateful to not have to recount the story himself. He told them about the lottery and how volunteers are solicited for off-world travel, which seemed to cause a lot of uneasy looks amongst the adults at the table. Cade talked about their experience in the hospital. After their exit interviews, they were held at the hospital until their families could be brought in. People from the park were being transported in a steady stream to Florida. Cade, Summer, and their families were kept at the hospital for three days before being loaded into a prisoner transport vehicle headed for Cape Canaveral. They had seen a few people try to escape the hospital only to be brought back and placed in isolation under heavy guard. It also sounded to Hunter as though they had a much more pleasant travel experience than he and April. The prisoner transport vehicle had seats and had not been overly loaded with people.

After dinner, they all walked to the evening informational meeting together. Nothing new was announced. The Detainment Center worker conducting the meeting reminded everybody that the sign-up sheets for volunteers would only be available for five more days. Again, Hunter noticed looks of concern being traded amongst the adults. The meeting was short and afterward everybody separated and went to bed except for April and Hunter, who found themselves playing checkers in one of the Center's lounges. They sat next to each other on a long couch. Hunter held the checkerboard in his lap and April sat close to him so that she could see and move her pieces. It wasn't the ideal situation for playing checkers, but they were making it work. April was being very quiet. In fact, she had said almost nothing since their tearful reunion with Cade and Summer's families and she was playing horribly at checkers.

Hunter wasn't very good at leading into awkward conversations, so he just blurted out his thoughts. "Look, I know you are thinking that maybe you should have brought your family, but you're wrong. You made the right choice. We made the right choice."

She began to tear up again. Her eyes were fixed on the floor, "But they look so happy together and I am so afraid that . . ." she choked on her words.

"That you will never see your family again," Hunter finished quietly.

She nodded as a tear rolled off her cheek. Hunter didn't know what else to say. She was probably right about never seeing her family again. The chances that either of them would ever set foot on Earth after leaving the Detainment Center were next to nothing. They sat silently and Hunter found his eyes also beginning to fill with tears as he thought about his own family. He set the checkerboard on the ground and slid closer to April, wrapping his arms around her. She cried on his chest and he cried into her hair. Crying together was becoming far too common, and he had a sinking feeling that things were going to get a lot worse. They sat like that until curfew came and they were forced to go to bed.

6 LOTTERY

The next five days passed quickly, and as Hunter feared, Cade and Summer's families decided to volunteer for the launch. Summer's dad tried to convince him and April to volunteer also. He argued that leaving was inevitable, escape was impossible, and that volunteering was the only way to ensure that they could stick together. Hunter understood Mr. Dees' reasoning. They had young children, and taking their chance with the lottery meant that one of his children might be selected and taken. As families, they decided that they would rather take advantage of what little certainty they had by volunteering. Hunter talked about the possibility with April, but both of them agreed that they would rather stay as long as possible. Both of them also secretly held out hope that some twist of fate would bring an end to this insanity and that maybe they could escape the life of slavery that awaited them.

Halfway through day ten, Hunter and April watched as all members of the Dees and Taylor families signed up to leave with the next launch. When the volunteer sheets were taken down in the evening, they were slightly more than three quarters full. Hunter liked their odds. There were roughly twenty-five seats to fill on this launch and the Detainment Center had grown more and more full each day, which made their odds look increasingly better. Despite their good odds though, Hunter went to bed feeling sick to his stomach. Tomorrow morning, they would announce the names of those that were drawn randomly to leave with this launch. What if one of them got drawn and not the other? He barely slept that night.

Next morning, he crawled groggily out of bed. He put on his finest pair of Detainment Center slippers and rushed off to the auditorium. When he arrived, he had difficulty finding April and the others. The auditorium was practically filled to capacity. It had been made clear to all OBs that this meeting was mandatory. ID bracelets were being scanned at the door and failure to attend would gain an OB automatic volunteer status for this launch. Hunter showed up early but so did everyone else. The auditorium was teaming with OBs and everybody looked exactly the same in their Detainment Center clothing. It was even hard to tell men from women at a distance. After nearly 10 minutes of searching, he found where their group was congregating, and he was glad to see that April had saved him a seat between her and Cade. By the time Hunter claimed his seat everybody else was already sitting except Mrs. Dees who was trying to put an end to a game of tag between Caleb and Sam. No sooner did she get control of her two children than attendants closed the doors to the auditorium and a Detainment Center worker, an older lady perhaps in her early sixties, stood at the pulpit and began to speak. Her comments were candid and to the point.

"Welcome. The following individuals were not admitted

to the auditorium at the appointed time and will be sent off world as members of the next launch by default: Kathan Highman, Jonathan Whipple, Nora Lively, Jane Patterson, Michael Wilcox, Lani Genson."

Hunter was caught off guard by the pitiless monotone with which she proceeded.

"We would like to remind all of those present today that failure to attend a mandatory meeting such as this at the appointed time will result in automatic assignment to the next launch. The following individuals have been chosen by random lottery to participate in the next launch: Niles Harper, Gale Knox, Joseph Lowery, Will Tate, Frank Howard, Braden Smith . . ."

At the reading of the name Braden Smith, Hunter heard a lady cry out from a few rows back and to the right. He turned in his seat to see where the cry had come from. A middle-aged woman began to sob as she threw her arms around the neck of a teenage boy sitting next to her. The lady conducting the meeting continued reading names, but Hunter stopped paying attention. He was positioned at just the right angle to see the face of the teenage boy. He must have been just a few years older than Hunter with sandy brown hair. He stared forward in shock and disbelief. His mother cried uncontrollably. A man that looked like the boy's father sat a few seats down and his face mirrored the same look of shock and disbelief. A few small children sat between them. Their little heads swiveled back and forth in confusion. Others sitting around the family looked awkward and tried not to pay attention to the woman's crying, but Hunter wasn't able to bring himself to look away. This little family looked like his own family. He couldn't help but look at their faces and see the faces of his own parents and brothers and sisters. He felt his heart pounding and anger rising out of his stomach. It shouldn't be this way. People should have a choice. Why wouldn't anybody stand up for what was right? People shouldn't feel uncomfortable and awkward because somebody else was suffering! They should feel indignant because that suffering was undeserved and unnecessary!

In the background, he could hear the droning voice of the lady that was conducting the meeting. How could she be so unfeeling and cruel? She read off names like she was taking roll for a math class. Hunter began to feel the urge to do something stupid. In all the strangeness and confusion of recent events, Hunter was discovering a new side of himself that he had never previously known. He was finding that he had a crazy, stubborn side to his personality that could come out whenever he got angry. That woman on stage, with her austere and disconnected manner was about to become the target of that anger. It was time to do something stupid! He began to turn around and get to his feet when he heard two words that stopped him instantly and drove all thoughts of the little family from his mind.

". . . April Lines." The old lady paused for a moment and then with only the least degree of formality, she finished. "Thank you. You are all dismissed." She turned and left. He looked at April and saw panic, fear and disbelief. Tears began to form at the corners of her eyes. She rotated her head until she was looking squarely at Hunter.

"Oh no," she mouthed, "oh no . . ."

Hunter didn't know what to say. The auditorium was emptying out around them. Cade and Summer's families sat rigidly looking at Hunter and April who stared wide-eyed at each other. All of their thoughts and fears were traded and understood as they looked at each other in horror. She was going without him. He was being left behind. They would probably never see each other again. He reached out to touch her hand. She stood up and quickly ran out.

"April . . ."

He spoke her name quietly and his hand lifted reflexively hanging in the air as if to reach after her. He watched her hurry into the crowd and then out of the auditorium. He didn't know what else to say. He felt like he had been punched in the gut. April was leaving without him and he would be alone. The relative peace that they experienced in the Detainment Center had lulled him into a false sense of security. They were being sold as slaves and they were being robbed of their choices. He would have to face the harsh reality that all of his freedoms would be gone soon and that he no longer possessed anything that could not be taken. Even his friends could be taken.

Hunter sat for a long time as the auditorium emptied out around him. Cade and Summer's families waited with him for a brief time. Mr. Dees gave his shoulder a squeeze as they left, and Mrs. Dees gave him a tearful hug. Cade and Summer whispered sorry as they walked by. He just nodded and was grateful when he found himself sitting alone in the auditorium. At first, he remained still to help himself control a growing sense of panic. Then he remained still to help himself control the anger that was building and then his emotions just faded off. He concentrated on breathing evenly and then he sat for a while thinking about his family and his life. Somewhere in the back of his mind, he thought he heard the curfew bell ring, but he chose to just sit and ignore it.

It was well past midnight when he felt someone sit down beside him. He didn't need to look to know that it was April. Somehow, he suspected that she might be wandering around after curfew and he hoped that she would find her way back to the auditorium. She slid her hand into his, their fingers intertwined, and she laid her head on his shoulders. They sat for a while saying nothing. He could hear her breathing and feel the slow rise and fall of her body next to his. It was relaxing.

"I'll find you," he said quietly. "I promise. I will volunteer for the next shuttle and somehow…"

"Sshh," she whispered, "I know."

They sat that way until they both fell asleep, slouching in their seats, her head still on his shoulder. As Hunter's thoughts faded into dreams, he began to form a plan. He would not give up his friend so easily.

In the balcony above Hunter, stood the dark silhouette of a hulking man. He had watched the proceedings of the meeting. He had watched as people cried out in despair. He had watched as the crowds left the room and he stood quietly watching Hunter sit for hours and hours. When Hunter and April finally fell asleep, he smiled to himself, thumbed his chin thoughtfully, turned and left the auditorium.

7 A PLAN

Hunter spent every possible moment of the next three days with his friends. He wasn't sure who had it worse, him or them. On one hand, they were leaving to face their lives as slaves to an alien race in just three days and Hunter would be able to remain, for a brief time, in the relative safety and comfort of the Detainment Center. On the other hand, though, his departure was just as inevitable as theirs and he would be facing it alone. He tried to convince himself that he was fortunate to be able to stay a little longer, but in his heart, he longed to go with his friends and not have to face such an uncertain future by himself.

In the brief moments when Hunter was not spending time with his friends, he roamed the halls of the Detainment Center searching for the face of a certain boy that he had only seen one time but that he was sure he could recognize. The hope that Hunter held out was small, but he was not about to give up so easily, and so everywhere he went he searched for the boy who he thought could solve his problems. It wasn't until the last evening before the launch that he spotted the young man leaving the cafeteria. He recognized the boy's sandy brown hair instantly. He told April, Cade, and Summer to go on without him and that he would catch up soon. April shot him a questioning glance that contained a small dose of irritation as he took off down the hall, but Hunter never saw it. He never looked back. He couldn't afford to lose sight of his quarry.

Hunter followed the young man at a distance watching carefully. The boy walked with his head down, shoulders slumped, dragging his feet. Hunter felt pretty bad for the kid. He had first-hand experience with losing everybody he loved. He found it curious that the young man was all by himself. He had expected to find him spending his last moments with his family. Hunter followed him through the hallways of the Center into the family dormitories. He watched as the boy used his wrist bracelet to gain access to a room on the left side of the hallway. He disappeared inside and the door slid closed behind him. For a long moment, Hunter just stood looking at the door. It took him some time to build up his nerve and smother his fears sufficiently to approach the door. He knocked three times firmly and then waited.

Within a few moments, the door hissed open and Hunter found himself staring into the teary eyes of a middle-aged woman. He recognized her also.

"Mrs. Smith?" Hunter tried timidly.

"Yes," she said. "I am Mrs. Smith."

Hunter didn't know how to begin this conversation and so he just blurted out his thoughts. "My name is Hunter Smith. I want to take your son's place on the shuttle tomorrow."

She stared at him incredulously, "What?"

"I know this sounds crazy, but I think that we can pull this off."

A man walked up behind Mrs. Smith, "Honey, who is it?"

Mrs. Smith looked over her shoulder, but she was speechless. Her mouth opened and closed repeatedly as she looked back and forth between Hunter and her husband. She obviously wanted to say something, but nothing was coming out. Hunter thought for a moment that she resembled a slow-witted goldfish bumping its nose against the glass enclosure of a fish tank.

"My name is Hunter. I want to take your son's place on the shuttle tomorrow." Mr. Smith's jaw dropped noticeably, and he looked even more dumbfounded than his wife. "Look," Hunter continued, "I was near you in the auditorium when they announced the results of the lottery. I saw your family when they called your son's name. I know that you don't want him to go, and I need to go very badly. All we have to do is trade bracelets. We are nearly the same height and probably pretty close to the same age with the same hair color and eye color. We even have the same last name." Hunter held out his arm. "I took my own bracelet off last night. It wasn't easy but it can be done." Hunter's wrist and hand were heavily scraped. "I put it back on this morning. I think that if your son . . ."

Mr. Smith held a finger to his lips and then he stepped

close to Hunter, "Sshh! Please step inside."

He leaned around Hunter looking up and down the hallway and pulled him inside. The door slid closed with a hiss. Their living quarters were about the same size as the room in which Hunter stayed but was arranged to better accommodate families. It seemed to Hunter that there were probably two or maybe even three families staying in this room. It made the tiny space look even more cramped than his own room. The boy that Hunter had followed sat on a bed against the wall. He had obviously been crying and now stared wide-eyed at Hunter. Mrs. Smith was also staring at Hunter with a desperate, hopeful intensity. Mr. Smith put his hands on Hunter's shoulders.

"We have to speak quickly. Our roommates will be back from dinner very soon. Do you really want to do this?"

"Yes. I need to take your son's place."

Mr. Smith looked as his wife and she nodded. He turned back to Hunter, "What do we do?"

"We need soap and water and a place where nobody will see us," Hunter replied.

"There is a family bathroom down the hall a little further on the left. We can lock the door behind us. Let's go now."

Hunter had been thinking about this plan an awful lot. "We don't want to draw attention to ourselves by all going into the bathroom at once and locking the door behind us. I will leave your room and walk toward the bathroom. If nobody is in the hall, I will go in and leave the door unlocked. You should follow behind me in thirty seconds. We'll probably need at least five minutes to get these bracelets traded. You and your son should both come. It will go faster if we have an extra pair of hands to help remove the bracelets."

"I'll come too," Mrs. Smith interjected.

"No," Hunter responded, "the more people that go, the more likely we are to draw attention to ourselves. All we need is three."

"We have to go soon," said Mr. Smith. "We don't have much time."

"Okay," Hunter started back toward the door. "I'm going now. Follow behind in 30 seconds."

The door slid open as he approached. He left the room and walked down the hall about 20 paces and discovered the bathroom on the left-hand side. The door displayed stick figures of a man, a woman and a child. He entered the bathroom letting the door swing shut behind him and began immediately working to get the bracelet off. In the bathroom sink, he let water run over his hands while he scrubbed soap around the bracelet. The unhealed scrapes on his wrist from having removed the bracelet the previous night began to bleed the instant he started trying to push the bracelet off.

The pain in his wrist was considerably greater than the first time he had done this. Hunter wasn't used to pain but desperation compelled him onward. He moved the bracelet over his hand in small increments. Pushing from one side of his wrist and then the other. As the band progressed it scraped off his partially formed scabs. With a final desperate effort, he pushed hard, and the bracelet came loose, dropping into the sink.

Even as Hunter removed the wristband, Mr. Smith and his son entered the bathroom. They locked the door and Mr. Smith led his son to the sink. Hunter quickly showed them how to lather the soap around the bracelet and Mr. smith began to pull on it. Fortunately for Braden the bracelet came off relatively easily leaving behind only minor scrapes. Hunter took the wristband from Mr. Smith and compared it to his own. Hunter's was slightly smaller, and he began worry that his bracelet wouldn't fit Braden. He handed his wristband to Mr. Smith who immediately began to try to work it around Braden's hand. Hunter lathered his own hand with fresh soap and managed to slide Braden's bracelet into place with relatively little effort. Mr. Smith was still struggling to get Hunter's bracelet to slide past Braden's hand. Both of them grunted and strained with the effort and Braden was wincing from pain. Hunter approached and grabbed the fatter portion of the other boy's hand. He squeezed and as he did the bracelet moved forward a fraction of an inch. He proceeded to move his grip on Braden's hand back by degrees squeezing as he went, and the bracelet slowly moved forward. With a final effort, it slid past the meaty part of his thumb tearing flesh as it slid onto his wrist causing him to cry out.

Braden's hand was covered in blood. Hunter inspected his own and realized that his was also a mess and both of them were dripping on the tile. He moved quickly to clean the floor with paper towels and the Smiths followed his lead. They washed their hands in the sink and wrapped their wounds in damp paper towels. The scrapes didn't seem nearly as bad once the blood was cleaned away. They flushed the bloody paper towels down the toilet and then paused to inspect their handiwork.

In the moment of inactivity, Hunter realized that they hadn't said a single word to each other since entering the bathroom. He turned to face the other boy, "Whatever you do, don't let anybody see the scrapes on your hand."

Braden nodded and Hunter offered him a handshake. He took it and they locked eyes. "Thank you," Braden said.

Mr. Smith moved up behind his son, "Yes, thank you. We were afraid that we would never see our son again."

"You shouldn't thank me until I am safely gone, and you are still safe here," Hunter replied and then he paused. "But, you're welcome . . . and thank you also." He turned to leave the bathroom but then paused and looking over his shoulder he said, "Also, don't forget that whenever you have to scan your bracelet, your new name is Hunter Smith. Good luck."

He turned, stuffed his wrapped hand into his pocket and left the bathroom walking quickly down the hallway and toward the exit for the family dormitories. He took his first easy breath as he rounded the last corner and crashed face first into a huge man. Hunter bounced off his chest, taking two steps backwards. He looked up at a sharp angle, taking in the man's familiar features quickly and mouthing the words, "Polka-dot-underwear Ken?"

"Hunter," he nodded. "It's good to see you again."

Hunter stood staring dumbfounded, without a response. "I need to sce your wrist, young man."

Hunter narrowed his eyes and shook his head. He took a step back preparing to run.

"I really don't think you want to run from me. Besides, where are you going to run? There is no way for you to get out of this Center except on a rocket ship. I suspect, from your response, that I already know what I will see, but I want you to show me."

Hunter considered his situation for a moment and he realized that Ken was right. Even if he ran, Ken would turn him in, and his plan would never work. He sighed in frustrated resignation, stepped forward and held out his wrist. The paper towels were soaked in blood and sticking to his wounds. Ken looked down, and almost unexpectedly, smiled. This was a response that took Hunter entirely by surprise.

"So, your name is now Braden Smith." How he knew about the bracelet's original owner, Hunter could not even begin to guess. Ken looked at him with a twinkle in his eye, "Honestly, I like Hunter better. Once you leave this planet, you should go back to using Hunter. Really, it fits you better."

"Are you going to turn me in?"

Ken, leaned in close and with a sly grin he said, "I plan on letting you do whatever you want. In fact, I'm going to help you a little." He stood up straight and reached into his coat pocket producing a small metallic object that looked something like an inhaler. "Here, let me see your wrist again."

Hunter held out his arm. Ken cradled his wrist, gently unwrapping the bloody paper towels, and began inspecting his hand. "Well, I give you points for determination, and your plan is clever, but you overlooked some very important details. I can help you a little. I will start by fixing the hack job that you've done on yourself."

He pointed the metallic object at Hunter's bloody hand. A series of green lasers shot from the device onto his wounds. Rapidly, they began to trace the areas of torn flesh and as they did his skin knitted itself back together. It tickled very badly but Hunter held still and watched in amazement as his wounds disappeared.

"I'm going to leave you now. I will need to fix some issues with the real Braden Smith. Let me give you some advice. Don't scan that bracelet unless you absolutely have to. The more you use it, the more likely they are to catch you. It is fortunate for you that your shuttle leaves tomorrow. Good luck and try not to die as a slave to the Leeber."

Ken turned and walked away. Hunter could hardly believe what had just happened. He wasn't even sure what it was that had just happened. He stood for a moment staring at his perfectly healed wrist and hand. He was utterly bewildered. He had been sure that his plan was ruined. He didn't understand Ken. He didn't know whose side he was on, but Hunter wasn't going to turn down help. He needed as much help as he could get. Standing around wasn't going to get him where he needed to be. He turned on his heels and headed for his room. It was almost time for curfew, and he needed to finish getting ready to sneak off the planet.

8 SNEAKING OUT

April stood in the back of a shortening line of people who were passing out of the Detainment Center security doors. She waited anxiously, impatiently. The line had been much longer when she arrived. Where was Hunter? The last time she saw him was after dinner when he had taken off toward the family dormitories following some teenage boy. Wasn't he even going to come say goodbye? Cade and Summer along with their families stood in line ahead of April.

Five more minutes went by, then ten more, and then fifteen. Cade's mom was going through the security checkpoint, followed by his siblings, then his dad, then him. April began to panic. Tears formed at the corners of her eyes. She looked out anxiously across the wide foyer in which they waited. The room was almost empty now. Only a few of the Center's workers moved about, and nobody was coming up the hallway. How could he do this to her? She thought he was her friend. In truth, she thought of him as her best friend, and now, she might never see him again. Maybe something was wrong. Tears began running down her cheeks.

She felt somebody touch her arm and turned to see that Summer was the only one left in line besides herself and she looked really worried.

"I'm sorry," Summer said.

April wiped the tears off her cheeks and sniffled, "Come on. Let's go."

April walked past Summer and held her arm so that the security guard could scan her bracelet. She was admitted through the checkpoint and Summer followed immediately after.

Hunter came running around the bend in the hallway just in time to see the door close and admit what must have been the last person in line through the security checkpoint. He ran up to the security guard and held out his harm.

"Hun . . . Hu . . . Uh . . . Braden Smith . . . Uh . . . reporting for slavery," He stuttered almost saying his real name. What would happen if he got caught at this point? Would they kick him out and go find the real Braden Smith? He finished with his best stupid grin. He was nervous. His palms were sweaty, and he could barely contain his anxiety. The guard looked at him suspiciously, shrugged and scanned the bracelet. He pushed a button underneath the table and the door clicked open. His passage through the security check point seemed far too easy. It was probably because they just didn't care. It wasn't like he was trying to flee the center. Hunter walked through into a long narrow hallway. April and Summer were about to exit the hallway through the opposite end.

"April! Summer!" he called out.

They turned and gave him the most puzzled looks that he had ever seen. Somehow, they managed to appear angry, relieved and completely confused all at the same time. Hunter jogged the length of the hallway. April began to open her mouth as she raised a finger to poke him in the chest.

Hunter spoke more quickly, "Look. I don't have long to explain. Please just trust me. I am going with you on the launch, but I am doing it disguised as another boy that was supposed to leave today. He has my bracelet and I have his. I need you to call me Braden, and I need you to tell everybody else to call me Braden. Please go into the next room and find the others. I will follow shortly. Very quietly, you have to let them know to call me Braden. My last name is still Smith. Nobody can be allowed to slip and call me Hunter, not even the kids. Now, please go quickly."

He began to push them through the door that exited the hallway. April tried to speak but he shushed her and continued to push her toward the door. Suddenly she threw her arms around his neck and squeezed him tightly.

"Thank you," there were tears in her eyes. She pulled away quickly, wiping them, and then exited through the door.

Summer was close on April's heels. As she left through the door she turned and gave Hunter a thumbs-up mouthing the words, "You rock!" he smiled in reply.

Hunter counted. He was nervous and counting helped to calm his nerves. He needed to make sure that they had enough time to speak with everyone and he had no idea what he was walking into. When he reached three hundred, he took a deep breath and went through the door. He entered a room that was too small to hold its one-hundred-plus occupants. Everybody was crammed together, and their attention was directed to a man who stood on a small riser at the head of the room giving out instructions over a microphone. Immediately he spotted his friends in the back of the room and began to squirm his way to where they stood. They spotted him as he moved clumsily through the crowd toward them and Hunter perceived a hushed excitement in their group as he approached.

Summer and Cade's moms gave him hugs. Summer's dad clapped him on the shoulder saying quietly, "Good work, boy."

Cade offered him a fist bump. "What's up . . . Braden?" he said in a whisper grossly over emphasizing the name, 'Braden.' Hunter just returned the attention quietly with a grin and a raise of his eyebrows.

April moved in close, sliding her arm around his waist. In response, he wrapped his arm around her shoulder squeezing lightly, and lowering his head he whispered into her ear, "I'm sorry that I took so long."

She squeezed him back in response. What he didn't tell her was that he had purposefully waited until the last minute. There hadn't been enough time to talk to everyone and he was sure that April would want to say goodbye so she would wait around as long as possible hoping that he would show up. It was a risky calculation on his part, but it had paid off. He managed to get April aside and use her to inform everybody else before anybody had the chance to call him by his real name in front of a Detainment Center worker. He regretted that she had worried so much, but he was kind of flying by the seat of his pants on this whole sneaking off the planet thing and, in truth, he was just glad that his plan seemed to be working. What would he have done had he not made it through the checkpoint? The thought almost made him nauseous. So, he pushed it out of his mind and turned his attention toward the speaker.

"The shuttle will blast off in 8 hours," he was saying. "In the meantime, each of you will prepare for space travel. Our shuttle will take you from Earth to a Leeber space station behind the moon. A trip to the moon would normally require two to three days. However, if everything goes well on the first launch attempt, you will be traveling for seven days. The Leeber are expecting our delivery in one week and you are being launched early to ensure that we make the delivery on time. Occasionally we encounter technical difficulties before, after, or during launch sequences. Should we encounter any complications that delay the launch, then we will have a few days in which to fix the shuttle. If the launch occurs on time, and we have no reason to believe that it won't, then you will be shuttled to the moon at a slower speed, which will allow us to conserve fuel. You will be transported in self-contained pods or SCPs. The interior of your pod will be only slightly bigger than a large human male. Are there any questions?"

Somebody in the front row asked, "What are we

supposed to eat?"

The man responded, "You will be connected to an IV that will provide you with sustenance and hydration. Are there any other questions?"

"How are we supposed to go to the bathroom?" This question came from a female voice somewhere in the back of the room. A wave of murmurs affirming the concern rippled across the crowd.

"Immediately following this meeting, you will be given some fluids to drink that will help relieve your digestive systems of all excess bio-organic materials. In short, you will not need to go to the bathroom."

This explanation was followed by another ripple of noise from the crowd. However, this time Hunter thought he could pick up on a mix of undertones ranging from discontentment to crude humor. The speaker looked up at a clock on the wall and cleared his throat loudly.

"It seems that we are out of time and now everybody is dismissed to move on to the next stage of pre-launch preparations. Thank you and good luck." The man quickly exited the room and a door next to the risers opened. An armed guard of about six men entered the room.

The next six hours were completely filled with various pre-launch tasks. The fluids that they were given performed exactly as the man said they would. They were each fitted with new clothes and boots. Hunter had to scan his bracelet numerous times. He was sure that he was going to be discovered but each time the bracelet worked exactly as anticipated. Before Hunter knew it, he was standing next to April in an enormous underground bunker larger than any stadium that Hunter had ever seen. They waited in the back of a line of one hundred people that stood parallel to a long conveyor belt that contained their personal transport pods. Cade and Summer's families waited in line also. They all stood silently except for Summer's youngest brother Sam, who was clutching his mother's pant leg and whimpering lightly. The conveyor belt was extensive and carried exactly one hundred pods. Each one was clamped perpendicularly to the belt by a set of hydraulic, robotic arms. The pods were painted a dull white and they had glass viewing portals near the top end. Each one looked as though it had been fashioned to accommodate the tallest and/or widest person likely to be encapsulated. Small sets of stairs were placed in front of each pod. Hunter could see that in the distance the conveyor belt turned upward running vertically along a wall disappearing into the ceiling above. It looked as though they would be carried to the surface and probably to the space shuttle in their pods. Hunter could hardly believe what was about to happen. He took a deep, steadying breath and even as he did so, all the pods opened with a hiss like the sound of a hundred startled snakes.

One Detainment Center worker was assigned to every two pods. The worker that was designated for Hunter and April's pods came forward, taking April by the arm. "Step forward, Miss." He was a young man with shortly cut hair, dressed in the drab gray scrubs typical to all the workers in the Detainment Center. He carried a satchel over his right shoulder that hung down to his waist. "I'll help you get secured into your transport unit."

She whipped her head around to look at Hunter in

desperation. He stepped forward and took her free hand looking at the man. "Can I help too?"

The worker gave a short nod, "Sure."

They helped April up the stairs. She laid down in the pod and the worker buckled her into a five-point harness. He then pulled out a disinfecting wipe from the satchel that was draped over his shoulder. Using the wipe, he swabbed a small section of her forearm and inserted an IV with a hose that ran into the inner shell of the pod. He taped the IV to her arm and then pushed a few buttons on a control panel beside April's left leg. A clear fluid began to flow through the IV tube.

"Whatever you do, don't pull this IV out. If you do, you will probably die from dehydration long before you ever reach the moon. Good luck."

He stepped back, pushed a few buttons on the outer control panel and the pod door closed. Hunter climbed up the steps and stood staring into April's view portal. She looked terrified. Hunter sat down on the pod straddling it and brought his face close to the glass. April tried to say something to him, but not even the tiniest amount of sound penetrated the glass between them. He put his hand to his ear to let her know that he couldn't hear. Then he winked and stuck his tongue out. In response, she rolled her eyes and shook her head, allowing the slightest smile to touch the corners of her lips. When their eyes met again, he mouthed the words, with very exaggerated movements, "It will be okay," and then he gave her a thumbs-up. She nodded in response.

"Sir, please climb off the pod." The voice of the young man came from behind him and Hunter realized for the first time that he must look ridiculous sprawled out on top of the pod as he was. He looked over his shoulder to see that the Detainment Center worker was glancing back and forth along the conveyor belt looking very awkward. "Climbing on the transport unit is not allowed. Please get off now."

Hunter shimmied backwards off the pod until he found his footing and could walk down the stairs. He paused to watch Mrs. Taylor helping one of her children into a pod. Hunter could see the concern and fear that she had for her family and he felt again a strong sense of indignation and anger at the situation in which they found themselves, but before he could fuel those feelings into anything more than a few vague thoughts, his worker took him by the arm, quickly helping him into his own pod, securing his harness and IV. Hunter observed that the worker didn't give him the same counsel to avoid removing his IV. The door on his pod closed and as it did, all sound from the outside world stopped and he lay in complete silence. Hunter did not believe that he had ever been in a place that was so quiet in his entire life. The only sounds came from his own breathing, the thumping of his heart, and the occasional soft rustling from shifting his weight around.

He lay in his pod staring out the portal at the steel beams of the high ceiling. He breathed in and out slowly and deeply and he considered his situation. He was successful. His plan had worked, and he was leaving the planet with his friends. He took a moment, as he lay in silence, to consider the events of the last few weeks. Who was Ken and why had he allowed Hunter to sneak away? Why had he healed Hunter? For that matter, how had he healed him? He reviewed carefully all of the events of his life since the night in Millennium Park and then he began to think about his family. It seemed to him that his old life had ended so very long ago. In such a short time, the memories of his home and his past were beginning to assume an almost dream-like quality. In this moment, he began to feel true terror. He realized that his greatest fear was not of the unknown future which he faced, but that he might forget his past, that he might forget his family. This single and sudden realization filled him with inexplicable horror. His body shuddered uncontrollably. He squeezed his eyes tightly together and he focused on just breathing in and out. He conjured a memory of his family in his mind and focused on it. He tried to remember the details of their faces. He thought about their personalities. He would not forget. He would never forget, and he would come back for them. Someday . . . somehow . . . he would escape, and he would come back.

Suddenly his thoughts were interrupted as the pod was jerked into motion. The conveyor belt came to life and the rafters overhead began to roll by. The movement along the belt felt quick and spasmodic like riding an old roller coaster. He was jerked hard against his harness as the belt turned upward and for a moment, he caught a glimpse of April's pod right before it made the sharp turn that carried them toward the exit in the ceiling. He watched the wall go by in the distance and the workers growing smaller on the floor, and then everything went dark as the conveyor carried him out of the large room. They steadily gained speed and flashes of piping and metal trusses flew by in a blur. The conveyor moved through a series of quick turns. Sometimes his pod was upright, sometimes he was laying on his back and at other times he found himself hanging upside down. Finally, they broke the surface and light filled his vision. Though they had only been under-ground in the Detainment Center for roughly two weeks, he had forgotten how good it felt to have the sun on his face.

The conveyor belt was now turned perpendicular to the ground and it ran upward at a steep angle so that all of the pods were upright but angled to the ground and they formed a long procession running into the sky. Hunter climbed steadily. He was twenty feet off the ground, then forty, then sixty… When the ascent finally stopped, he found himself suspended hundreds of feet in the air. He leaned his head forward to look sideways from the view port and he could see that the conveyor belt and pods turned and flowed into an enormous rocket ship. He watched as the first pod was lifted from the belt by a robotic arm and placed into docking stations on the ship's fuselage. After the pod was secured deep inside the rocket, a second pod was placed over the first more towards the exterior and then both rotated counterclockwise like the cylinder on an old-style revolving pistol. Each time a pod was removed from the conveyor belt, Hunter was jerked forward closer to the rocket.

Hunter and April traveled in the last pods to be loaded onto the rocket. The robotic arm lifted Hunter's pod from the conveyor belt with surprising precision and care. He was placed in the inner compartment of the rocket facing outward. His eyes were still adjusting to the dimmer lighting inside the fuselage when April was placed immediately over Hunter with her pod facing inward. Hunter realized, with hope and surprise, that they had been loaded in such a manner that they were facing each other.

He found himself starting face to face with April, separated by less than a foot of air and glass.

April looked very frightened and disoriented and then her eyes met his. He couldn't help but smile and she couldn't help but smile back. It seemed strange that Hunter would be so excited about such a little thing, but he felt suddenly like he wasn't alone. April was going to make this trip with him. He had a friend and a traveling companion. Three weeks ago, he would have felt completely ridiculous and probably very embarrassed to stand and stare face to face with a girl for one minute let alone one week, but the site of her made him feel hope. She made him feel happy. He was beginning to be able to read her facial expressions, and he could see that she felt the same way. With very slow obvious movements, he mouthed the word, "Hello."

She mouthed back, "Hi, Lumphead."

He stuck his tongue out and crossed his eyes. She laughed. He laughed back and then everything went dark.

...

Ken watched from an observation deck as they loaded Hunter's pod into the shuttle. He was being shipped in tandem with that young lady. Her name was April Lines. Curious, he thought. He barely knew anything about this young man. The boy would probably end up dead in the mines of Olum or eaten by a Draaken, or even worse, he would learn how to live as a slave and become beaten down, bitter, and utterly worthless.

He watched as workers on the launch pad secured panels

over the fuselage. The OBs would have to leave their world in darkness. What a pity, he thought. It was such a beautiful day. Earth had the most pleasant sun of any planet he had ever seen. It was just the right distance away. He didn't particularly care for Florida, but it wasn't such a bad place to be in November. Perhaps it didn't matter that they would be surrounded by darkness as they left their planet. Most of them would lose consciousness from the g-forces exerted during the launch. By the time they awoke, their artificial lighting systems would have engaged.

He rubbed the stubble on his chin thoughtfully. He hated these launches. They represented the end of so many precious lives. Nonetheless, he would attend every single one that he could. In a way, all of this was his fault, and it was his responsibility to keep searching. He had to be so very careful. If he made the wrong choice, he might just destroy everything. 'That's what happens when you play God,' he said to himself. 'The problem is that you are just playing. You aren't very good at it, and you make too many mistakes. People all around you pay for those mistakes with their lives. If you aren't careful, you end up ruining the whole Universe and then what are you left with?' He mentally shrugged off his pessimism, tucked his hands into the pockets of his long trench coat and watched as the primitive, liquid-fueled rocket engines engaged and slowly lifted the great monolith into the air. 'Hunter,' he thought, 'I hope to see you again soon. I hope that you are the one that I have been looking for.'

9 LIFT OFF

Almost immediately after the panels were locked into position, Hunter felt the deep rolling shudder of the rocket engines as they came to life. At first, he could feel movement only as a slight increase in gravity that pulled him downward as the shuttle lifted slowly into the air, but the pull increased steadily at first and then exponentially. In a matter of seconds, their whole world was shaking violently, and the forces caused by acceleration pulled mercilessly downward. His pod rattled and jerked in response to the explosions that lifted them toward space, and the very air around him beat against his body. He thought that something must be going wrong. It simply could not be possible that the violence of this moment was part of any normal human experience. He had never imagined that pain could be caused by the simple act of movement, but he now felt like his whole body was going to be shaken to pieces. At the very instant when he felt like he could not last another moment, a second bank of rocket engines engaged and the g-forces that racked his body were doubled. Hunter screamed into the darkness and then he lost consciousness.

Hunter awoke to weightlessness and dim lighting. His vision returned slowly, and it was followed by a dull headache. He tried to blink through his blurry sight, and he struggled to remember where he was and what he had been doing. As his vision returned slowly, memories came back. He remembered the last few weeks of his life. He remembered the launch and the brutal g-forces. He moaned and shook his head as if that act could scatter the disconcerting memories before they had a chance to fully piece themselves together.

The first thing he saw was April's wonderful face behind two layers of glass. She was sleeping and lay perfectly still, held motionless by the absence of gravity and the natural posture of her body. Her breath condensed on the glass creating a brief damp haze that obscured the features of her chin and mouth before rapidly receding after each exhalation. He had nearly forgotten what her face looked like when she was not worried. She looked peaceful and innocent and beautiful. Her face looked like it did not belong in the world of fear and uncertainty of which their lives had now become a part. In the state he saw her now, Hunter felt like it would be impossible that she should awake to anything but a life where she could live without fear or hatred or pain. He wished, for her sake, that she could remain just as he saw her now.

The first signs of wakefulness that returned to April's face were the worry lines that creased her brow and wrinkled the corners of her eyes. Hunter sighed. What had he expected, for her to sleep forever while he stared on like some weird creeper? As her eyes fluttered open, he put on his best casual smile. She would probably feel pretty disoriented and it might help if the first thing she saw was him grinning back at her like an idiot. He watched as she struggled to focus her vision and was pleased to see that some of the worry and fear drained from her expression when she found his face.

"Hey there, sleeping beauty!" The sound of his voice was startling against the overwhelming silence. He knew that she would not be able to hear him from her pod.

Her face took on a quizzical expression and she mouthed, "What?"

He considered for a moment and decided that he did not want her to know that he had just called her sleeping beauty and so with exaggerated movements he mouthed the words, "Good morning!"

She smiled and exaggerated back the words, "Hey, Lumphead!"

He laughed out loud and watched her smile broaden. The jovial moment faded into an awkward silence where neither of them knew what to mouth.

"Let's play a game," he tried. She watched his mouth carefully and returned his sentence with a confused look. She put her hand to an ear, and he tried again more slowly, "Let's . . . play . . . a . . . game."

She smiled in recognition and responded, "O . . . K . . ."

"Funny faces," he mouthed. With considerable effort, Hunter managed to convey the idea that they would play a game of making faces at each other to see who could be the most ridiculous. It took almost an hour to explain the rules and then the game lasted all of about ten minutes. They decided unanimously that Hunter was the winner, though he was really impressed by April's effort. She had put up a respectable showing.

Their first day in space was filled with a lot of awkward moments where all they could do was stare at each other. They noticed that the lighting in their pods increased and faded to simulate the passage of light during a normal day. At least, Hunter thought, they would be able to keep track of how much time they spent in space, but it seemed to him that the days and nights spent in the pod were longer than Earth days and nights and it felt like they were getting longer every day. He shrugged it off and figured that life just felt slower when you had nothing to do. Hunter watched on the first night in space as April's face faded in the dimming light. When there was barely enough light to see, she mouthed the words, "Thank you."

"Good night," he responded. Then everything went dark and he hoped against all his fears that the lights would turn on again in the morning. He stayed awake for a long time after the lights went out.

Hunter woke up to the dim light of an artificial dawn and the dull ache of hunger pains. He looked at the IV that was plugged into his left arm and took a small amount of comfort in the slow and steady flow of clear liquid that moved through the tube. At least, he thought, I won't die from starvation. I'll probably just go crazy from it. April's eyes fluttered open about fifteen minutes later.

They spent most of day two developing their lip-reading skills. During an awkward silence when neither of them could think of anything to say Hunter came up with some very clever tricks that he could perform with his own spit in zero gravity. April rolled her eyes in disgust, but she also couldn't help but smile. They had two arguments that resulted from misinterpreted words and Hunter managed to successfully execute three knock-knock jokes. It took almost twenty minutes to tell each joke. By the end of the day, they could have very slow conversations. Hunter found that if he watched her lips very closely, he understood when to interject and make comments. April was by far the more talented at reading lips. Apparently, she and Summer had practiced quite a bit during classes at school. For Hunter, it really stretched the limits of his concentration. By the end of the day he wasn't sure which was worse, his hunger pains or the total mental exhaustion and mild headache from concentrating on April's lips all day long.

Hunter slept in until his pod was too bright for him to remain unconscious. He woke to find April smiling at him. He was getting good at reading lips, but now he wished he could read minds. She winked and mouthed, "Good morning." He yawned and stretched and then they just stared at each other for a while. He was surprised to find that he didn't feel awkward. He took the time to observe the finer features of her face. He noticed, for the first time, a few small freckles along her chin line and cheeks. When he looked her directly in the eyes, he saw subtle movements in the direction of her vision and realized that she was studying his face also. Suddenly, he felt self-conscious and could not help but smile.

"What?" she mouthed.

"I noticed that you were looking at me," Hunter responded.

To anyone not trapped staring at another person for days at a time, this might have seemed like a ridiculous thing to say, but April caught his meaning. "I couldn't help but notice that you have nice features," she smiled and blushed.

"I'm okay with you inspecting me," he said, "so long as I can go on inspecting you."

She nodded shyly and so they went on looking at each other for most of the morning. It was very peaceful, but by midday the gnawing hunger was maddening, and they took to telling each other children's stories to help them forget about their discomfort. Hunter made an attempt at Goldilocks and the Three Bears. April followed with a spectacular telling of The Three Little Pigs. Then Hunter recounted epic moments from soccer games. April told funny stories about her family and so they went on back and forth for the rest of the day. Hunter almost forgot that his stomach felt like somebody had cut the bottom out of it. When the artificial twilight finally came upon them Hunter was staring intently at April's lips while she recounted a story from her sixth-grade science class about the first time she had ever dissected a frog. Absently, Hunter wondered if April was speaking out loud or if she was just mouthing the story. He had taken to just moving his mouth in word patterns to speak with her, but she looked so natural that he felt like he could almost hear or maybe see her voice in the air. He strained ever harder to see the movements of her mouth as the light in their pods steadily disappeared. Moments before their pods would become too dark to communicate, she abruptly ended her story and mouthed the words, "Good night. I love you."

His eyes went wide. His heart jumped into his throat and then everything went dark. Sleep came very slowly that night as Hunter turned the image of April's lips forming those words over and over again in his mind. Had she really said what he thought she had said? Did she mean it the way he wanted her to mean it? He stared into the darkness for a long time and couldn't help but wonder if maybe she was awake also looking into the blackness in his direction wondering whether or not he might still be awake. He smiled at that thought. He fell asleep wishing that morning could come sooner.

It was still dark in Hunter's pod when the exterior panels of the shuttle ejected, flinging outward and allowing the light of the sun to flood into the pod compartments. Hunter awoke with a jerk, startled by the explosion of the panel ejection charges. The first thing he saw was the confused and scared look on April's face as she tried to come awake and make sense of the noise and shaking that had pulled her abruptly from her sleep. The shuttle shuddered and rumbled. April's vision seemed to clear, and they made eye contact. She opened her mouth and began to say something, but Hunter didn't have time to make sense of even the first syllable before his pod was jerked violently in a quarter turn rotation and then jettisoned into space.

Hunter spun end over end drifting through space. The sun was brilliant and blinded him each time it flew through the viewport of his pod. In less than a minute, he began to feel dizzy and sick. He closed his eyes and the nausea subsided.

Unable to see, he found that he couldn't even feel the rotation of the pod. The only indication that he was spinning through space came from the brightening and darkening of the pod interior that he perceived through his closed eyelids. He focused on breathing steadily and on keeping calm though his heart raced inside his chest. He heard the noise of small thrusters engaging and felt the forces of inertia as his pod righted itself, changed directions and accelerated. Shortly, the thrusters disengaged, and all sense of motion stopped as his speed through space became constant. So he waited, which seemed to be a common theme in his new life... waiting... and trying to not to freak out.

He drifted through space for hours staring out at the stars. He had never felt so alone in his entire life. The last three days with April felt like they went by fast compared to this. The absence of her face staring back at him through the viewport almost made him sick. He couldn't help but wonder if he would ever see her again and if he did, then on what terms. The images of what their new lives as slaves would be like haunted him in the lonely silence. All he could imagine came from his limited understanding of the history of slavery on Earth. Would they be beaten? Would they have to wear chains? What would their jobs be? Hunter couldn't imagine why an advanced alien civilization needed slaves. Would they have to work in mines or on farms? Did the aliens have some sort of labor that was so horrible that they refused to do it themselves?

Abruptly, a dark shadow came into his viewport and he realized that he was entering some sort of vessel. The thrusters engaged again, and he felt the pod slowing until it drifted lethargically across an enormous dark hangar. His eyes adjusted to the blackness and he began to perceive other shapes that floated in the darkness, which he realized were pods, like his own. The thought occurred to him that somewhere April floated in that darkness. He hoped she was okay. He hoped that she wasn't too frightened. All of a sudden, he felt very glad that neither of them was afraid of the dark. They would have gone mad these last three days. He realized that he was also glad that neither of them was claustrophobic. Then suddenly he chuckled to himself as he wondered whether or not science had any sort of official designation for a fear of being taken into slavery by an alien race. He knew he shouldn't be laughing, but what else could he do? His whole life was now out of his control. The only choice he had left was to decide how to feel, and at that very moment he chose to feel amused. So he chuckled to himself and he waited.

After nearly an hour of floating in the hangar, it began to grow darker, and Hunter realized that the door that he had drifted through was closing. In moments, the room was completely dark until lights on the ceiling of the hangar engaged and Hunter felt the pod begin to descend in the direction that seemed to be downward. He bumped softly against the hanger floor, bounced once and then settled lightly. No sooner had his pod settled, than he began to feel a pressing weight settle over his whole body. It steadily increased until he was having problems breathing and he realized abruptly that he was experiencing the effects of gravity returning. His pod lay on the floor of the hangar for about fifteen minutes.

Hunter heard a low clunking noise that was followed by the hissing release of pneumatic pressure, and the lid of his pod swung open. He found himself staring up into the reflective face shield of a very tall humanoid soldier. The figure leaned down, unfastened Hunter's harness, removed his IV and grabbed him by the shoulders. The soldier's hands were enormous, and his grip was crushing. He lifted Hunter from the pod and shoved him in the direction of a row of 20 large, rectangular, metal containers. He stumbled forward, tripping over his feet and almost falling. His legs felt so weak that he could barely walk, and his head started to swim from standing up so quickly. His heart was pounding hard inside his chest and his whole body felt like it had atrophied. He hadn't even considered the possibility that a few days without gravity could cause his body to grow so weak. It was all that he could do to stumble forward and not fall flat on his face.

As he walked toward the steel containers, he began to look around. The hangar in which their pods had landed was ginormous. They settled haphazardly around the massive room and people were being pulled from the pods and pushed in the direction of the transport containers. Tall alien soldiers moved amongst the humans, barking commands in an unfamiliar language and herding them like stumbling, lethargic animals. Hunter recognized the sleek futuristic uniforms from the raid at Millennium Park. On one hand, Hunter was glad he hadn't been taken as a slave to the Cravos. On the other hand, he hadn't liked the look in the eyes of the Leeber soldier from the park, and he was pretty sure that life as a slave to these people wasn't going to be very pleasant either. He already felt like they were being treated more as animals than sentient beings.

As the humans shuffled forward, Hunter began to scan each face looking for his friends. He found Cade first who gave him a tired nod. Then he found Cade's mom and then

April who was walking with Summer's youngest brother Sam huddled against her. She gave him a very weak and worried grimace when they met eyes. He kept scanning the crowd, but he was having trouble finding everyone. He worried that maybe some of them hadn't made it. They all looked scared and strained. The lack of gravity had not been good for any of them.

Steadily they were herded in the direction of the steel containers. Hunter recognized that these metal boxes were probably going to be their latest mode of transportation. He wondered how long they were going to be in them, and he hoped that they came with lights, food and bathrooms. Two of the containers were open at the ends with ramps that allowed access. The aliens pushed them towards these two boxes. Hunter realized suddenly that there were a hundred people in their group. That meant that roughly fifty would be placed in each container. He did not want to find himself separated from his friends, but the crowd was beginning to close in around him and it was becoming harder to find his friends in the mix of pressing bodies. He started to panic when suddenly someone grabbed his arm and began to drag him sideways through the crowd. He looked up to find that Summer's dad, Mr. Dees, was pulling him through the crowd to where their families had grouped themselves together. Mrs. Dees and Mrs. Taylor were counting heads and it looked to Hunter like they all survived the pod ride-o-death that had brought them this far. They moved forward as a group, shuffling slowly and placing themselves near the end of the mass of bodies.

Together they entered the second container, walking up the lowered ramp. The entrance was closed by raising the ramp almost immediately after they were all inside. They experienced a moment of total darkness that was followed by the activation of dim lighting placed along the upper corners of the transport container. Now that he was inside, Hunter could see that the walls were lined with 3-deep bunk beds. The floor was bare metal, as were the ceiling and walls. A very large screen, like a computer monitor, was set into the far wall. Two doors were placed on either side. The screen activated and Hunter found himself staring at the tall muscular figure of an alien soldier. Instantly, he recognized the cold, chiseled features of the soldier he had seen in Millennium Park.

"Humans," he spoke with a rich and unfamiliar accent, "I am General Harn. You have been taken as servants of the people of Actaeon 9, given up by your own race as a price for our protection. Today you are made our slaves. You are made our property. We will not pretend to be benevolent in our relationship with you. You are inferior both mentally and physically to the race of Actaeon. To live and die and breed in our service and in the furthering of our causes will give your lives greater purpose than you have before known. Your species has done you a great honor by giving you to us. You will learn what is your place among us and you will wear out your lives in our service. Resistance and rebellion are not tolerated. You may decide to learn this now or you may learn by resisting and being punished. It does not matter, though; you will learn obedience and compliance, or we will dispose of you. That is all."

The video had seemed pre-recorded, kind of like a welcome-to-slavery orientation video. The General's manner was frank and cold. Hunter did not like the casually dispassionate tone in which he had said he would dispose of them. He was no judge of alien character, but Hunter was pretty sure that this guy was a total jerk.

The screen activated again. This time, they were addressed by a slender female figure with the same accent in a high pitch. "My name is Eesha. I will provide you with information that is important to your comfort and safety during travel and that will help you assimilate into your new life as a servant to the people of Actaeon. First, human style bathrooms have been provided on the left and right sides of this monitor."

She gestured and Hunter suddenly felt like he was watching an airline stewardess. He snickered to himself and shook his head. All of this was too much to take in.

"Food and water are dispensed from the square recesses near each bed. Each of you will receive a ration of three cups of water and 4 hishop biscuits per day."

Did she say hiccup biscuits?

"Hishop biscuits each contain eight hundred calories and all the vitamins and minerals necessary to sustain human life."

Hunter didn't think that hiccup biscuits sounded very tasty, but then again, he was really hungry and probably would have enjoyed eating dirt had she offered. He imagined that maybe they would taste like granola bars. That would be nice.

"You will spend 95 Earth days in your transport container. This is equivalent to roughly 49 days on Actaeon 9. The lighting in this container, just like the lighting in your pods, is designed to simulate the lighting and length of days at Actaeon 9's capitol city where you will arrive in 49 Actaeon days. Gravity on Actaeon 9 is 1.5 times that of gravity on Earth. Over the next 37 days, gravity in your container will be steadily increased to simulate the actual gravity that you will experience once on the surface of Actaeon 9. You are currently experiencing gravity that is 1.2 times that of Earth's gravity. You will notice that each bed has been fitted with manually engaged belt restraints. These restraints serve the purpose of securing transport occupants during times of anticipated movement or shaking of your container. Your transport container will occasionally be moved using cranes or other such devices. During these times, it is highly recommended that you utilize the belt restraint to ensure that neither you nor your children are damaged during transport. Flashing yellow lights will engage approximately fifteen Earth minutes prior to anticipated situations during which you will need to be restrained. Thank you for your cooperation."

The alien lady disappeared, and Hunter heard hissing sounds followed by a series of clunking noises. He looked over at one of the square-shaped food cavities that was located near each bed. A small, square, tan-colored hishop biscuit lay in the bottom of the cavity. Breakfast was served.

10 ACTAEON 9

For 95 Earth days or 49 Actaeon days they lived in a metal box. Most days in the transport container were very uneventful. They ate, they slept, and they waited. Periodically they were warned that they needed to secure themselves in their beds and so they did. Hunter and April practiced reading each other's lips as a game. The container in which they were transported was not uncomfortable. At least they had bathrooms and food, though the term 'food' had to be applied pretty liberally to include the dry tasteless biscuits that they were given.

They spent most of the 49th day secured in their beds while their transport unit was jostled from one location to another. The constant jerky motion was enough to make Hunter nauseous from motion sickness. Shortly after the first alarm sounded for them to secure themselves, erratic g-forces let them know that they were entering the atmosphere of a planet, which was followed by violent shaking. It reminded Hunter of his experience in the pod as they left Earth, though not as bad. He couldn't help but feel grateful for whatever dampening technology the

Leeber used to control g-forces during their transition from space to the planet. After their apparent landing on the planet, their transport container was moved around numerous times over the course of the day until finally all movement stopped, and they sat waiting in nervous anticipation for many hours.

After the exhaustingly long wait, a low steady alarm began to ring inside their container. It continued for about five minutes until the hissing release of pneumatic pressure sounded abruptly. The hissing was followed by metal clanking noises and then the transport unit door folded down, offering a walkway to the ground and giving them their first view of Actaeon 9. It was nighttime, and if the artificial cycle of days experienced in the transport unit was representative to actual time on Actaeon 9, then it was sometime close to the twenty-seventh hour.

It was raining heavily. Somehow this surprised Hunter. Rain felt familiar, and he hadn't expected anything to be familiar. The sky, as far as could be seen, was textured with massive charcoal gray clouds with underbellies lit by flashes of lightning that stayed high in the atmosphere. Low waves of rolling thunder shook the air and a light wind slanted the rain as it poured down in heavy sheets.

Their transport unit had been deposited on a steel landing platform that was roughly the size of a football field and suspended hundreds of feet in the air. Despite the dizzying height of the platform, the dark silhouettes of many other structures and enormous trees rose up around them to create an astounding and breathtaking night skyline.

The singular experience of stepping onto a new world for the first time, combined with the spectacular beauty of the scene that was laid out before him would create a high definition memory in Hunter's mind that would stay with him for the rest of his life. He felt like he had never seen anything beautiful before this moment and that if he had ever used the word 'beautiful' to describe something, it had been a gross misinterpretation of the meaning of beauty.

He tried to relate what he saw to things he knew from Earth. The trees might have been described as giant cottonwoods like those found along riverbanks in Arizona but they must have been hundreds of times larger and he could only see them as silhouettes. The platform on which their transport unit had been deposited might have been described as a shiny aircraft carrier deck. The buildings were similar to skyscrapers, except each one looked as if it had been artistically sculpted to compliment the skyline. Lights from windows in the buildings sparkled through the rain. Aircraft lights moved across the sky like fireflies. From the landing platform, they could only see a very small portion of the City of Aernos, but everything they could see looked to have been made to appear beautiful, and every small detail had been created to add to that beauty. Even the clouds in the sky, the thunder, the rain and the wind were elements painted into the scene by a master artist to add majesty and power.

Hunter forgot for a moment that he had been traded into slavery. April moved up next to him and slid her hand into his and they stood gaping at this beautiful alien landscape that would be their prison. In that instant, they were awed, and they were terrified.

Their moment of awe was interrupted by a loud and low-pitched clank that was followed by the whirring of what could have been an electric motor. Their transport unit began to tip, and Hunter realized that they were being dumped out into the rain. He felt as if they were being herded like animals and their transport unit suddenly gave him the impression of a space-aged cattle-hauling truck. He had seen plenty of those in Arizona, and if you hitched any of these 'transport units' to the back of a semi-truck it would serve perfectly for hauling cows.

As the slope of the transport unit floor increased, Hunter reconciled himself to the inevitability that they were all going to get very wet. He gave April's hand an encouraging squeeze, pulled her to his side wrapping an arm around her shoulders, and led her down the ramp and into the rain.

It was bitter cold. Had Hunter not been so enthralled with the scenery he might have noticed the chill in the air the moment the transport unit door opened. Now that he was in the rain though, he could not ignore the fact that it was very, very cold. The rain poured down so heavily that both he and April were almost completely soaked by the time they reached the end of the ramp.

He held April tightly trying and failing to shelter her from the sheets of pouring rain. As they stepped off the end of the ramp, they turned to see the other members of their transport unit following them down. Hunter could see that the unit was continuing to tilt and was passing through a nearly 45-degree angle. The last member of their group was just stepping out of the unit before the increasing slope would have dumped them out onto the ramp.

A frantic voice sounded out over the rain and Hunter began to look around. Dozens of transport units had been placed in lines along the suspended platform. They were each in various stages of unloading their human cargo. From the end of the ramp, he could see into the nearest neighboring container where a middle-aged lady was backing away from the ramp and moving deeper into the increasingly tilting cargo unit. A man who might have been her husband tried to coax her forward. Others from their container had paused halfway down the ramp turning to watch the scene. She shook her head frantically yelling, "No" over and over again. As the container tilted more and more, it became obvious that she would not keep her footing for much longer.

Even as the thought occurred to Hunter, the woman slipped. She fell to her back and slid rapidly toward the container exit, bowling into the man who had been trying to coax her onto the ramp. He fell forward over the woman and then both of them rolled off the edge of the ramp. Hunter hadn't noticed until that moment that the topmost part of the ramp must have been 8 feet above the steel platform. He winced as he watched them fall over the edge, landing in a tangled heap on the steel ground. He heard the sound of bones breaking over the rain and uncomfortable shivers ran up his spine.

Hunter reflexively began to move toward the man and woman when he caught sight of a soldier approaching from between the containers. The tall alien man approached quickly in long purposeful strides. He knelt down inspecting them and then with a gesture that was effortless he grabbed the man by an ankle, rose to his feet, and flung him off the platform. The man pinwheeled through the air like a rag doll. Then the soldier took one casual step and kicked the woman in her midsection sending her flying from the platform as well. Hunter heard their screams as they disappeared into the darkness. He stood helpless and paralyzed. He could not believe that he had just seen human life discarded with as little regard as throwing away a broken kitchen appliance. Before Hunter could regain his capacity to think, the soldier strode away back between the containers.

Hunter was stunned and shaking. He looked down to find April clinging to his arm, her eyes wide with horror. He looked back at the now empty spot where the couple had fallen and was sick to his stomach. Their lives belonged to unknown captors and they were valued like animals. They would only be kept alive so long as they were useful. Hunter couldn't feel the cold or the rain anymore. He was in shock and everything around him suddenly felt sinister, dark, and foreboding. Had he just thought that this world was   beautiful?

11 SLAVES

They stood out in the rain for most of the night and tried to find shelter around the transport units, which had closed automatically after dumping them onto the steel platform. They huddled together as groups trying to stay warm, but after fifteen minutes in the rain Hunter felt like he had been frozen clear to his bones. After many hours of exposure, he was sure that he was going to die. He shivered uncontrollably, seated on the ground, pressed between April, Cade and others in a huddled mass of bodies. April's shivering was even worse than Hunter's and neither of them had spoken so much as a single word for hours. Despite his hatred for and fear of the aliens he was desperately anxious for his captors to come and take them out of the cold and the rain. He wondered what had happened to the soldier that had killed the elderly couple. Surely someone would come and get them soon.

It was only as the first rays of sunlight began to crest the horizon that a ship landed on the platform. The rain had diminished to little more than a drizzle, but everybody was soaking wet from the night's downpour. Hunter's face was tucked between his knees, which he had pulled to his chest in an attempt to stay warmer. Stiffly, he raised his head in response to the roaring engines of the ship. He was having a hard time thinking straight and so he was only vaguely aware of the soldiers that filed out of the vessel.

They moved quickly across the platform and began marshaling the humans to their feet. Hunter was grabbed by an arm and hoisted to a standing position. His legs felt weak and he stumbled to get control of his balance. Now that he was standing, he noticed that several ships had landed on the platform. They were constructed of smooth silvery metal and stood on long runners that suspended them about 15 feet off the ground. The underbelly of each vessel carried a large square cage made from dense metal grating with circular holes. Each cage had one side that was hinged and lowered to the ground to allow access and form a ramp that sloped upward into the steel basket.

With very little encouragement from the soldiers, people began to shuffle toward the ramps. Like animals, they didn't have to be told what to do. They understood where their captors wanted them to go and so they moved mindlessly in that direction. Hunter wanted very badly to resist but he was so cold and tired that even shuffling slowly along with the crowd required more effort than he cared to muster. He wondered if this was what it felt like to be beaten into submission. If so, then he thought that he had given up far too easily. In the movies, one might expect the hero to resist his enemies with his final dying breath, but Hunter didn't even know how to resist. He could try throwing himself off the platform just to spite his captors, but that seemed like a very stupid plan, and so for the moment he just continued to shuffle along, and he told himself that he would search for better opportunities.

Somehow Cade and Summer's parents managed to subtly control the direction in which they all shuffled, keeping their group together and ensuring that they were all locked into the same cage. No sooner was their cage full than the soldiers quickly closed the hinged ramp and their vessel began to lift off the ground. With stomach lurching speed the ship gained altitude rapidly, soaring high above the treetops and skyscrapers. The wind whipped Hunter's wet clothes and whistled in his ears. This might have made the cold unbearable, but it was tempered by the rising Sun and it actually seemed to help dry his clothing. Hunter was pressed against the wall of the cage and he gazed out over the enormous city that spread beneath them. The sun rose to his left and reflected off the underbellies of clouds left behind by the night's storm. Again, he was struck by a sense of beauty and wonder at this new planet and his feelings waged war inside of him. This planet was not his home. It would never be his home, and no matter how beautiful it looked on the outside, this place was terrible. The people that inhabited this place were terrible. They robbed him of his true home and family, and he hated them for it. In the isolation of his own thoughts, flying high above the City of Aernos, his feelings came together, and he promised himself that he would not die on this planet. He would see his family again. Somehow, he would get out of this.

After about a half hour of flying above what seemed to be a nearly endless sea of sleek skyscrapers and massive trees that fought for control of the skyline, Hunter noticed a change in the texture of the City's landscape and architecture. Trees became shorter and sparser. The architecture responded in kind as buildings became smaller and more spread out. They were colorful and artistically crafted using a lot of what looked like glass in their exterior construction. Hunter could now make out city streets with pedestrian traffic far beneath them. As far as he could tell, there was very little, if any, vehicle traffic moving through the streets.

Shortly after flying over this more urban section of town, their aircraft began to descend. In a matter of minutes, they were skimming just sixty or maybe seventy feet above the ground. When they had flown high in the air, it appeared to Hunter that they were moving slowly, but now that they flew close to the ground, buildings and people seemed to flow by in a steady, rapidly paced blur. It almost made Hunter nauseous and gave him a headache to try to keep an eye on the scenery as it streamed by.

They approached a broad, oddly shaped building that Hunter might have described as a football stadium. Their craft banked sharply backwards, stopping quickly and coming to hover above the large structure. Like a football stadium, the building was open in the middle exposing a wide, dirt courtyard. The ship descended steadily throwing up clouds of dust, and Hunter noticed that the other vessels containing humans were landing in the courtyard as well. In a matter of moments, their cage was thrown open and they were being pushed across the open yard and into the mouth of a dark, expansive hallway that sloped downward into the ground. They moved along the poorly lighted hallway, pushed by soldiers around various turns until their path opened into a large room with marginally better lighting. Here they were separated, men from women. Cade and Summer's parents seemed almost prepared for this as they quickly passed their little girls to the moms and the boys went with the men. Hunter managed to give April's hand a quick squeeze as they were pulled away from each other.

Without delay, the men were pushed through one door and the women another. They walked down a short hallway and found themselves waiting in a damp, empty and poorly lit room. It smelled to Hunter like old, burnt meat. The floor was rough and sloped unevenly. In the corner of the room sat a low metal table. The walls were bare and dark. The ceiling was about eight feet tall and much lower than others that Hunter had seen so far. Two doors, opposite each other, provided access to the room. After being herded into the room, the doors were closed and locked and here they were left to wait. This might have provided a good opportunity for them to talk amongst themselves, but everybody was far too tired to talk. They found spots on the floor and against the wall to sit and rest. Hunter sat next to Cade. They exchanged worried looks as they sat in silence but all they could do was wait. After about fifteen minutes, Hunter curled up on the hard floor and fell fast asleep.

He was awakened about an hour later when one of the doors swung open and a regiment of more than 20 soldiers holding long sleek batons entered the room. Quickly they forced the men to their feet pushing them into a mass against the wall opposite the metal table. A young man, in perhaps his early twenties, was pulled from the group at random and pushed toward the table. An older gentleman called out after the young man but was silenced by the quick strike of a soldier's baton. The baton made a sharp cracking noise and released a brief flash of light when it made contact with the man's shoulder. He crumpled to the ground instantly and lay shaking spasmodically.

Three of the aliens grabbed the boy, dragging him to kneel in front of the steel table. Two of them held his arms while the third pressed and held his head sideways against the table exposing his left cheek. A fourth soldier stepped forward holding a short rod with a flat, perpendicular head that was molded to form an intricate design. In horror, Hunter realized that he was holding a branding iron. The soldier with the rod used his left hand to stretch the skin on the young man's cheek so that it was flat. He held the rod face down at head height in his right hand and Hunter thought he saw the soldier press a button along the length of the shaft with his thumb. Within moments, the head of the branding iron began to glow bright red and he lowered it toward the boy's exposed cheek.

Suddenly, distant but clear, blood chilling screams could be heard coming from outside the door. The screams startled Hunter and rattled his nerves. He was still groggy from being drug out of sleep and he had been engrossed with trying to make sense of the scene that was unfolding before him. He looked at Cade and both of them recognized with shock that they were hearing the screams of a young lady. Dread and sickness came over Hunter as he realized that they were branding the women in a nearby room. In the very moment that this thought occurred, the young man began to scream, and Hunter's gaze was jerked away from Cade to watch in horror as the boy kicked, thrashed and screamed beneath his captor's grasp. Hunter felt sick and his nerves felt unhinged. He wanted to turn away, but all he could do was stand and watch as they tortured the boy. The smell of burning flesh began to fill the air and from somewhere behind him, Hunter heard retching.

As the metal rod was removed from the boy's cheek, his frantic yelling subsided quickly into low whimpers and his body went limp. The two soldiers that had pinned his arms to the table lifted him and began to drag him from the room. His head drooped, his feet dragged behind him, and his chest heaved deep exhausted breaths. Hunter could clearly see the brand on the boy's cheek. Though he could neither speak nor read a single word of the Actaeon language, he knew what the mark meant. It meant that they were slaves. As Hunter watched them half carry, half drag him from the room, his initial shock began to subside. Fear gave way to consternation and in a moment, his consternation turned to pure hatred and anger. His initial confusion subsided, and determination blossomed in his mind. Ever since his pathetic attempt at resistance in the loading docks, he had allowed himself to be herded about like a mindless animal. He was done being pushed around.

Two more soldiers stepped forward preparing to grab another human. The whole crowd of men pulled away bunching against the wall except for Hunter. He stepped forward. Animals ran from things they feared. Only a thinking being could recognize certain events as inevitable and choose to face them bravely. Hunter could choose courage over cowardice. He could not escape his fate. The only real choice that Hunter had was how to face this. The soldiers paused for a moment, caught off guard by his unexpected behavior. Hunter took advantage of their hesitation and walked between them. He approached the metal table and knelt, grabbing the table legs and placing his right cheek flat against the cold, metal surface.

He felt the presence of the tall alien with the branding iron step up next to him and he could swear that he heard the man chuckle. He closed his eyes and focused on breathing steadily. A massive hand set itself against his cheek and spread his skin flat between the outward pressure of thumb and forefinger. He could feel the warmth of the iron as it approached his skin and then his cheek was on fire. His body convulsed and he wanted to tear away from the pain, but he gripped the table legs fiercely holding himself steady. The soldier that branded his face seemed to be holding the iron to his cheek for much longer than he had with the previous boy. Tears ran from Hunter's eyes and he breathed violently through clenched teeth. He would not give up. He would not try to pull away.

When the iron was removed and he felt the soldier's hand begin to lift from his face, Hunter spun, slapping the alien's hand away and jumped to his feet. His actions again took his captors by surprise and they paused, waiting to see what he would do. Hunter turned to face the tall soldier that held the branding rod and he screamed in defiance. Then he spat on the alien's face mask and with a motion that was so quick and smooth that Hunter could not even recall what happened later, the soldier backhanded him. Hunter was lifted off his feet and thrown against the wall. His head slammed backwards hard and he fell to the ground face first and unconscious.

12 HEADACHE

Hunter awoke a short time later with a brutal headache. He found himself stripped naked and lying on a cold metal floor. He crawled to a kneeling position and straightened up, looking blearily about. The room seemed to be made entirely from metal, and the floor sloped gently toward a drain hole in its center. Cade was sitting next to him. He had also been stripped. He sat with his back against a wall and his knees pulled to his chest. A few other men were spread around the room. Each man had been stripped of all clothing and bore a brand on his face. Hunter sat back against the wall next to Cade. Tears ran down Cade's face and Hunter could see clearly now the brand that had been burned into his cheek. The mark was about the size of a silver dollar. It was a symbol or perhaps two symbols made from a single flowing line like English cursive. The inner portion of the line was black from the burning and outlined by red inflamed skin. Hunter reached up and gingerly touched his own left cheek and as he did so, he realized that his right cheek hurt also. He had been branded on both sides of his face. He raised his two hands tracing the brands and wincing from the pain. After a moment, he turned his attention back to Cade. His red hair was a crazy mess. He was dirty. He looked completely exhausted and miserable. He found that as he looked at his friend, Hunter's own problems felt lighter. His ineffectual act of resistance had given him courage and he wanted to share some of that courage with Cade. Hunter shuffled a little closer.

"Well, now that really sucked," Hunter said with a sarcastic smile and half a chuckle. Cade responded with a sharp whimpering laugh and Hunter tried again, "Are you ready to escape?"

This time Cade genuinely chuckled. Hunter continued, "I mean, I have watched a lot of sci-fi movies and I think that really should be our next move. Don't you?"

Cade gave him a sideways look and then wiped his nose. "Sure. We just need to steal a spaceship and fly home. Right?"

"I think that's the general idea," Hunter began, "but we should steal some clothing first, and at this rate, I think I am probably just going to get myself killed."

"Yeah, that was pretty stupid," Cade responded, "but I guess that it was also pretty epic. I think that you are one hundred percent crazy, man." He actually smiled a little.

"Yeah," Hunter began, "and here we always thought that

you were the crazy one. Turns out that I just needed to be abducted by aliens to bring out my true nature." An awkward silence followed until Hunter thought to ask, "What happened after I got slapped stupid."

Cade grinned, "Well, we all stood around shocked, and nobody really knew what to do. Even the aliens were all like... Whoa. Then while everyone was distracted, that guy over there," Cade indicated with a nod, "walked up and knelt down in front of the table just like you did."

The man that Cade had indicated sat cross-legged in the corner. He might have been fifty years old. He was thin with brown hair and wrinkles in the corners of his eyes. His head was tipped back against the wall and his eyes were closed. Hunter could see clearly the inflamed brand on his left cheek.

"They branded him and then they gave you a second brand on your other cheek. I don't know what those marks on your face mean, man, but that second one can't be a good thing." He hesitated, looking at Hunter's brands and then he continued his story. "After that, everybody just started forming a line and we went in turn. We put the smallest kids in the back of the line with their Dads. I was the fourth one to go after you. Nobody wanted to scream or cry after you did your 'Mr. Super Cool Rebel' thing. We could still hear the women screaming from the hall, but it didn't feel so crazy after we got all organized and stuff. Seeing as how you were like passed out you probably don't remember the trip here. We are pretty far from the branding room and I don't think we could hear if somebody was screaming. At least we can't hear the girls from in here. The hardest part was imagining my mom being held down and branded." Cade choked up at this remark and then shook it off. "After they brought me in, I flopped myself down next to your drooling and unconscious body. You were breathing, so I figured you weren't dead," He looked at Hunter, "but honestly, your face is looking pretty beat up, man."

The door opened, interrupting Cade, and two soldiers came in with a young man held up by both arms and stumbling between them. He was probably in his early twenties with straggly blond hair. They stood him in the middle of the room and cut his clothing off with scissor-like instruments. They tossed his clothing into a pile in the corner with everybody else's, and then left the room closing the door behind them. The young man stood in the middle of the room for a moment looking around dazed before he staggered off to the side to find a section of wall where he could sit.

Hunter sighed, "Where's your dad?" he asked.

Cade shrugged, "He went to the back of the line to help Summer's dad with his kids."

Hunter laid his head back against the wall and sighed, "Yeah, this definitely sucks . . . I'm going to take a nap."

"A nap?" Cade asked. "How do you do that, man? You're naked, sitting on a metal floor, with your back against a hard metal wall, and you are going to take a nap? You're nuts."

Hunter yawned, "It's easy. Watch. You may even want to take some notes. I mean . . . this takes real skill that only comes from many long years of sleeping through math class . . ." Hunter paused, "Besides, I've got a splitting headache and I am trying to not think too hard about what they are doing to the girls." He closed his eyes, but it took a long while before he could escape consciousness. He tried desperately to fight off images of April being branded. Was that her that they had heard screaming? Could he even recognize her screams? It was nearly a half hour before he began to doze fitfully.

Hunter awoke to the sound of a whimpering child. Summer and Cade's dads sat against the wall with Summer's little brothers huddled together crying. The room was now almost completely full of men sitting against the walls and a few had found places in the middle of the room. Each bore the same slave mark on his left cheek. None of them had been marked with a second brand like Hunter. He hadn't noticed how many children had been in their group, but now that they were all whimpering and crying, he could see that almost a third of those in the room looked younger than 10 years old. He sat forward and looked at Cade, "Did I miss anything?"

"Not really. I think they're all done. At least, this looks like everybody that was with us. It's been about 10 minutes since they brought in the fathers and sons. It was pretty sad watching them bring in the kids and dads. At first, I was afraid that the kids would come in screaming, but I think that most of them were just in shock. None of them really made much noise until just now."

Hunter rubbed his eyes with the palms of his hands and sat back against the wall again. "I know I've already said this before, but man, this really sucks." That comment ended their conversation. It was all that really could be said.

They were left alone again for about two hours during which time nobody really said much. People shuffled their weight trying to find more comfortable positions on the hard metal floor. Occasionally somebody coughed or moaned. Most of the children stopped crying. Hunter suspected that they were far too exhausted to make much noise. Most of the men just sat and stared blankly at the floor in front of them. Hunter couldn't help but wonder again if this is what it meant to be broken. This life of slavery was giving him a lot of time alone with his thoughts. What would he have been doing if he were home right now? He might be playing video games. He might be playing soccer. He might be at school or even sleeping. He wondered what time it was back home. What was his family doing? He tried not to follow this line of thinking too deeply. If he thought too much about his family, it began to feel like he was being torn apart from the inside out.

So, he began to think about his captors. Up to this point, it almost felt like they were being handled by robots. He was beginning to develop a very one-dimensional view of the 'People of Actaeon'. He said the words in his head with no small measure of disgust and sarcasm. What do you call it when you mix disgust and sarcasm in a single phrase? Discasm? Sargust? Yes, that was it. He looked upon the aliens with a great degree of sargust. He chuckled to himself ever so slightly. Cade, who was sitting next to Hunter, had his legs pulled to his chest, his hands were clasped around the front of his shins and he was resting his forehead against his knees. He lifted his head when Hunter chuckled and gave him a very strange look. Hunter realized that the room was so quiet now that even the small amount of laughter that had stayed in the back of his throat stood out starkly against the silence. He cleared his throat in an attempt to cover up for his chuckling. Cade just shook his head in response and placed his face back against his kneecaps.

Hunter returned to thinking about his captors. What did he really know about them? Most of the aliens that he had seen so far were soldiers and they had all been wearing helmets. He had seen the face of the soldier at Millennium Park, who, it turned out, was an alien general. What was an alien general doing at the park? Aren't generals supposed to watch battles and give orders from back in a command center somewhere? Hunter had witnessed, up close and personal, as the general fought with and killed an opponent using his bare hands. The disgust and disdain with which the alien had looked down at Hunter was still a little disturbing in his mind. Again, in the video while traveling to Actaeon 9, Hunter had been disturbed by the General's cold, intense mannerisms. Humans, it seemed, were little more than bugs or maybe animals to this man. Were all the aliens on this planet like the general and his soldiers? Hunter hoped that he never had to deal with this alien again. He realized suddenly that he still thought of them as aliens. In truth, on this planet, Hunter was the alien. Did that mean that he should start thinking of all of them as natives? In his mind, he heard the words of an old movie, 'The natives are getting restless,' and he pictured all of the tall aliens . . . well, natives . . . in war paint and loincloths. He had to suppress another chuckle. He didn't want everybody to think that he was going crazy.

As he considered the People of Actaeon, he decided that he knew next to nothing about them. They couldn't all wear helmets all the time. The City of Aernos, from the little he had seen, was very beautiful. This meant that they had to have architects and artists. Somebody had to build those beautiful buildings. Somebody had to keep the streets clean. Maybe they had restaurants like back on Earth. Did they have cars? Did they all ride around in flying machines? What did they eat? He couldn't imagine that they lived off hishop biscuits like he had been fed so far. Perhaps not all of them were bad? He couldn't decide if this were a question or a statement in his mind. On one hand, he detested the thought. On the other hand, it gave him hope. He wanted to think of them all as monsters. The problem was though, that if they were all monsters - if they were all like the general - then what hope did any of the humans have? Their lives would be miserable until the day they died on this far-away planet. No, he had to hold out hope that he would find kindness also among the people of Actaeon. He was proud of himself for this line of thinking. Somehow, it felt like the right thing to think. His dad would have wanted him to think this way. The memory of his dad choked off his thoughts. Even if the people of Actaeon turned out to be better than he feared, he still had to get home. This was the real hope that he held. Someday he would see Earth again. Someday, he would let his family know that he hadn't died. No other end to his life would ever allow Hunter to have peace, even if he had no idea how he could ever get the power to make it happen.

The door to the steel room opened and a group of soldiers entered. The first two to enter held pistols. They approached men who had seated themselves closest to the door, grabbed their wrists and held their hands up placing the barrels of the guns against their palms. The pistols fired with a small pop and each man jerked and yelped. The soldiers continued around the room shooting everybody once in the right hand. Other soldiers approached a panel on the wall that Hunter hadn't previously noticed. From the panel, they unrolled thick heavy hoses and it seemed to Hunter that they were preparing to wash all the humans down with whatever liquid would spray from the ends of those hoses. Hunter hoped that it was just water. A soldier grabbed his hand and with a quick motion pressed the pistol barrel against his palm and fired. His whole arm spasmed in response and he jerked his hand away. When he looked at his palm, he found that he had an inch-long linear cut that appeared to have been cauterized to avoid bleeding. Next to the wound, he thought he could feel a flat disc about the size of a dime. It tingled and Hunter thought that he could feel tiny movements around the edge of the disc underneath his skin. The nerves throughout his whole arm and shoulder burned and his hand hurt like somebody had driven a knife through his palm.

When Hunter looked up from his hand, the two soldiers that had been shooting people were finishing up their handiwork. 'Handy work?' Hunter chuckled to himself again, but nobody noticed. Everybody was preoccupied nursing their palms and rubbing their arms. Some of the children cried. Hunter rolled his shoulder and found that most of the tingling sensations had dissipated, and his whole limb was beginning to feel normal again.

Suddenly a man cried out and Hunter felt splashes of liquid against his feet. He whipped his head around to see that the soldiers with hoses were spraying down a middle-aged, balding man who had fallen to the ground and was clutching at his face and eyes. The liquid from the hoses put off pungent, acidic vapors that burnt Hunter's nose.

They began to work their way rapidly around the room. The pressure from the hoses was forceful enough that it knocked people off their feet. The men tried to protect the eyes and faces of the children, but it was almost impossible against the torrent of burning liquid that blasted from the hoses. Hunter could swear that he heard the soldiers laughing from inside their helmets. He began to reassess his previous thoughts that maybe not all of these people could be bad. When they reached him, he ducked his face into the crook of his elbow and crouched low against the pressure. After the hosing-down, Hunter's skin tingled and burned. In a very short amount of time the soldiers had finished their tour of the room and were preparing a second hose. This time they were sprayed with water. Again, Hunter had to brace himself against the pressure from the hose, but the cool, cleansing water offered welcome relief from the acidic, burning liquid that covered his body.

Once the washing was done, they were taken into an adjoining room where they were made to choose clothing from stacks of pants and shirts. Hunter found himself wearing baggy brown trousers and a matching shirt. Both articles of clothing were made from material similar to burlap that was so abrasive it felt like it was going to rub his nipples completely off and give him rashes in the unmentionable regions of his body. Between the clothing and the acid wash, his skin would be raw for weeks. Hunter pointedly noticed that they were not offered shoes. He hoped that he wouldn't find himself being pulled barefoot behind a wagon. He saw that in a movie once. It didn't look like much fun. From the clothing room, they were taken to eat a pathetic and hasty meal of water and hishop biscuits. Next, they were given what Hunter thought must have been shots from a space-age-looking hypodermic needle. In one room, they were held down while their teeth were brushed. In another room, their heads were shaved. Hunter felt like some poor sheep when a massive alien put him into a headlock and sheared off all his hair with a set of alien hair clippers.

All of these events transpired without a single word from their captors. They were pushed, pulled, kicked and shoved, but never did their alien slavers talk to them. Occasionally the soldiers held brief conversations amongst themselves in a language that Hunter could not understand, but even these conversations were limited to the exchange of just a few short words. If the humans tried to talk amongst themselves, the soldiers struck them with batons. Truly, Hunter felt more and more like an animal. He traded worried glances with Cade and watched as Mr. Dees struggled to keep track of and protect his children. For the first time, Hunter began to notice other families. Men tried their best to shelter boys from the more brutal treatment, but many were struggling just to stay on their feet. Hunter himself found that unless he was sitting or lying, he had a hard time breathing. The increased gravity and constant brutality were taking their toll on everyone. Nobody was offering resistance because they were all struggling just to keep from falling on their faces.

They trudged forward laboriously until finally they found themselves waiting in a long hallway with small square doors. The hallway must have been twelve feet high, and the doors were stacked three on top of each other. The soldiers began opening doors and stuffing people inside one at a time. Hunter was grabbed right away and pushed into a box on the lowest of the three levels. The door was closed and locked immediately, and he found himself sitting in a cube made, on four sides, from steel grating. The door through which he had been pushed was solid and made from heavy gauge steel. On the opposite side of the box was a heavy-duty glass door. The box was perhaps barely larger than four feet square. Through the glass door, he could see that his box was one of many that lined both sides of a long hallway, which was very wide, perhaps 15 feet. Hunter could see inside some of the boxes that lined the opposite side. Many of them were empty. Some of the boxes held captives dressed in the same abrasive and nondescript clothing that he wore. Their heads were also shaved, and Hunter realized with a start that they were all women. He thought he recognized some of them from their group, but it was difficult to be sure. They all looked so completely different with their heads shaved. The skin on their cheeks was flushed and raw from the brutal cleaning that they had received. Many of them cried and huddled in the corners of their boxes. Others just sat stoically staring forward.

The back door of the box directly across from Hunter opened and a small whimpering young lady was dumped inside. The huddled form lay sobbing, curled up in a ball. Part of her face was covered by her hands, but Hunter could also see part of her left cheek and one eye that was squeezed shut. He realized in sudden horror that he recognized the face. It was April. Her cheeks were flushed and red. Her scalp looked raw and some blood from a nosebleed had been wiped across her cheek. Tears welled up from her tightly closed eyes and her body convulsed slightly as she sobbed into her hands. Hunter scrambled to his knees and pressed his fists against the glass door. She hadn't noticed him, and he began to pound on the glass. He yelled her name, but she didn't respond. She couldn't hear him. He sat back against the metal door and began to kick at the glass. Then he began to truly scream her name. Suddenly her exposed eye fluttered open and she raised up on one elbow. Hunter sat forward again, bringing his face up against the glass. At first, she stared at him without recognition and then suddenly her eyes seemed to focus, and her face became alive with realization. She didn't smile though. She scrambled to her knees and pressed her hands against the glass.

April looked at Hunter with a desperate intensity. Tears still poured from the corners of her eyes. Hunter was shocked by the transformation that she had undergone, and he was suddenly very grateful for their time in the rocket ship staring at each other day and night. Had he not become so intimately familiar with her face; he would not have recognized her. She had fresh signs of bruising around her right eye and her cheek was burned with the strange alien symbol. One of her wrists looked swollen and raw. A little bit of fresh blood trickled from her nose and her shaved head nearly transformed her whole appearance. Hunter completely forgot that his own face was extremely bruised and burnt. He noticed that without hair, she looked younger. She was shaking and Hunter could practically feel her panic. She looked like a caged animal and her eyes begged him for help. Her desperation was truly palpable, and it washed over him, tearing away all pretense of calmness or mental fortitude. An ominous sense of helplessness welled up inside him and tears of anger began to form in the corners of his own eyes. What had they done to her?

He wanted to scream but that would only add to April's terror. He had to do something to help her. He breathed deeply. He held her gaze for a long moment and he mouthed the words, "I love you." He did not know if this was the right thing to say but she began to cry openly, and uncontrollably. Her head slumped against the glass. Her whole body went limp and she wept. Hunter watched her cry for a very long time. He did not look away though his own tears came freely. April eventually slumped to the floor and curled up into a ball. Over the course of hours, the lights in the hallway grew dim and eventually went out leaving them in total darkness. He sat staring into the blackness in her direction. With all his will, he cursed this alien planet, and he cursed these people. In the fury of his anger, though, he lost some of his desire to escape. At this moment, with an image of April broken and crying, freedom from slavery felt secondary to a more dark and hateful longing. Hunter felt true loathing for the people of Actaeon and he wanted revenge.

The lights came on abruptly the next morning and Hunter awoke to the muffled sound of alien voices. He sat up immediately and looked for April. She lay curled on the floor with her back to the glass. She seemed to shudder and cringe against the glaring light that now filled the hallway. The voices drew nearer and shortly two tall women walked into view. The first had straight, black hair that flowed to the middle of her back. She was close to 6 feet tall with long, lithe arms and legs that were supple and graceful. Her face was angular but beautiful. She wore gray pants that might have been compared to a pair of women's slacks on Earth and a laboratory style overcoat. The other woman was only slightly shorter with a more curvaceous build. Her hair was a dusty blond color and she wore it on her head in a pattern of elaborate braids with interwoven flowers. Her feet were bare, and she wore only a single piece, brightly colored gown that came down below her knees. Her face was heavily tattooed with alien symbols. Hunter literally jumped when he saw her eyes. They were solid black with no distinguishable differences between her pupils and irises. They seemed to be made of pure liquid darkness. She inspected the caged humans as she strolled casually with the other woman who pointed and offered explanations. They were followed by two soldiers and a shorter balding man who wore slave's attire and bore a branding mark on his face. Hunter supposed that he must be human.

The entourage walked back and forth along the hallway numerous times, stopping in front of various cages discussing the human slaves. As he watched them come and go, Hunter realized that the curvaceous lady with the dark eyes was shopping for slaves. She had looked briefly into his cage but dismissed him and moved on quickly. Her gaze made him shudder and he was relieved that she did not linger on him as she did with others. He wondered if his extra brand had revealed him to her as a troublemaker. After numerous trips back and forth, and a great deal of what Hunter thought might be haggling, the lady with the long black hair gave commands to the two soldiers and they began to pull humans from the cages. Hunter watched in horror as they were dragged stumbling down the hallway, and he realized that this would shortly be his fate as well. He would have to watch as April was dragged away, or she would have to watch as he was dragged away. He wondered where Cade and Summer were. They had to be locked in these cages as well. Their parents and brothers and sisters also had to be somewhere in this hallway. He had such a limited view from inside his cage that he doubted he would even see them as they were taken away.

After taking away a handful of humans, the group of aliens left the hallway. Hunter looked in at April. She rolled over and sat up. Her eyes look so tired. They were bloodshot and red from crying. He couldn't help but wonder if she had been awake, crying all night. She looked at him and he mouthed, "How are you?"

She stared blankly back and then mouthed, "I can't do this."

Hunter was again grateful for the time that they had spent on the rocket ship together. Reading each other's lips gave him something to focus on. Perhaps he could help her. "I'm sorry," He replied. "You can do this. I will help you."

"Hunter," she mouthed. "You saw what they did this morning. Pretty soon someone will come and take one of us. You won't even be around to help me."

He had wondered if she noticed the activity in the hallway. "I will find a way, even if we get separated," he responded.

She just nodded and laid her head against the glass, closing her eyes. Hunter sat back, relaxing against the metal rear door of his cage. He had only been sitting for a few minutes when again he heard muffled voices in the hallway. Shortly the tall alien lady with long black hair came into view. She was accompanied by an even taller lady in a form fitting jumpsuit with dark auburn hair. Though this lady was well over six feet tall she was proportioned like a shorter human. Her face was round, and pretty. Her eyes were shrewd and discerning. She looked carefully into each cage, inspecting the occupants meticulously. She reached April's cage and paused for a long time. Hunter's heart was in his throat. The tall alien tapped the glass and made a comment to the others that were with her. The soldiers moved to open the cage. Before Hunter knew what he was doing, he was pounding on the glass and yelling frantically. They couldn't take her. He couldn't allow this to happen. He screamed even louder and drew the attention of the soldier that was about to open April's cage. The alien slapped the glass of Hunter's door in an attempt to cow him. Hunter continued to scream, and the soldier reached for a baton on his belt. The tall lady stopped the soldier with a muffled command and a raised hand. She knelt down and inspected Hunter carefully. Then she looked across the hall at April and back again at Hunter. He had stopped screaming and pounding the glass, but he stared the woman down with a violent intensity. She narrowed her eyes and he saw her gaze as it fell upon his branded cheeks. Grinning ever so slightly she held up a finger and wagged it at him as if to say, 'Tsk, tsk, bad little slave.' Wasn't that a human gesture?

She seemed to consider for a moment and Hunter watched as a smile formed on her lips. The look that she gave him was more frightening than anything else he had experienced yet. This woman was forming a plan for his future and Hunter did not like what she was thinking. She tapped on his glass and issued a command. The soldiers pulled both him and April from their cages. As Hunter stood up, he saw that other traders were doing business down the corridor. He watched as a middle-aged woman was being dragged down the hall.

She started to scream and reached for a nearby cage.

"My children!" She screamed frantically. It took Hunter a moment, but he recognized Mrs. Dees. "Please!" she screamed. "No! No! No!"

They were now dragging her as she kicked and thrashed. Hunter was being pushed the opposite direction down the hall. He had to look over his shoulder to see what was going on. The soldier who pushed him slapped him across the cheek to force him to look forward. In front of him, April was being pushed by another soldier. Hunter saw, strapped to the soldier's thigh, a sheathed knife. Before he even gave it a second thought, he snatched at the knife, pulling it free from the sheath. The blade glowed green with energy. He spun slashing wildly and drove the knife through the hand of the soldier that had been ushering him down the hallway. The man screamed as two of his fingers were severed from his hand and blood sprayed across the white hallway floor. Hunter shot past him, taking off at a dead run toward Mrs. Dees and the soldier that dragged her away. The alien looked up in surprise as Hunter leaped over Mrs. Dees and barreled into him. Releasing his captive, the soldier tried to raise his hand protectively, but he was too slow, and Hunter drove the knife into his shoulder. It sank in with surprising ease. Something about this blade allowed it to cut very easily through the soldier's armor and into his flesh. He screamed and fell backwards. Hunter tumbled with him and came up sitting on the man's chest. He tore the knife free and raised it high above his head preparing to plunge it down again, but he paused. What was he doing? He was about to kill somebody. He hated these people. They took everything from him, but could he really do this? His breathing was ragged, and it came in gasps. He was not a killer. He did not want to become a killer. He was afraid of how he felt. He was afraid of what he would become if he took this man's life. In an instant, hatred overcame fear. He screamed and started to bring the knife down with all his force. However, even as the knife began to fall, he was hit in the back of the head with such force that he instantly lost consciousness. Had he remained awake for even a moment longer he would have also felt his body being thrown mercilessly against the wall. He would have felt his ribs break and his shoulder dislocate. He would have heard April's screams of terror. Fortunately, all he heard or saw was blackness.

13 ANOTHER HEADACHE

Hunter finally awoke when his head bounced off the floor of the wagon for the ten-thousandth time. The first thing he noticed was his brutal headache. His next sensation came from a vicious pain in his ribs and right shoulder. The combined distraction provided by his injuries caused him to only barely notice that his face was bouncing up and down in a puddle of his own drool. He rolled over and moaned. He had the feeling that he was moving in some sort of primitive vehicle that jumped and bounced spasmodically as it was pulled along. He didn't want to be awake. He wanted to go to sleep and escape the pain, but the violent bouncing magnified his torture exponentially. So, he opened his eyes, rolled onto his side, coughed once, and threw up.

Being beaten to the point of unconsciousness and vomiting felt like it was becoming a regular part of Hunter's daily routine. Fortunately, he was near the edge of the wagon and most of his puke spilled off the cart and onto the ground. Once he was done retching, he found himself staring through bars across a flat barren expanse of desert. The terrain consisted primarily of sandy washes, bare dirt, and low growing shrubs. It looked a little like the desert from his home in Arizona. A blue outline of distant mountains framed the whole scene and through his sickness and pain the familiarity of the terrain brought a mild sense of nostalgia. He choked it back. This was not Arizona. It was nothing like Earth and he hated this place.

He lay on his side long enough to catch his breath before using the bars to pull himself to a kneeling position. His head swam and he was hit with a second powerful wave of nausea that made him feel like he was going to throw up again. He leaned his head against the bars, closed his eyes and focused on breathing steadily until the sickness passed. He took a deep breath and then rotated awkwardly until he sat with his back against the bars. He tilted his head back, closed his eyes, and gingerly felt at his left side. Something did not feel right. He thought that maybe some of his ribs were broken. He could barely move without causing muscle spasms and sharp pain along his left torso. His shoulder ached terribly, and his forehead burned. He reached up, tenderly feeling the skin above his eyebrows and was surprised to find that he had been branded with yet another mark. He moaned softly. This could not be a good thing.

Hunter tried to think. What had happened? What had he done to get himself into this predicament? He remembered the cages and April. His heart lurched as he thought of April being branded and beaten. He remembered being removed from the cage. He remembered a knife with a glowing green edge. He thought of Mrs. Dees screaming and being dragged away. He remembered sitting on the chest of an alien soldier, resolving to drive the green glowing knife into the face of the man. And then... and then... Pain? No, not pain, but rather . . . obliviousness. He blacked out. He couldn't remember anything else. He brought his hand to the back of his head and found a very large lump. He must have been hit from behind. How did he get here? Where was here? He opened his eyes and began to look around.

He found himself in a wagon with two other men that he didn't recognize. They wore the same slave's clothing that he had been given. They sat stoically, bouncing with the motions of the cart and staring flatly at Hunter. Each of them bore multiple brands on their cheeks and forehead. Criminals? Troublemakers? Was he a criminal? Well if he was, then at least he was in good company. He managed a weak smile and a nod for each of them. Somehow their flat stares seemed to grow even flatter.

Hunter turned his attention to the crude means of transportation in which he found himself. The cart bottom was fashioned from thick sturdy planks. It was roughly square and enclosed by steel bars and a roof made from the same wooden planks. The steel bars in the back of the cart were framed and hinged and looked as if they could be lowered to form a ramp that would provide access in and out of the rolling cage. The cart was being pulled by a large hairless animal with leathery gray skin. From the back, it might have been a rhinoceros but from his position Hunter could also see drooping tusks that curved back from the animal's head. As closely as he could tell, nobody was controlling the animal. It just plodded forward slowly and steadily. He couldn't help but reflect on the primitive nature of this mode of transportation. Why was he being pulled in a wagon? Hadn't he been abducted by a highly advanced alien civilization? This felt like he was taking a nightmarish trip through an old Conan the Barbarian movie.

It felt like it was well over a hundred degrees and a bright sun hung at a 45-degree angle to the horizon. Hunter wondered vaguely if the sun were rising or setting. He imagined that it would become much hotter if it were cresting high into the sky. The ghostly form of a large moon loomed opposite the sun. Hunter scanned the desert and was surprised to find that other carts were being pulled along in paths parallel to their own. One cart caught his eye. It moved in a path that was parallel to Hunter's own wagon and was filled with people. Somebody in the cart was waving frantically. Hunter's vision was blurry. He blinked, and squinted, straining to make sense of the waving figure. He recognized with a start that it was April. "April!" He tried to yell her name, but it just came out as a croak. His mouth was so dry. He swallowed hard and tried again. "April!" It only came out as a small yell, but she might have heard him.

"Hunter!" His name came back from across the desert and the little figure on the cart in the distance waved more vigorously. He acknowledged her by waving his own arms broadly. They stared for a while across the expanse at one another, but there was nothing else that they could do. The carts were close enough for Hunter to recognize April but too far for any sort of meaningful communication. After a few minutes, he turned around and sat back against the bars of the cage. At least he knew where April was and that she was okay… kind of. That was worth something.

He again found himself staring at the two very grim-faced men who shared his wagon. He eyed the multiple brands on their cheeks and foreheads. Hunter had yet to see his own brands. One of his, he imagined, looked just like the marks on everybody else's left check. He saw this brand on the faces of the men. They however, like Hunter, bore numerous additional brands. The man who sat to Hunter's left was lean and tall. His head was shaved in the customary slave fashion. His face was long and angular like his body. He looked Hunter over with such intensity that Hunter became uncomfortable and turned his attention to the other occupant of their cart. He was short, with thick muscular arms. His face looked like he had lost far too many fights. This man had so many brands on his face that Hunter doubted any more could fit. When they made eye contact, he smirked in a manner that was just as un-nerving as the other man's intense stare. Hunter looked back and forth between the two figures. In his mind, he named them Skinny and Beefy.

"Anybody got some water?" It came out as little more than a croak and ended with a cough.

Skinny indicated with an eye motion and a slight nod to something above Hunter's left shoulder. He shifted his weight painfully and looked up. A water sack with a hose hung from the cage. He took the hose, inspecting it. It looked as though it were made from rubber and it had a bulbous end that was pocked with teeth marks. Hunter took the end of the hose and bit down. His mouth was almost immediately filled with a bitter, salty liquid that burned his throat as he swallowed. He coughed, spraying a little of the liquid onto the floor of the cart.

Beefy chuckled and with a Russian accent commented,

"How do you like that, little rebel?"

"What is that stuff?" Hunter coughed again and wiped off his chin.

Skinny chimed in, "That, is Alien Gatorade." He had a slight southern accent, maybe Texan. "Boris over there," he raised an eyebrow and nodded at Beefy, "Managed to sneak a little moonshined vodka into the mix."

"What?" Hunter was trying to shake off the persistent, bitter taste in his mouth. "That stuff's terrible."

"Drink up, son. It tastes terrible but it'll keep you alive. Well... maybe. You're looking pretty sorry and I'm not sure if anything's gunna keep you alive. At least, you won't die of dehydration. You see, Boris and I have a bet going on. If you die, he wins."

"Boris?" Hunter said blearily and he looked at Beefy, "Is that really your name?"

"Cowboy over there," he nodded at Skinny, "He calls me Boris." He shrugged. "It works. You can call me Boris too."

Hunter looked at Skinny, "And should I call you Cowboy?"

"Name's John, if you don't mind. Now drink, boy."

Hunter bit down on the hose again, but this time he was a little more careful. Liquid poured slowly into his mouth and with considerable effort he managed to swallow a few times without coughing it back up. It still burned his throat and it was indescribably bitter, but it was also refreshing, and it did make him feel better. He closed his eyes again and rested his head back against the bars taking several deep breaths and fighting down another wave of nausea. When he lifted his head and opened his eyes again, he found that they were still staring at him.

"I told you he wasn't dead yet," John observed.

"Bah! Give him a few more hours and he'll be a corpse for sure."

"You know, Boris, you can be downright insensitive sometimes."

"I am not being insensitive. I'm just being realistic. Look at him. He is a complete mess," Boris snorted. "He will probably die in the next 10 minutes.

Hunter just shook his head, "Where are we? How did I get here?"

"My friend, we are on a one-way trip to the encampment of the Dragon Raiders," John began. "As for how you got here, well . . . you must a done something real stupid. Now understand, I know a thing or two about doing something real stupid because I did something real stupid myself to end up in this cart. You though, the way you was all beat up, I think you might a done something even stupider. The aliens that threw you in here didn't seem to much care if you lived or died. I suspect they'd have just thrown you away, but you was still breathing and our cart was closer than the dumpster. Boris and I been arguing for two days now about what we was gunna do with your body if you died and started to stink up our wagon."

"Wait a second," Hunter started, still trying to shake off the bleariness of his thoughts. "Did you say that I've been in this cart for two days?"

"That's right, boy. Sun's gone down and come up twice since they tossed you in with us."

Hunter sighed, rubbed his face and laid his head back again.

"In all honesty," John continued, "Neither of us really thought you was gunna live. I just bet in your favor so that we'd have something to bet on. If you keep on living, Boris is gunna have to give me one of his meal rations."

Hunter chuckled. There wasn't any real humor in his laughter though. It was hollow and short. It was more like the chuckle that might come from a man as he begins to go insane. He lifted his head again, remembering John's previous statement. "What are the Dragon Raiders?" Hunter asked. The two men eyed each other, and Hunter saw an understanding pass between them that sent chills up his spine.

"It is a death sentence," Boris said, eyes focusing on Hunter and then he shrugged, "but it sounds like a good enough way to die."

"I don't know how much I agree with my friend. I think I could come up with better... less excruciating ways to die." John leaned forward, giving a sideways glance to the stout Russian man. "You see, all we really know is just rumors and stories, but the stories that people tell don't sound good at all. They say that the aliens want something that's guarded by flying reptiles, maybe a mineral or resource of some kind. It's said that they feed live humans to the monsters as a distraction so that they can take whatever thing it is that they're looking for. Amongst all us humans, this place is called the Dragon Raiders. The only slaves that they send to the Dragon Raiders are ones that have done something real stupid, like us," he smiled making a broad gesture, "and we... never come back."

Hunter slouched back against the cage, John's last words ringing in his ears. Well, that's just dandy, death by monster. He sighed. Maybe Boris would prove right, or maybe he would luck out and die before they arrived. Hunter was suffering from a massive jumble of emotions. Sometimes he was full of hatred toward his captors. He wanted revenge against the people of Actaeon so badly that he would kill every single one of them if he could. At other times, he felt like he was being consumed by desperation, and all he wanted was to escape and get away. He was like a trapped animal and he just wanted to run. When he thought of his family on Earth, he just ached and felt like his guts were being ripped out. Now though, he felt a new emotion that could replace them all. As he considered John's words, he began to feel like he didn't really care whether he lived or died. It was like hopelessness only without the pain. He saw it behind John's eyes, and he saw it in Boris also. How long had they been on this planet? What had it taken to break them? Was he broken?

"Now you see, Cowboy," Boris said, "notice the look in his eye. This boy, he knows he's going to die, and he is beginning to not care. He is like a member of our little club now."

"Yeah, I see it," John responded. "Too bad though really. Nobody as young as him should be as bitter as you and me. Pity that."

"How long until we get there?" Hunter changed the subject. He didn't want to face what he was becoming. In the back of his mind he knew that the emotion he was feeling wasn't truly an emotion at all. It was a total lack of emotion. He knew that this was how it felt to give up and for April's sake, for the sake of his friends and his family, giving up was not an option.

"Well, friend," John responded. "Neither of us have ever come this way, but I think we're getting close." He pointed in the direction that they traveled.

It strained Hunter's vision, but in the very far distance, he could see an oasis of trees and maybe structures. He looked about and noticed that all the wagons seemed to be converging on this location. Some of the other carts had drawn nearer as they moved toward this single point. He looked carefully at the little town and thought he could make out the forms of buildings and streets. Despite being able to see the town, though, they still traveled many more hours before it was close enough to make out details. Slowly their wagon moved forward, and the three of them settled into glum silence as they each considered their impending fate. Very little conversation was exchanged as they watched the oasis steadily grow larger.

As they drew close to the small town, Hunter could see

that the buildings were single-story, sturdy, simple structures with flat rooftops, made from wood and metal. The large gray animals that pulled their wagons seemed to grow anxious and increase their pace as they drew near the oasis. They lumbered more earnestly, and Hunter was jostled as the cart bounced over the rutted desert landscape. He ground his teeth together and clutched at his ribs as pain shot through his body from being bounced about by the increased movement. His wounds were painful and sharp, but he was growing increasingly more confident that his ribs weren't broken. The extreme and sickening pain he had felt when he awoke in the wagon had subsided considerably and he was beginning to think that his wounds had not been nearly so bad as he had originally feared.

In a matter of minutes, a large pond situated on the outskirts of the oasis came into view. It was apparently fed by a water source from the oasis interior and had been prepared for animals such as the creatures that pulled their wagons. Two of the wagons had already pulled up to the pond and the large gray-skinned animals began to drink thirstily. Hunter's own wagon pulled in next to the others. Within minutes, seven carts sat in a line along the shore of the pond while their animals drank.

Hunter's wagon was situated near the middle of the line. He thought he saw April's cart pull in near the far end, but he was unsure because of the three carts between them that blocked his view. After drinking steadily for almost five minutes, the animals began to back away from the pond. They stayed in the immediate area, but one at a time they began to meander about munching on the grass and sparse vegetation that grew in the arid soil. After nearly an hour of grazing, his animal lay down and began to snore heavily.

They waited many hours through the heat of the day until several humans with shaved heads, dressed in slave's clothing, approached the wagons and began leading them into the heart of the oasis. April's wagon was the first to be led away. Hunter could only sit and watch her go. She waved and he waved back. Once more he watched her leave and couldn't help but wonder if he would ever see her again. His own cart sat for many more hours after the others left. Hunter had nothing to say to his cart buddies and they offered nothing but silence in return. Only after the sun began to sink low over the distant mountains did a slave wander lethargically out of the little town to approach his cart. Without a word, he took the reins of the big animal and began to lead the cart into the oasis.

A single main road passed through the little town. Numerous small roads jutted out perpendicularly and were lined by low flat-topped buildings that formed alleyways. The slave led their cart down the main road. Hunter watched as numerous alleyways passed, searching anxiously for sight of April but without luck. Each alleyway looked like all the others. Every building was nearly a duplicate of the building on either side. It all seemed so monochromatic to Hunter. It was small but he felt like he could easily get lost in the maze of alleyways and buildings that all looked alike. The main road through the little town was about two miles long. Hunter couldn't help but wonder what purpose a town such as this could serve. It was literally sitting in the middle of nowhere, surrounded by desert in all directions. The slave led their cart to the edge of town, slapped the large gray-skinned animal on the flank and then walked away. Their animal began to trudge forward on its own heading away from the town and into the wilderness.

Hunter slumped against the wagon wall and gazed into the distance. He could see clearly for miles and yet he could identify no obvious destination. The sun dipped low in the sky, and another moon was rising on the opposite horizon. Thin clouds hung above distant mountains. The setting sun painted the underbellies of the clouds with gold accents. In a way, the whole scene was very beautiful. Hunter lowered himself carefully to the bouncing floor of the cart, where he could lay on his side and use his arm as a pillow. He did not close his eyes but positioned himself so that he could stare through the bars of his prison and watch as the miles of desert rolled by.

☐

14 DRAGONS

Hunter's eyes were still open when the first rays of sunlight broke the darkness, and their wagon rolled to a stop. He had wanted very badly to sleep, but the jostling of the wagon, and the stress in his mind would not allow him to relax enough to catch even the most fleeting moment of slumber. He sat up blearily and looked around. His two cart buddies groggily began to wake and sat up also. Their wagon had stopped at the edge of a small village. Hunter scanned the area in the growing light. The little encampment consisted of no more than a few dozen huts, a guard tower and one flat-topped building. The huts lined a single dusty road that ran through camp. The building sat at the end of the road, and the guard tower was situated immediately to the side of the entrance to the encampment. The animal that pulled their cart seemed to know exactly where to wait.

It was only a few minutes before their cart was approached by an Actaeon soldier and three slaves. In the dim light of early morning, Hunter could only make out their dark silhouettes. The soldier passed his hand over the locking mechanism along the top of the cage. A series of clicks sounded, and the cage door was released. The soldier stepped back, allowing the door to drop heavily to the ground. Hunter couldn't help but muse over the obviously sophisticated locking mechanism that was attached to a crude cage on wheels, pulled by a lumbering gray-skinned animal.

Hunter was surprised when the soldier simply turned and walked away. He headed in the direction of the flat-topped building without a single word. The three shadowy figures that appeared to be slaves approached the cart. One of them stepped forward as the apparent leader. His skin was as black as ash and, and the whites of his eyes shown like burning coals. With a soft French accent, he began to speak.

"Welcome. My name is Adam. I am sorry for you that you have come to this place, but we are glad to have new brothers. Follow us and we will teach you what you need to know until you die." The man turned and walked away from the cart, flanked by the other two slaves. Hunter exchanged uneasy glances with John and Boris. They hesitated, uncertain of what to do next. The Frenchman paused and looked over his shoulder. "Do not worry. You will not die today. Tomorrow . . . tomorrow is another story. You might actually die tomorrow." Hunter thought he could hear a smile in the man's voice. "Follow me, please. I would like to get a little sleep before the sun comes up." He turned and continued walking.

Boris and John looked at each other one last time, shrugged and left the cart. Hunter followed cautiously. As soon as they left the cart, the animal seemed to know exactly what to do. The cart door closed automatically, and he lumbered slowly away. They walked along the road that ran between the huts. Hunter found himself looking back and forth as they passed the humble little habitations that he assumed must be the homes of slaves. Some of them had doors. Some of them had dirty, patched lengths of cloth that acted like curtains to provide privacy for the hut occupants. Some had no door at all and gave off the appearance of being abandoned. They were all formed from large, crude, earthen bricks.

When they were about halfway up the road, the three men turned and entered one of the huts. They left the door to the hut open, and Hunter could see a low, steady light that dimly illuminated the ground in front of the small building. John and Boris entered. Hunter followed. The doorway was short enough that John had to duck to avoid hitting his head, and the top of the doorframe was just barely taller than Hunter. Inside the hut, the three men seated themselves in a line on the ground. The floor was dirt, and the whole building consisted of one small, square room. A sleeping pallet was arranged in one corner of the room. A small chest sat next to it and a dim lantern hung from the low ceiling. Hunter could see no other furnishings or personal items. The room was tall enough that any man could stand up straight, but it gave the impression of being so cramped that Hunter found himself slouching his shoulders.

"Please, sit with us, brothers." Adam sat in the middle of the room flanked by his companions. Hunter's eyesight adjusted to the dim lighting and he nearly jumped in surprise. One of the men was missing an arm from the elbow down. Adam was scarred with a deep slash that began behind his left temple and ran along his face to the point of his chin. All three of the men, like Hunter, John and Boris wore numerous brands on their cheeks and forehead. Hunter struggled to not stare at Adam's scar or at the man with the missing arm. Boris sat down. Hunter and John followed his example.

"Welcome. As I said earlier, my name is Adam. Sitting on my left is Stephen." The man who was missing half his arm nodded. "On my right is João." The man on his right nodded. He had dark hair, dark eyes, and olive skin. "It is our job to welcome you to the Dragon Raider's encampment, introduce you to your new job, and to explain the rules. The rules are simple. Do your job and nobody will care about anything else. If you do not do your job, then the Leeber will kill you. You have undoubtedly heard about the Dragon Raiders. Some of what you have heard is probably true. Some is probably not," he paused.

"You have most certainly heard about the dragons. The Leeber," he explained, "call them, 'Artog.' We call them dragons. Their eggs are very valuable. They are small, about the size of quail eggs from Earth, but the shells are made from smooth transparent crystal. You can see the baby dragon on the inside. They are very beautiful. The Leeber, they kill the baby dragon so that the egg never hatches and then they use it for jewelry. They are very hard to obtain. To own one is a symbol of great wealth and status on this planet."

The more that Hunter learned about his captors, the less he respected their superiority. It seemed to him that they suffered from many of the same weaknesses as humans, not the least of which included vanity.

The Frenchman continued, "The dragon, he is an independent creature. They will not lay eggs in captivity. They will not eat food that they don't kill themselves. They make their homes on the sides of cliffs and on mountains. They live in colonies of nests and they will not stay in an area that is vulnerable to attack. A single colony of dragons may contain a few hundred nests. If their eggs are continuously stolen, they will move the colony. Harvesting their eggs is a constant and delicate balance. The dragons need to live in an area with plentiful food. They also want food that fights back. The Leeber want to harvest their eggs but if they harvest too many, the dragons will leave. To keep a dragon colony stationary, they must control their food supply. They must keep them entertained, give them something in which to find sport and they must not harvest too many eggs."

A fierce light came into his eyes, "That is where we come in. We harvest the eggs and in doing so we provide the dragons with entertainment and with a part of their food supply." Adam's arm swung up and he pointed at a 45-degree angle toward the wall. "About 5 miles that way is a drop-off to a great canyon. A colony of dragons lives on the walls of the canyon. Every 10 days we travel to the canyon to try to harvest the eggs. Each time we go, we are told exactly how many of us must die before we are allowed to return. The only way that we can return sooner is if we capture an egg. Sometimes, we return with an egg. Many times, we do not. Often, more of us die when we successfully capture an egg than when the dragons simply defeat us by eating their quota."

"Why do you even try to capture eggs then?" Hunter

interrupted. "Couldn't a certain number of people just run away? You could just return empty handed every time."

"What is your name, young man?" Adam asked. There was no malice in his voice. Adam looked to be in his early forties and his tone was almost fatherly.

"Hunter," he responded.

"Hunter, our captors are not fools. They watch us very carefully. You will find that we have many freedoms here that other slaves do not, but when it comes to harvesting eggs, they will kill us and replace us if we don't do our jobs. They need to keep the colony of dragons happy. They carefully calculate how many of us are needed for food. As well, we are given a quota of eggs to fill. If we do not fill our quota, they will kill us."

He paused seeming thoughtful for a moment. "Hunter, you must also know that we have pride in our work. We are not afraid to die, and we are proud that we are not afraid to die. I do not want to be mean or cruel, but I am an honest man. Tomorrow, we will try to harvest an egg. We will teach you all that we can in the short time that we have about how to survive, but there is a good chance that all three of you will die. You are the newest members of our team. You are inexperienced, and you have no time to train. I do not want you to die but this is the reality that you face. If, by chance, you survive tomorrow, then you might survive for a little while. I have survived 30 harvests, but I do not expect to live much longer. I am skillful and I am careful, but many times I have survived only by luck. Please understand also that if you refuse to go on a harvest, the Leeber will kill you. The tracking device that was injected into your right hand contains a toxin that they can release remotely. If this happens, you will die in a matter of minutes. I have seen them use this to kill other slaves. I have seen many men come here and die. So . . ." he said leaning forward. He took a moment to look each of them in the eye. "Good luck, my brothers. May you die well. Go now. João will help each of you find an unoccupied hut with blankets. You should try to sleep a few hours before we harvest."

Hunter's mouth was dry. "Die well," the words echoed through his head. What kind of a good luck wish was that? Whatever happened to 'live long and prosper?' Hunter, John, and Boris followed placidly as João led them from Adam's hut. João was nearly wordless as he helped them find their new abodes. When he did speak, it was with broken and heavily accented English. Hunter couldn't help but wonder where the man was from.

In a matter of minutes, Hunter had been left to himself, alone in a dark, unfurnished brick hut. A small pile of dirty blankets lay in the corner. The tattered remains of a cloth curtain offered a small amount of privacy from the outside world. He found himself turning circles within the cramped confines of his new home until he stopped, facing the door. Without thinking, he exited the little hut to stand in the street. He walked slowly to the location where their cart had stopped. He looked back at the row of little buildings and then out across the dry, lonesome desert. The horizon had begun to glow with the rising sun. He wondered how April was doing. He had a sickening feeling in his gut that he would probably never see her again. According to Adam, his odds of surviving past lunchtime were pretty poor. Would she even hear about his death? Did he even care anymore? He considered the question and realized that he did still care. That thought gave him a small measure of comfort.

After a few moments, he discovered that he was beginning to grow tired, and so he sat down in the sand, crossed his legs, and sighed. How might he have viewed this world differently had he not come here as a slave? He loved the desert where he grew up on Earth. Might he have been able to appreciate the similarities in this world and his own? He tried, for a moment, to look at the scene before him with the same wonder and awe that had captured him when he stepped from the transport container and into his first moment on Actaeon 9. This desert was beautiful in its own way. The sand shimmered in the starlight. Mountains rose up on the distant horizon. The shadows of a few small animals scuttled across the terrain. Unfamiliar sounds caressed the air, the types of noises made by small insects. Little bushes grew in clumps and patches. In the distance, the silhouette of a small bird beat its winds in flight. A soft breeze brushed his skin. The gentle edge of a falling moon pulled soft, silver light in its wake as it dropped behind the skyline. He tried very hard to appreciate the pure and natural beauty of the alien landscape, but it was all dulled by the fear, hatred, and shame that filled his heart.

Hunter laid back and gazed up at the dwindling stars. In a way, he was glad to find himself at the Dragon Raider's camp. It was nice to not have alien soldiers breathing down his neck. It seemed that they would pretty much leave him alone until he got eaten. He began to feel exhaustion settle over him and his eyes itched to close. Under threat of his imminent death, he shouldn't have been able to sleep but he was so very tired that he doubted he could stay awake for long even if he tried. Besides, what was the point in worrying? He might as a well get a little sleep before facing down the man-eating dragons. He closed his eyes and within seconds, was fast asleep.

Hunter was shaken into consciousness a few hours later. It was Adam. "Look at you," he smiled, "too good for our accommodations? Come. It is time." He stood and walked away.

Hunter groggily rose to his feet and dusted himself off. Men were coming out of huts and forming a line in the street. They stood shoulder to shoulder with near military posture. Their legs were spread, and their hands were clasped behind their backs. Most of them stood with lifted chins. The display truly surprised Hunter. Awkwardly, he took his place at the end of the line attempting to imitate their stance. There were at least forty men in the line. Most of them had excessive branding on their faces. There was a broad range of ages from teenagers to old men, though by Hunter's best estimation, he was probably the youngest one present. Adam walked away from the group towards the square building. A flat paneled door slid open as he approached, and a soldier stepped out to meet him. Hunter could not hear their conversation. They spoke briefly, and Adam returned. He walked in front of the men with a commanding presence and he began to speak. "At least three of our brothers will die today. This is the way of it. Regardless, we will do our job with pride. If you are blessed to be among those that die, then know that all of our hopes go with you. Fight well. Die well!"

The men all echoed his last words. "Fight well! Die well!" They called out in chorus three times.

"We leave in five minutes," Adam added. "Those of you who know what to do, you are dismissed. Anybody who is new, stay close."

Most of the men dispersed. Hunter remained for what he hoped would be some sort of introduction-to-fighting-dragons speech. Avoiding death was top on Hunter's to-do list for the day. Seven other men did not leave after the dismissal. John and Boris were among them. Adam beckoned them together and began to speak. "Some of you have been here long enough to train with us. Some of you have not. None of you have experienced a raid. All of you should be determined to survive today, and at the same time you must be prepared to die. For now, the best thing that you can do is stay hydrated and eat some food so that you keep up your energy." He pointed between two of the huts. "Over there you will find water bags and biscuits. Grab a bag and two to three biscuits. Do not eat or drink so much that you feel heavy. You will have to run today. Go now. We begin our walk to the canyon soon. We will talk as we walk and perhaps you can learn more about how to not die. Now go!"

Hunter grabbed a water bag and three biscuits. Within minutes they had all begun their walk across the desert. He found out as they walked that they called themselves Raiders for short. They had a simple authority structure with Adam at the top, with two assistants, João and Stephen, whom Hunter had met the night before. Well... he thought of it as the night before, but it had really been earlier that morning. Adam, João and Stephen made sure that the group remained together as they walked. The Raiders set a brisk pace and the new guys found it difficult to keep up. The atmosphere of the procession seemed genuinely happy, almost jovial. Men slapped each other on the back and told jokes. Only the new guys seemed like they were walking to their deaths. Had they not all been dirty, stinky, dressed in rags and looking heavily underfed, any outsider might have taken the group for touristy sightseers.

Hunter was having a hard time participating in the jovial atmosphere. He walked just a little apart from and behind the group with a few of the other men that were also new to this whole being-fed-to-dragons experience. For the most part, his eyes remained fixed to the ground about 10 feet in front of his march. John and Boris had separated themselves from the group as well and appeared to be whispering back and forth. In the back of his head, he wondered what they might be discussing, but at the forefront of his thoughts, he imagined his impending doom. He was deep in thought when a hand clapped him on the shoulder dragging him out of his sullen thoughts. Hunter found himself staring into the smiling face of a dark-eyed teenage boy of about 17 years. The boy's face was almost completely covered in branding marks. It was the most that Hunter had ever seen on one person's face. It was as if the young man wore a mask of twisting flowing lines that bubbled up from his skin.

"How you doing, kid?" He had a thick New Jersey accent or maybe it was New York or Brooklyn. Hunter couldn't identify exactly where it came from. He knew there was a difference between the eastern accents. He just couldn't tell the difference. "You look like somebody whose favorite kitten just got run over by a taxi."

Hunter grimaced, "Oh, I don't know. I guess I'm letting this whole being fed to flying lizards thing get me down."

"Ah, it isn't so bad. I've seen a few guys get eaten. Usually the beasties bite your head off right away. I don't think you feel much pain."

Hunter started to chuckle, but then he noticed that the young man wasn't smiling. He seemed to be considering the matter ponderously. He might have been giving serious consideration to what it was like to be eaten. Hunter swallowed his laugh with a hard gulp.

"So… what's your name?"

"Hunter."

"Hunter? Hey, that's a good name for what we're going to do. You may not even need a nickname. I'm Jerry, but everyone just calls me Brooklyn, Because I'm from Brooklyn." He smiled and offered Hunter his hand. Hunter shook his hand. "Adam asked me to talk to you. He thinks you'll stand a better chance at survival if you're a little bit calmer. He also wants me to tell you a little bit about what to expect." Brooklyn paused for a moment. "First of all, how you doing? I mean really. How you doing?"

Hunter stared at the ground. He was considering how much he really wanted to open up to this guy. The young man looked and sounded sincere and he just walked along patiently, keeping pace with Hunter and waiting for a response. After a time, Hunter sighed. "I don't know. I'm confused. Sometimes, I feel like I want to fight. Sometimes, I feel like I want to run. Sometimes, I just wish I could die and not have to keep doing this." He rubbed his eyes with the palms of his hands and paused from speaking. When he continued, he found himself telling his whole life story. Brooklyn just listened. He nodded occasionally. He asked a few questions about Hunter's friends and family but mostly he just listened. Hunter told him about the night in Millennium Park. He talked way too openly about April. He told about how he had earned the brands on his face. He wasn't sure why he was opening up to this guy but as he did, he felt the stress of his whole life lightening just a little. The story of all that had happened to him seemed to leave his lips like one great, long sigh. When he was finished, silence hung in the air for several long minutes.

Brooklyn broke the silence when he nodded approvingly. "Not bad, Hunter. That's a pretty good story. If you die today, you can say that you lived a good life. April sounds like a pretty special gal. I bet she'll be okay."

"How can you say that? All of this is... is... horrible." Hunter felt his temper flare with annoyance. How could this guy say that Hunter had lived a good life, as if all that had happened to him was just dandy?

Brooklyn saw Hunter's annoyance and grinned a small but knowing smile. "You see, Hunter, you're a Raider now and we see things differently than most people. You might notice that most of us have got a face full of branding marks. Here, every extra mark is like a badge of honor. Every extra mark that a fella's got on his face means that that fella hasn't given up on life. It means that he fought for what was right. Sure, we're probably gunna get eaten by dragons today, but who cares. I'll fight them beasties with everything I got and if they eat me, I'll try to choke them on the way down. We've all got to die someday. This is a good way to die. Most people ain't so lucky. They die from cancer or in their sleep."

He paused again seeming to reflect upon what it would be like to get eaten by the dragons and then he continued, "Hunter, you should be proud of them marks on your face. I ain't never heard of no one stealing the knife from an Acky and attacking them. That's pretty impressive. It's probably why you already got a rasha mark when you've only got three marks total. You are probably one of the youngest members of the Raiders ever." He gave Hunter an appreciative glance.

Hunter's annoyance faded and his curiosity piqued, "What do you mean by a 'rasha mark'? Do you know what all of these brands mean?"

"A rasha mark," Brooklyn went on, "means that you are so dangerous, you ain't good for nothing but dragon food. Anybody with a rasha mark gets sent to a job where they are going to die quick. The brands you've got on your face tell the Ackys who you belong to and what you're good for. The first one on your left cheek just means you're a slave. From there, the brands go in a pattern, left cheek, right cheek, forehead, chin, left temple, right temple and so on. Some of them are the mark of your owner. We've got no clue what most of them mean but everybody recognizes a rasha mark. It's what got most of us sent here. Now sure, some fellas get sent here that ain't never done nothing to deserve getting themselves sent here. Sometimes the Acky's just need Raiders and they ain't got no troublemakers to feed to the dragons so they buy whatever cheap slave they can get. Usually, those guys get eaten faster than anybody.

It's like they ain't got enough fight in them to survive here. Adam always tries to help them though. He tries to help everybody. Pretty decent fella for a snail-eating Frenchy."

Brooklyn went on talking almost without seeming to breathe. Hunter was happy to just listen and relax into the steady pace that Adam had set for the group. "The dragons," Brooklyn was saying, "will all be in their nests at this time of day. It seems like a bad idea to attack when they are all at home, right? But really it is best to do our raids in the middle of the day. Dragons usually hunt in the mornings and in the evenings. They are a little bit calmer during the middle of the day. They also don't hunt well as a group. One dragon by itself is pretty hard to avoid. Put a bunch of them together though, and they just start fighting over their food. It's total chaos, like when a bus full of tourists pulls into a buffet."

Hunter was almost caught off guard when the young man stopped talking and their whole group came to a halt. They had arrived at the base of a tall embankment. The ground in this area was hard packed and rocky with low growing grass. The hill rose about fifty feet in front of them and stretched for hundreds of yards in both directions. It seemed to Hunter that they were at the base of a wide plateau.

Adam gestured for them to come together around him. As they drew close, he began to speak in a whisper. "We have received orders that we are not to abandon the harvest until we have either captured an egg or three of us have been fed to the dragons. There are three of us here today who have no training. John, Hunter, and Boris," he nodded to each of them as he spoke, "you will probably all die. The dragons will sense that you are weaker and less capable. They will target you." Hunter's stomach turned upside down and he felt like he might vomit. "But . . . there is perhaps something that we can do to help you. We can give each of you a partner, someone to follow. You must try to do what they do. When they run, you run. When they stop, you stop. If they are quiet, you must be quiet. If they give you instructions, you must do as they say, without hesitation. Do you understand?" Each of them nodded. "Boris, you are with João. John, you will run with me. Hunter, stick with Brooklyn." Brooklyn gave Hunter a small nudge and a thumbs-up. Hunter returned the thumbs-up with more enthusiasm than he really felt. "Today we are going to run a scramble formation. We are in silent mode until detection. Now go."

Brooklyn took Hunter's arm and looking him directly in the eye, held a finger to his lips. The Raiders began to spread out along the plateau, and he led Hunter along the embankment a short distance before pointing up the slope. Hunter took his meaning and began to climb the embankment. They were slow and careful, trying to make as little noise as possible. They crested the top of the plateau and Brooklyn looked down the line towards Adam, who concentrated intensely, staring across the flat open plain. Hunter followed his gaze and thought he could see in the distance a point where the flat steady ground dropped off into what might be a canyon. It was very difficult to tell with his perspective coming from no more than a few inches above the ground.

He looked back at Adam. His hand was raised in a gesture that seemed to suggest waiting. He held this posture for several long moments, until for no reason apparent to Hunter, he closed his fist and climbed onto the plateau. The rest of the Raiders followed suit, moving with great stealth. On the plateau, they began to run. Brooklyn made a gesture and mouthed the words, "Run like this." Hunter read his lips and experienced a flashback to his time on the shuttle with April. He had spent so many hours staring at her lips as they mouthed conversations back and forth. He now found that he could read lips naturally. Brooklyn wanted him to run in more of a crouching position, and Hunter realized that his foot falls were making too much noise. He imitated his running companion and began to concentrate on using the softest, quietest steps possible.

They trotted steadily in an unhurried crouch for a short period. It was easy for Hunter. He was young and athletic. His ribs still ached slightly from his injuries, but he had little problem keeping up. Despite the unnerving situation of trying to steal eggs from man-eating, flying monsters, he began to settle into a calming rhythm. He almost lost his rational fears, until a soul-rending chorus of screeches swept across the plain. The deafening cacophony nearly caused Hunter to stop running. Brooklyn seized him by the shoulder and screamed "Run!" Hunter ran. He ran straight at a rising wall of beating wings and undulating reptile bodies.

In moments, the first of the dragons leveled their course, flying low over the plateau, and before Hunter could even begin to process the oncoming danger, he found himself swallowed up in a frantic fight for his life. The dragons came in low and fast, grabbing and slashing at the raiders as they swept in. Adam, despite his age, had out-distanced the other men and was the first to meet the onslaught. He ran directly toward the first two dragons that led the flurry of attacking creatures. With mild adjustments in his course he placed himself at the perfect distance between the two animals so that they beat each other with their wings as they tried to reach him. He dashed between them, one of them stretching out a long snout to snap at the air inches from Adam's head. The whole exchange lasted only moments and neither Adam nor the dragons slowed their frantic pace.

Brooklyn shoved Hunter hard changing their course rapidly as a ball of teeth and claws cut between them. Hunter stumbled and scrambled to keep his feet. After the dragon ripped between them, Brooklyn swerved, and they were running shoulder to shoulder again. Somebody screamed. It was a frazzling, blood-curdling noise that stopped too abruptly, and Hunter knew that somebody had died. His mind went wild and he ran furiously. Within a second he was outrunning Brooklyn, and then his feet were caught up and he fell flat to the Earth as a set of claws raked his back, tearing his shirt, and digging shallow gashes into his skin. He screamed and looked back. Brooklyn had hold of his ankles. He had tripped Hunter by diving and grabbing his feet just in time to save them both. Without exchanging a word, they scrambled to their feet and ran.

Screams came from all around, mixing with the chaotic screeching of the dragons and the pounding of blood in Hunter's ears. He was surrounded by pandemonium, and it was all that he could do to track Brooklyn. Later he would barely be able to remember what happened beyond Adam's dash between the first two dragons.

They never made it to the chasm. Somehow the other

raiders knew when their death quota had been met and their race toward the chasm had turned into a mad dash for safety. Hunter lost all track of time and space. He felt like his life was, had always been, and would always be running from monsters. He didn't come to himself again until Brooklyn grabbed his shoulders forcing him to stop. When he looked around, he found that they had stopped in a deep and narrow gully. Shadows passed overhead accompanied by the screeching of frustrated beasts. Hunter threw up, and then he threw up again. After throwing up the third time, he rolled over in the sand, closed his eyes, and passed out with drool running down his chin.

He slept without dreams and was awakened many hours later by Brooklyn.

"Hey kid. Good news. You're alive. Come on. It's all clear. Let's get you out of here."

Hunter stood up wordlessly, feeling like a zombie. He wiped his face with the back of his hand and followed as Brooklyn pulled him along. Their return to camp was slow and somber but Hunter noticed that the other men were not weighed down by the experience. As they trudged the distance to camp, he found that both Boris and John had been killed. Hunter's stomach turned over and he threw up again, losing a few of the biscuits that Brooklyn gave him early in their walk. He felt frazzled, like he had been shaken to his very core. He couldn't believe that John and Boris were both dead. He hadn't known them long, but he had liked them. It was hard to face the fact that they were just gone. It forced him to face the stark and terrible reality that any of his friends could be already dead. Human life meant nothing on Actaeon 9. He took some comfort in knowing that he had been the most rebellious and he was still alive. Didn't that mean that they were probably still alive also?

By the time they arrived in camp, Hunter was mentally and emotionally exhausted. He felt like a wrung-out washrag and found himself seated in the dirt outside his hovel, staring blank-faced at the ground. He was numb. He didn't think that he could feel anything or that he would ever feel anything again. It was as if some primal self-defense mechanism had kicked on inside his brain to prevent him from going insane. It was more than just his emotions though. He found that he didn't even want to form a coherent thought. Doing so might lead him to think about what had happened today. For that matter, it might lead him to think about everything that had happened to him in the last three months. The constant stress of his new life was taking an irrevocable toll on his sanity. All he really wanted was to just quietly slide into oblivion. He had never felt so dark in his entire life. Someone plopped down in the dirt next to him.

"I'm not nearly as smart as Adam." It was Brooklyn. "I do, however, know a thing or two about feeling so worn out… so tired… so utterly fed up with all this garbage that you just want to die," he paused, "sure looks likes you feel that way right now."

Hunter turned his head to stare at the young man and noticed again all the branding marks that covered his face. He scanned the marks absent-mindedly. Brooklyn noticed and grinned crookedly. The smile brought some life back into Hunter and his brain began to work again.

"You are wondering where I got all these brands from."

There was a little bit of pride in his voice. "You are wondering about what epic adventures are behind these marks."

Hunter nodded.

"Well, I got a great story to tell. Thanks for asking." Brooklyn launched into a lengthy tale about his exploits as a slave and Hunter couldn't help but be distracted by the grand story that Brooklyn told. He could tell that the young man had recounted this story many times and that he liked telling it. It turned out that Brooklyn had been a slave almost as long as it was possible to have been a slave. He was now eighteen years old and he had been a slave since he was ten. His whole family had been taken after surviving a train crash. They had received the same interview as Hunter, and then they were shipped to Actaeon 9. The whole family was purchased together and worked as slaves for a farm on the other side of the planet. Brooklyn actually seemed fond of his first years on Actaeon 9. He had three brothers and a sister.

It wasn't until he was fourteen that disaster struck. His older brother Charlie, then 18, had been overly rebellious and so their owner sold him back to the central slave trading system. Brooklyn was devastated. Charlie was his hero. He choked up when he talked about his brother. He did the only thing that he thought was possible. He started trying to escape. Every time he got the chance, he made a run for it. Back then, he explained, the central slave trading system hadn't placed trackers in the hands of slaves. It was still difficult to escape, and you could never be free for long, but as a fourteen-year-old boy, Brooklyn didn't care. His mom and dad tried in vain to stop his countless escape attempts, but nothing could deter him. He had to get free and find his brother. He recounted numerous stories of his escapes. Hunter suspected that he exaggerated most of them, but it was still very entertaining to hear Brooklyn tell them. Some of his escape attempts seemed adventurous, dangerous, or even terrifying. Others seemed almost funny. He had once tried to escape by burying himself in a manure cart that was being taken away for dumping. Hunter actually laughed while he listened to this story.

He never did get very far in his escape attempts. One day, he heard that his brother had been killed in a mining camp. He lost his temper, attacked a guard, and earned himself a place in history and a job with the Dragon Raiders.

That night they held a ceremony for the fallen raiders. Hunter was caught off guard by the humanity and determination shown by this ragged group of men. It seemed to him that almost everyone else he had met since arriving on Actaeon 9 was beaten down and had given up. In contrast, these men faced their fates alternating between smiles, quiet severity, and grim determination.

They gathered around a campfire, talking idly in pairs and small groups. Some of the men laughed softly as they spoke. Others seemed engaged in serious conversation. Hunter marveled at the casual manner of the Raiders. None of them appeared distressed from the day's labors or losses. For Hunter, the deaths and the chaos of that day still felt very real. He was not sure that he would be able to sleep that night without having nightmares. He wasn't sure that he would ever be able to sleep again without having nightmares. Adam stood up before the group and cleared his throat.

"Welcome. We are all tired. It has been a long day, and so I am especially grateful that all of you are here to honor our fallen comrades."

Adam then proceeded to give a brief but passionate speech about what it meant to be a Dragon Raider. He spoke of honor and of duty to each other. Death he said was lighter than a feather, duty heavier than a mountain, and sacrifice the key to true happiness. His words moved Hunter. Two days earlier Hunter had wondered whether or not he even cared to live, but now, in Adam's words, he found something to live for. He wanted to be a man of principles. He wanted to face the inevitability of death with courage and determination. Hunter looked about and saw, shining in the eyes of his fellow Raiders, the same light of determination. Heads nodded in agreement and some of the men even raised their fists and called out passionate affirmations.

Adam spoke of the fallen Raiders and of the importance of remembering them. He recounted stories about the two men who had died but whom Hunter did not know. Hunter could not help but be touched by the stories. Some of them were moving. Some of them were funny. Adam shared information that he had known about the families of the two men. One of them was named Frank and had a grown up in Boise, Idaho. He was 35 years old and had a wife and two children. They had also been taken by the people of Actaeon. Frank hadn't seen his family for more than a year. He was sent to the Raiders after his third attempt at escape from a farming operation on the other side of the planet. Hunter could not believe how much

Adam knew about each of the men and he shared their stories with an honest reverence that brought tears to the eyes of those who listened.

As Adam neared the end of his speech, Hunter's thoughts began to wander, considering the things that he had heard. He began again to remember his own life before coming to Actaeon 9 and to think about his friends and family. What would be said about him when he was eaten by the dragons? He took a small measure of comfort knowing that he would be remembered by these men. It was truly only a small amount of comfort, but better than nothing. Perhaps, if he had enough time with the Raiders, he could come to take great comfort in knowing that this little group would honor his death. Perhaps it would be sufficient to help him not live out the last days of his life in fear.

He was snapped abruptly back to the present when Adam spoke his name. "Hunter, would you speak on behalf of Boris and John?" He saw the surprise and fear in Hunter's eyes, "I think that you are the only person who spent any time with them," Adam encouraged. "Please, help us to remember these men."

Hunter wanted to say that he barely knew the two men. He wanted to say that he was only 14 years old and that he didn't know what to say, but the words stuck in his throat. He realized that he wanted even more to be part of this group. He was drawn to their comradery and their compassion. He wanted to be like them, and he wanted to honor the memory of these two men. He stood up. His mouth felt like it was full of chalk. He moved to stand in front of the group. He swallowed hard and cleared his throat.

"I shared a wagon with John and Boris," Hunter paused for a moment, considering how to continue." I was hurt pretty badly when I got thrown into the wagon and they gambled with each other about whether or not I would survive my injuries. The stakes were set at one meal's ration. I'm so glad that John won the bet." He chuckled and he heard a few of the listening Raiders chuckle back in response. As he spoke, he felt like he was gathering courage and it came easier. "Boris always called John 'Cowboy' and I don't think that Boris was Boris's real name. . . I barely knew them, but I liked them. I think that they must have been good men because they were sent here. I think that only the best men on this planet are sent to be Dragon Raiders. I appreciate that they helped me feel at ease on our trip here. John was from Texas and Boris was from Russia. I imagine that they had families. I wish . . ." Hunter choked on his words. He swallowed. "I wish I could have known them better. I wish that I had more to say," he sighed deeply. "I will remember them." He concluded and his voice rang with determination. Hunter sat down.

Adam stood again. "Thank you, Hunter. Well spoken. Let us all pray and then go to bed. We have a hard day of training tomorrow."

Hunter was again caught off guard. Wasn't prayer kind of pointless? Didn't the existence of all-powerful aliens sort of disprove the existence of God? The men stood in a circle wrapping their arms around each other's shoulders and bowing their heads. Hunter followed along not knowing what else to do.

"João," Adam spoke again, "could you say the prayer tonight?"

The olive-skinned man nodded and then in his native tongue began to pray. Hunter had no idea what he was saying. He did notice however, that the prayer was spoken passionately, and Hunter could tell that the man was not simply reciting something that he had memorized. Everybody said amen when João was done speaking and then they separated, each man returning to his respective hut.

☐

15 RAIDERS

Brooklyn gently shook Hunter awake as the sky began to lighten from a distant rising sun. Hunter had slept fitfully through the night, his rest marred by frantic nightmares, flashing images of hungry monstrous creatures that snapped and swiped at him. Though Brooklyn shook him gently, Hunter sat up sharply, a whimpering cry escaping from the back of his throat. His forehead was slick with sweat, and he trembled slightly. Brooklyn reached out to put a hand on his shoulder.

"Hey kid, it's okay; it's just me. I know the first night after your first run can be pretty rough. The good news is that you are still alive. Come on, today you are going to start to learn how to not be afraid. It's time to train."

He helped Hunter to his feet and led him out of the hut and to an open space of ground off the main road. Most of the raiders had gathered to the area and milled about chatting idly. Hunter slid into the group, tucking his hands into his armpits and waiting. Brooklyn broke away to speak to some of the other men. In short order, Adam called for their attention and put them to work doing calisthenics. After a light warm up, the men ran. After they ran, they stretched. After stretching, they went through a series of heavy calisthenics, and then another one. They practiced dodging and rolling techniques. They ran sprints. They took breaks for water and biscuits, but mostly they just kept going and going and going.

By the time they stopped, Hunter found himself so completely exhausted that he had nearly forgotten his grief and fear. His thoughts had slowed to a crawl and a peaceful stupor had settled over his emotions. The sun was low on the horizon, the heat of the day washing away as twilight settled on the camp. The moment Adam dismissed the group, Hunter began to stumble toward his hut, but was tapped by a hand on his shoulder.

Brooklyn interrupted his peaceful mental stupor, "Not so fast, kid. You're coming to dinner."

Hunter gave him a smirk. "I think I've had about all the biscuits and water I can take."

"Nah, this ain't no biscuits and water. Come on, you'll see." Brooklyn led him toward the camp's fire pit.

Hunter was surprised to see a large pot of steaming stew brewing on the fire. As he came closer, he was drawn in by the rich aroma of the food and the warmth of the fire. Men strode in laughing, clapping each other on the shoulders. He found his mouth watering.

"What's in the stew?" he asked.

"Some local vegetables, herbs, and maybe a few of those little six-legged rabbit-looking things."

Hunter hadn't realized it, but his life as a slave had completely kept him from noticing simple things like animals. Of course, there had to be animals running around on this planet, probably all sorts of animals, but he had been focused on nothing but his own misery. He had a difficult time thinking about anything but his own pain and fear. He couldn't help but glance around, suddenly wondering what animals or insects might be in his immediate vicinity. He didn't see anything particularly interesting.

Brooklyn misinterpreted his expression. "Don't worry, there ain't nothing weird. It tastes amazin'. Nobody makes six-legged-rabbit-and-vegetable stew like Henry. Let's get in line."

They managed to wedge themselves into the middle of a rapidly forming food line. The line went quickly, but it felt like a lifetime with the savory smell of meat and vegetables filling Hunter's nose. When he finally got to partake of the stew, it was like Heaven did a dance on his taste buds. He didn't think that he had ever eaten anything so amazing in his whole life. Along with the stew, they served a lightly sweetened, earthy tasting tea. A year ago back home, Hunter probably would have been highly unimpressed by the meal, but at this moment, he could not imagine anything ever tasting so good. The stew and tea had been prepared in abundance, and Hunter ate until his belly was swollen. He ate until he thought he might be sick if he took another bite.

As the night went on Hunter found himself enjoying the company of the other men. He began to get to know more of the Raiders. He joked and laughed with them. They sang songs around the fire. He learned that the Raiders came from a broad range of ethnicities, religions, and ages. Hunter was by far the youngest, and this earned him no small measure of fame amongst the men. They all wanted to know what he had done to earn his death sentence with the Raiders, and they often whistled and slapped him on the back when he told them.

Hunter enjoyed the attention. He loved the food. The comradery was amazing, and he felt somehow that a tremendous burden was being lifted off his shoulders. When he finally made it back to his hut, he was utterly exhausted, but he felt warm on the inside. He felt like he wasn't alone anymore. He fell asleep the moment he lay down.

Waking up early the next morning was easy. He was still sore from the previous day's training, but Hunter looked forward to the work. He was surprised at how much he enjoyed the exercise. He could lose himself in the rhythm of his own running. He found peace in the strain of doing sets of pushups. Even the biscuits tasted better when you were tired, and at the end of his second day of training, he was excited to spend more time around the fire with the other Raiders. His third day passed in very much the same manner, and his fourth, and his fifth. Two weeks passed with very little variance in his daily schedule. He trained hard. He pushed himself more and more each day. He was getting very good at running. He got stronger each day, and he learned quickly.

On his sixteenth day with the Raiders he awoke for training, no longer needing Brooklyn to drag him out of bed. When Adam stood in front of the group, though, he didn't give them instructions for exercise routines. Instead, he announced that they would be making a raid on the canyon. They had received orders to retrieve a minimum of three eggs. They were not to return without at least three eggs, and they were to do so at all costs. For the raiders, this was a very big order. It was very uncommon that they were ever sent to acquire more than two at one time. After Adam's announcement, Brooklyn explained to Hunter that it might be very difficult to achieve this goal without taking serious losses. There was a gleam in his eye, though, and Hunter saw determination and bravery in Brooklyn's face. He couldn't help but be bolstered by the young man's spirit. They were to grab provisions and set out immediately.

Everybody moved quickly. Unlike Hunter's first experience heading for the canyon, this time he could feel the energy in the air. It wasn't just fear clouding his mind anymore. He definitely felt fear, but this time, he also felt excitement. He didn't want to die, but he didn't feel helpless. He was in much better shape, and they had taught him tactics for evading the attacks of the dragons. He now knew what to expect when he reached the canyon wall. They had practiced climbing techniques so that he would be able to move around in the canyon. He only had two weeks of training, but Hunter had learned quickly. Some of the other men had complimented him as being naturally talented for this sort of work. He actually found himself grinning a little. Adrenalin began to pump through his veins. He could do this.

Time rushed by in a blur, and it seemed like only a moment had passed before Hunter found himself again cresting the embankment to gaze across the plateau at the distant canyon and to jog toward his impending doom. He hadn't even begun to feel fatigue, but his excitement caused him to breath harder than was necessary. He trotted in a crouch, without making even the faintest noise. They made it much closer to the canyon than their previous run before the dragons roared to life. He couldn't help but wonder if he had been much noisier and clumsier the first time and had alerted the dragons earlier. If so, then he felt bad for having endangered everybody's lives.

When the wave of dragons hit, Hunter was ready. He avoided the first attack by flinging himself to the ground and rolling to the side. It wasn't fancy, but it worked. Claws passed within inches of his head. He was up and running in an instant. Another dragon was already sweeping in low with claws outstretched to bury into his chest. He changed directions without hesitation, diving perpendicular to the creature's path, rolling through a summersault to come up running at a full dash. He flung himself into the chaos and his training took over. Hunter truly was good at this. It was not that he moved with any sort of grace or fluidity, he just moved fast, and he kept moving. His fear disappeared. He never felt the burn in his lungs or his legs. He wasn't even consumed by the fight for his life. He was completely lost in the task of evading attacks and reaching the canyon wall.

When he did reach the canyon, he nearly flung himself triumphantly over the cliff. He had to throw himself to the ground splaying his arms and legs to stop quickly enough, and still he nearly slid into the chasm. He scrambled frantically, legs and waist dangling over the edge. When most of his body was back on safe ground, the next part of his training kicked in and he scanned the rim of the canyon for fissures or outcroppings that would give cover or allow safe access into the canyon. In less than a second, he discovered a deep crack that stretched out from the canyon wall, and he was up and running. He slid like a baseball player, falling into the crack as a diving dragon snatched at the empty air through which Hunter had passed.

The crack was very deep but narrow, and Hunter easily managed to support his weight by wedging himself awkwardly between the walls of the fissure. He paused for a moment, tilting his head against the dirt wall. He breathed deeply and closed his eyes. His heart pounded in his chest. For a moment, he was sheltered and safe. As he regained his composure, and his brain began to think again, he realized that he could easily hide in this crack. The dragons couldn't reach him. The other raiders couldn't see him. He opened his eyes and looked around. The walls were heavily textured. He could probably find comfortable handholds maybe even a place to sit. It would be easy to wait out the raid and then sneak back to camp in the dark. He could tell everyone that he got lost or pinned down. Nobody would know differently.

He wondered how the other raiders were doing. He could hear shouting and screeching coming from above him. Some of it was distant. Some of it was close. Once the race toward the canyon had begun, Hunter lost track of everybody else. He knew that others were running around him, each caught in their own struggle to avoid being clawed, bitten, or eaten, but they were like shadows in his memory, images on the fringe of his perception. He had no idea how well anyone else had fared in their efforts to reach the canyon. How did Adam manage to keep track of other raiders while he ran? Somehow, he seemed to know if anybody had been killed and how many had been killed.

As the moments grew longer. Hunter grew anxious. He worried about his new friends. They had taken him in, made him feel welcomed, trained him. Brooklyn had risked his life for Hunter on their first run. In the mere two weeks that he had been with the raiders, they had given him a way to deal with his loss and his fear. They had given him a purpose. He realized that if he hid in the crack, he would give up that purpose. Fear would rule over him. More of the raiders might die. What if he could end their raid sooner by finding one of the three eggs that was needed? He couldn't just hide when it was within his power to help his friends, and besides, the worst that could happen was he could die. The thought made him chuckle just a little bit. He steeled himself and allowed his new sense of purpose to take over again.

Hunter swiftly descended the crack about fifteen feet and then moved laterally to look out over the canyon. He stuck his head out tentatively and then sucked back in as a dragon flew by. He tried again and it was clear. He found that he had a good vantage point to see both directions along the canyon. The walls were craggy and uneven with many outcroppings and rugged-looking trees. It should be easy to move along the wall without falling. Leaving the safety of his crack, though, would make him an easy target for the monsters that soared overhead and that flew low through the canyon.

Hunter could see numerous nests tucked into various crannies along the slopes and outcroppings of the canyon walls. He had been told that the eggs they were seeking were small and difficult to spot from outside the nests. As well, he knew that not all the nests would have eggs. He would just have to pick a target and go for it. Even as he had this thought a scream broke his concentration and a man fell past him. His arms pinwheeled in the air, and Hunter watched in horror as one of his fellow raiders plummeted to certain death. Before the man had fallen more than fifty feet, a dragon swept in and speared the man through the neck and torso. His screams were cut off by a grotesque gurgling. Hunter looked away and pulled back into the crack.

When he looked out again the horrific scene had moved on. He swallowed his disgust and began to search determinedly for a target. He had to find an egg. He had to help bring this madness to an end. A glint caught his eye. About 15 feet down and 60 feet over, Hunter saw a nest. A single gnarled tree stretched out over the nest and he thought he could see a small dark crystalline egg glinting from its center. His eyes traced the canyon wall and he realized that he could get fairly close to the nest with relative ease, but he would have to leap across a wide gap to actually reach the dirt landing where the nest had been placed. The jump was wide, and it wouldn't be easy, but he couldn't see any more promising options, so he went for it.

Hunter crawled out of the crack, and using the abundant handholds and footholds, he crossed the canyon wall swiftly. At one point, a dragon flew dangerously near and he plastered himself against the rocks, but the creature moved on without noticing. In the distance he could see other raiders trying to scale into the canyon. He saw another one plucked from the wall and torn to shreds. He tried not to think about it. He let his arms and legs work and within a few minutes, he found himself poised at the edge of a daunting precipice.

There was an egg in the nest and the dragon was gone, but the jump would be difficult. He was able to stand on a small ledge and face the nest's landing, but he had no room to run. He would have to jump from a standing position. He knew that he didn't have much time, so he chose to not think about the distance or the consequences of not making the jump. He crouched and leapt. For an instant he felt suspended in the air. He could see his trajectory, and he was aware that his feet would not make the edge of the landing. He focused on what he could grab with his hands. He fell below the level of the ledge, and his chest slammed into the cliff wall. His legs curled under the landing, and he grabbed at an outcrop protruding from the rock. The stone held and his movement stopped.

He pulled himself slowly and laboriously onto the ledge. His ribs ached from slamming into the cliff wall, but he ignored it and went straight for the egg. As he snatched it from the nest, he only had less than a second to notice a rapid flickering shadow of a dragon that was about to bury its talons into his back. He flung himself to the side. The dragon slammed into the nest. Hunter slid off the landing, and only caught himself with his one free hand. He dangled from the edge. Not wanting to give up the egg, he quickly stuffed it in his pocket, and brought his hand up to strengthen his faltering grasp. By the time his hand reached the edge, the dragon had reached him. It extended a long claw and attempted to stab it through Hunter's hand. He jerked his arm back and the spike buried into the Earth where his hand had been. Hunter hung again from only one hand.

He looked up at the beast, and it looked back. He found intelligence behind its eyes, and he also found the cold blood thirst of a predator and the hot rage of a mother whose egg was being taken. Eye contact lasted only for an instant before the animal went for his other hand. It was trying to use its long claws to pin him to the ledge. Hunter had to let go. He moved quickly, grabbing with his other hand to switch his hold on the ledge, but he missed. The world slowed down, and Hunter fell. The dragon dove over the edge, maw gaping, but gravity moved faster than the monster, and Hunter fell out of reach.

He didn't remember the first impact, or the second, or the third, as he bounced down the steep slope of the cliff. He didn't remember crashing through outstretched tree branches, or freefalling the last 10 feet and slamming into the ground. The dragon had chased him as far as it could, grasping and clawing, but never quite reaching him, until Hunter's unconscious body had tumbled between two rock faces and could no longer be seen or reached.

16 WAKING UP AGAIN

"Hey, Spot! I think he's waking up."

Hunter sluggishly struggled to fight his way free from unconsciousness.

"You probably shouldn't eat him. After all, we could just cut off his hand. It would be nice to have another friend around here."

Were they talking about him? Who were they? Did that voice have an English accent?

"Okay, I'll make you a deal. If we decide to cut off his hand, then you can have it. In fact, why don't you bite it off right now? Just consider it a treat for being such a good little dragon."

Hunter thought the voice got all cutsie-wootsie when it said, 'Good little dragon.' Cut off his hand? Bite off his hand? He couldn't think straight. He was in so much pain. They couldn't be talking about Hunter. Who would want to bite off his hand? Did he say dragon?

"No, I don't think he is one of them. I know he smells funny and all, but he's way too scrawny, and he's dressed like a slave. Tell you what, Spot. Why don't you just bite his hand off right now before he wakes up all the way? He's much less likely to put up a fight if you get him while he's still drowsy."

Bite his hand off? Hunter felt something warm and wet begin to lick at his left hand, and suddenly he was wide-awake. He sat bolt upright and his whole body screamed in pain. Hunter scuttled pathetically backwards away from the large, sleek form of a dragon that had apparently been prepared to bite his hand off. His shoulder ached. His ribs burned and his whole body was covered in scrapes and bruises. The dragon took a step towards him.

"Now you've done it, Spot. You've gone and took too long. You've lost the element of surprise." A young boy of perhaps 11 or 12 stood next to the monster. When he put his hand on the dragon's neck it seemed to calm down. The beast swung its head around to look at the boy. It snorted and then swung back to stare hungrily at Hunter. In particular, it seemed to be staring at his left hand. "I suspect he's not going want to let us take that hand without a fight. Let's see if we can talk him into just giving it up freely." The boy talked to the monster as if Hunter were not present.

He cleared his throat, "Hello, sir, my name is . . . um . . . well . . . I'm Dragon Boy. This is my dragon. He wants to eat your hand. Actually, he wants to eat all of you but I'd rather he only ate your hand. So . . . if you don't mind . . .

well . . . let's have it then. We don't want to keep Spot waiting. Hold it up. This will go quickly. Come on now. Have at it."

Hunter clutched his hand possessively and his eyes shot back and forth between the boy and the monster. He was scared to the point of panic and could only just barely stammer out the question, "Who… who… who are you?"

"I told you. I am Dragon Boy and this is my dragon. His name is Spot. I thought about naming him Puff, but he don't blow no smoke or fire. He is covered in spots though."

Hunter looked at the dragon. His body was lean and black, spotted with silvery patches. "You - you can talk to it?"

"Now be careful," the boy's eyes narrowed. "This dragon speaks English and he don't like being called an 'it'. I'd hate to have to let him eat you. I haven't had no human company in a long time, and it seems like it would be downright rude of me to feed you to my dragon."

Hunter thought it was his imagination, but Spot seemed to narrow his eyes as well. "I'm sorry," he came back quickly, "I just… well… this is the first dragon that I have… uh… met, and I'm just a little nervous. You know… with all this talk about eating my hand." Hunter found himself wishing he could back away again, but his whole body ached and throbbed, and he was afraid to move.

Spot took a step forward. The boy took a step as well.

"I'm afraid that Spot here is going to have to eat your hand now. So... let's have it."

Hunter began to panic, "But – but – but why?"

The boy stopped, "Because you've got a little device in your hand that is going to tell them where we are." The boy held up his own hand and Hunter could see that it had been grotesquely mangled. "You see, I had mine ripped out when I fell off the cliff. You however, were not so fortunate. We could try to cut it out, but if we aren't quick enough it will release a toxin into your blood that will kill you in minutes. You should just let Spot here take care of it for you. He doesn't mind the poison one bit. Just think, after your hand is gone, you'll be a free man. You could hang out with us and kill stuff."

Hunter paused, "But what if I don't want to be free?"

The question seemed to hit the boy like a sledgehammer to the stomach. "Why wouldn't you want to be free? Only a crazy man would want to go back to living with them snot-nosed aliens." The vicious tone in his voice and the look of open disgust on the boy's face caused Hunter to recoil even further. He narrowed his eyes again and his voice grew dangerous. "Spot thought you smelled funny. You don't look like an alien but I'm beginning to think that maybe he was right." The boy reached to his waist and Hunter noticed for the first time that he carried two crude, but very wicked-looking hatchets. "There's something off about you. Maybe you're some kind of alien sympathizer. You're like their little human pet or something." He deftly pulled the hatchets from his belt and took a step forward, "I think that I might have to let Spot make a meal out of you after all." Spot seemed to grow very excited by this comment. He wagged his tail anxiously and crouched low, ready to pounce.

Hunter painfully squirmed backwards until his back was against a rock wall. "No. No. That's not it at all. It's just . . . it's just . . ." he stammered, "it's just…" he grew quiet and a touch of hopelessness entered his voice, "I have friends that I can't leave behind. I want to be free. I hate this place. I hate these people, but I can't stay here and leave my friends behind." The boy paused and seemed to consider Hunter's comments. Hunter continued, "Believe me, at this point I think that I would gladly give up my hand to escape, but I don't know if I can just run away. I don't know what I am going to do. I don't know how I can help anyone, but I have to try." He paused again slumping backwards against the wall. "It might just be simpler for Spot to eat me." Hunter slid to the ground and buried his face into his hands.

Hunter sat with his eyes closed for several long moments. He anticipated being eaten at any moment. It wasn't such a bad fate, he decided. He wondered if it would hurt much. Maybe Spot would start by biting his head off. Would the dragon take requests? Did he really understand English? It felt like an eternity and then suddenly his face was pulled from his hands by a warm, wet tongue that licked his whole head. Spot licked him again before turning around to shuffle away and Dragon Boy came over to sit down beside him. Hunter's face was practically dripping with dragon drool. "Well," the boy began, "I can't very well feed you to Spot what with you looking all beat up and sad. I can't say that I rightly know what to do with you, though. I don't imagine that they are going to come for you right away. They wouldn't want to upset the balance of their precious dragon colony. Maybe I'll just wait until tomorrow to feed you to Spot."

An awkward silence followed until Dragon Boy asked the question, "So I've told you my name. What's yours?"

Hunter gave him a sideways glance and a smirk, "My name's Hunter, but yours isn't really Dragon Boy."

"Most certainly is. My mum gave it to me when I was born. Nice to meet you, Hunter. Show me what you found."

Hunter decided to let the boy's obvious fabrication go uncontested, "What do you mean?"

"You fell from the cliff and landed in the exact same place that I landed about two years ago. That means that you must have been trying to take an egg from . . ." He glanced uneasily in the direction that Spot had gone and in a whisper, he said, "from Spot's mum."

"Spot's mom?" Hunter began but Dragon Boy shushed him anxiously.

"Ssshhh! Don't let Spot here you say that." He continued in a very low whisper. "He thinks I'm his mum. You see, there's a spotted black dragon that makes her nest in a little nook beneath a single tree that grows out from the canyon wall. It was about two years ago or maybe a little less, when I was a member of a dragon raiding party, and I spotted her nest. I climbed down and stole the egg that was in that nest, but then I fell bouncing off the rocks all the way down to here. I was hurt pretty bad and I almost died. My tracker was ripped from my hand during the fall and so, well… it seemed like a chance for freedom. As soon as I was conscious enough to realize what happened, I made up my mind that I was never going back to being a slave. I would rather die from my injuries or even starvation than go back to being a slave. I lived here near the entry of the cave for months. It was terrible. I had nothing to eat but small animals that I killed with rocks and some nasty tasting plants that grow up the cave wall. I was lonely and half-starved, I was. It was getting so bad that I had half a mind to kill myself." The boy became suddenly very intense, "But then it happened. Spot's egg hatched. Suddenly, I had myself a friend and it wasn't so bad. Spot got bigger real fast and pretty soon he was going out to get food for the two of us. About a year ago, he got big enough to ride. Now I'll tell you what, riding a dragon is about the funnest thing I've ever done."

Hunter interrupted, "You mean to tell me that he lets you ride him? That's incredible."

"I know, right? That's why I've started calling myself Dragon Boy. I think it's a right good name. When I'm old enough to grow facial hair, I'm going to change my name to Dragon Man."

"Wait a minute," Hunter interrupted, "I thought you said that your mom gave you that name."

He paused, realizing that his ridiculous fabrication had been uncovered and he smiled, "She did . . ." he began slowly, "well at least I am pretty sure she meant to. She was an awful smart lady. In fact, I think she could right see the future and she knew that one day I would become a dragon rider. She just didn't want me to feel awkward around the other kids. You know. Most boys got names like Timmy or Harry. A fellow with a name like Dragon Boy would have a right difficult time fitting in," and then without losing so much as a single beat he continued, "so, like I was saying. Spot thinks of me like his mum. I think he knows that I'm not his 'real' mum." The boy used his fingers to make quotation marks, "but I think that he might also be just a little bit sensitive about it. If you know what I mean." He elbowed Hunter and gave him a knowing glance.

Hunter chose not to question the boy's innate sense that Spot was more than just an animal and that he had feelings and was capable of rational thought and human-like emotions. He didn't want to make Dragon Boy feel suspicious again. He was still just a little afraid that the young man might change his mind and decide to feed him to Spot. So instead, he reached into his pocket and pulled out the egg he captured. "Is this what you're asking about?"

The boy's eyes lit up with excitement, "Yeah . . . now look at that. You've got yourself a right valuable piece of treasure there."

"I know. I was told that the aliens love these things."

"Now don't you even think about giving that to no alien." The boy had a dangerous tone in his voice. "If I even think you plan on giving that up, I'll let Spot make a right tasty meal out of you, I will. When that egg hatches, you'll have the most loyal friend you ever found. You'd be a right big fool if you gave that up."

Hunter was stunned by the boy's severity and he sat in silence for a few moments while he turned the egg over in his hand. This was the first time that he had ever seen a dragon egg close up. It seemed to be made from light gray crystal. It was surprisingly small and shaped perfectly like an egg, round and bulbous at one end and slightly tapered on the other. It was perfectly smooth and perfectly symmetrical. Inside Hunter could see the hazy form a very tiny reptile. "Well, then . . . how long until it hatches?"

"Now that is a tricky question and I don't think that there is a right definite answer. I had Spot's egg for maybe three months before it hatched but I don't know how long it sat in the nest before I took it. I used to stare into that little egg for hours when I had nothing to do. The lighting in this cave was very poor, but I thought that I could occasionally see Spot move just a small bit. He moved so little though that sometimes I thought he must be dead. It wasn't until I got the courage to step out into the sunlight one day to have a better look that he actually hatched. I went out right before the sun come up. I didn't want any of the dragons in the canyon to see me. I was afraid that they would eat me. I was planning on dashing right back into the cave as soon as I got a good look but then the sun rose up. Light began to stream down the canyon, and as it did Spot started to move. You see, this canyon points right at where the sun rises so it didn't take long at all before the ledge in front of my cave had a good amount of light shining on it. I felt awful nervous, but Spot was squirming around inside the egg so much I got downright curious and forgot that I might get eaten at any moment. Before I knew it, he hatched. He was born right in the palm of my hand."

The boy looked nostalgically at his palm. "I'm not sure if

he would ever have been born if I hadn't taken him out into the light. First thing he did, was to eat up all of his own eggshell. Gobbled it right up he did and licked my hand like he was licking a plate clean. Now that I can go exploring with Spot, I've noticed that the other dragons keep their eggs covered until they want them to hatch. I'm not sure what makes them ready to hatch but I am pretty sure that they need light to do it." He seemed to think for a moment, "Not just light though. There's something else. Spot was waiting to hatch. I think he was waiting for me. I can't quite explain it, but when he hatched... I think he recognized me from all that time I spent staring at him in the dark." The boy paused for a moment seeming introspective. "Spot's the best friend I ever had. He'd give his life for me and I'd give mine for him." There was resolve and determination in the boy's voice.

Dragon Boy's last statement hung in the air, and they sat in silence for several long moments. Hunter couldn't help but feel a little bit jealous. The boy seemed to truly have a deep affection for his dragon. Hunter could really use a friend like that right now. He looked longingly at the egg as he rolled it between his thumb and forefinger. Who knew? Maybe it would hatch for him. Maybe he could have a ferocious, flying, man-eating pet reptile. He smiled a little at the thought. He couldn't help but feel like he was living in a half sci-fi, half fantasy novel. For a moment, he felt hope swell up inside of him. Maybe things could work out okay. Maybe something incredible could come from all this craziness. Then he remembered that he had to go back to being a slave. He could never keep a pet dragon while he worked as a slave. For that matter, he would probably end up dead in a week or so when he was sent back to try to harvest more eggs. Spot's friends would eat him and then his story would end. He tucked the egg back into his pocket. Maybe turning it over to his captors was the wisest idea. Could he hide it from them? What would happen if he never brought it out into the sunlight?

"So . . . Spot speaks English?" Hunter asked, in part to hide the thoughts he had entertained of turning the egg over to his captors.

The boy looked at him suspiciously. Hunter couldn't help but feel like the young man could read his mind. He seemed to consider Hunter for a moment before shrugging off whatever suspicions he was entertaining. "Well . . . not exactly but I'm pretty sure that Spot can read my mind. I think he knows what you are saying, because I can speak English and I know what you are saying. I can read his mind too . . . I think. Well, at least, I am pretty sure that I know how he is feeling. Dragons don't have very complicated feelings. Most of the time he is either hungry, angry, or content. Come to think of it, though, that pretty much describes me too. Sometimes he gets happy. He is especially happy when he manages to snatch up a coney. That's what I call the little six-legged, furry, rabbit-looking things. They live in holes along the rim of the canyon. He also likes to sunbathe in the mornings. He really enjoys sleeping. I like eating conies too."

The boy continued to babble on and Hunter couldn't help but smile to himself. He was pretty sure that this kid could talk more than anyone he had ever met and he couldn't help but think that 'Dragon Boy' was just a little off his rocker. He talked about conies, hedge rats, stink snakes, moth lizards and so many other things that Hunter lost track. It seemed that he had given names to almost every animal on the planet. After nearly fifteen minutes of listening to Dragon Boy babble on, Spot, the hand-eating dragon, lumbered back into the chamber. He curled up next to them and laid his snout on the ground with one large eye staring directly at Hunter. It looked as if the dragon still had hopes for snacking on his appendages. To say that he felt a little unconformable beneath the piercing stare of that one large eye was a gross understatement.

Dragon Boy talked on for hours and Hunter sat listening. The young man knew a great deal about the area in and around the canyon. He spoke of adventures and of things that he had learned while flying on his dragon's back. Hunter learned that Dragon Boy was actually 12 years old, though he appeared younger. He couldn't get him to share any other details from his life on Earth. It actually seemed that the younger boy was happy with his current life on Actaeon 9. Hunter couldn't help but be jealous and long to have such freedom. Couldn't he just stay with Dragon Boy and Spot? Perhaps they could organize a resistance. Perhaps, the egg that he harvested would hatch. If he had his own dragon, then maybe he could save April. If he went back to the Dragon Raiders, he would probably just get eaten. On the other hand, staying meant that he would have to let Spot eat his hand. It would probably hurt . . . like . . . a lot! But what was he going to do if he went back to being a slave? How long could he stay here before they came after him or just got tired and pushed their kill-the-kid button? These thoughts swirled around and around in his head.

"And that is how you cook a bottle bug," Dragon Boy smacked his lips together. "They are absolutely delicious." He cocked his head at the dragon. "Spot says it's time to go hunt for some food. Right then. We'll be back after dark." Dragon Boy stood up. "You should get some sleep. You look like a mess. You can sleep right here if you want. No need to thank me for my hospitality. Spot and I will bed down in the library after we get back." Without another word, he turned and walked out, pet dragon close on his heels.

Library? Hunter wondered what type of room in these damp and dreary caves might pass for a library. He looked around the rocky room where he now sat alone. The floor was relatively flat and covered with powdery, well-trampled dirt. Soft light filtered into the cave from the entrance. He realized that it was getting darker. The sun was going down, and the cave would be completely dark soon. As he inspected his surroundings, he noticed that they must have drug him into the cave. The entrance curved away from the interior of the room. Light managed to filter in, which meant that he was relatively close to the interior of the canyon, but there was no way that he could have just fallen and landed here.

There was a crude pallet fashioned from ragged blankets in the corner. The boy had said that Hunter could sleep here. Did that mean he could use the blankets. It was beginning to get cold. Hunter crawled to the corner and laid himself out on the bedding. He hoped that Dragon Boy wouldn't be upset. If so, would he find himself being eaten as a midnight snack for Spot? He wasn't sure whether or not he cared. As he stretched out, he realized that every part of his body ached. His ribs protested sharply with each movement. His head swam just a little as he laid himself down. He could not help but worry that he might have suffered permanent damage. He did not believe that it would be possible to sleep with so many aches and pains, but once he closed his eyes, unconsciousness came rapidly.

17 DRAGON BOY

Hunter awoke to the smell of food. When he opened his eyes, he found some meat and roots laid out on a flat rock before him. A crude water skin was set beside it. Dragon boy squatted in the corner, his lips turned up in a smirk.

"Maybe I'll call you Snoring Boy. You make so much noise when you sleep, I was afraid that the aliens would find us for sure."

Hunter sat up and stared at the food. The plate contained a surprisingly large helping. It looked and smelled delicious. "How? . . ." he began, "where? . . ."

The boy laughed, "Spot killed some conies and I picked some roots. I cooked it all in the kitchen." He smiled broadly.

"Can I . . .?" Hunter began.

"Well, it's not there for staring at."

He needed no more urging and dug into the food ravenously. The meat was not seasoned but it was good. The roots were moist and flavorful. It was a good meal, and Hunter didn't even notice that the water was brown.

"Not bad. Right?"

Hunter nodded. His mouth was stuffed with the delicious meat and vegetables.

"You eat like you haven't had a decent meal in forever."

Hunter shrugged sheepishly; his mouth still too full of food to respond. Dragon Boy flopped back and watched him eat. Though the helping of food had been large, Hunter consumed it all in moments. He was tempted to lick the stone plate but thought better of it and placed it aside with a contented sigh.

"Thank you. That was amazing."

"Yeah, I am a pretty incredible cook, if I do say so myself," the boy smiled, obviously enjoying the praise.

"Where did you get the food? How did you cook it?"

"Spot killed the coney. I've got a kitchen. It is down the hall from the library." Dragon boy continued as if this explanation needed no additional clarification. "Spot and I have been thinking about it and we both agree that he shouldn't eat you. Honestly, it was Spot who came to your defense. He thinks that you smell a little like one of those nasty aliens and you'll probably give him indigestion. Look, here's the thing though. You've either got to give up your hand or you've got to go back. I've given it some consideration and I think that Spot and I will be just fine. I don't think they will come after you. I think they'll just push the button that kills you and I think that your time is running out. I was almost a little surprised to find you still alive this morning."

Hunter considered the boy's words. He looked at his hand and shuddered. It was unnerving to think that at any moment some alien could dispassionately press a button on a remote control and then Hunter's life would just end. Would it hurt much? He tried to not to fixate on the thought. "I don't know. I can't make sense of anything," he began to reason out loud. "If I go back, nothing will change. I don't know if I'll ever have another chance to escape. I'll probably be dead in a week. If I stay, I'll have to let Spot eat my hand. I think I'm open to that . . . but would that really stop them? They know that I am alive right now. I am sure that they probably even know exactly where I am. What else does this device in my hand tell them? Do they know that I ate food this morning? Why haven't they killed me yet?" Hunter paused for a moment trying to reason through the problem. "If my hand were gone, is there anything that might still draw their attention?" He looked up at Dragon Boy, "You said that your tracker got ripped out of your hand. How exactly did it happen?"

"I don't know. I guess it happened when I fell but I was knocked unconscious just like you. I don't know how long I was out. When I woke up, my hand was a bloody mess and the tracker was gone. I was awful sick for three days after and my arm swelled up like a balloon. I think that maybe some of the poison got into my blood."

"Do you have the tracker?" Hunter asked.

"No, I never saw it after that."

The more that Hunter thought about his situation, the more he was surprised that they hadn't killed him yet. "I think I have to leave. Even if my hand is gone, they might come to check. In your case, it probably seemed that you died the instant you fell from the cliff. They know that I'm alive. They may know other things that I have been doing. They might not be killing me because they want to know what is going on down here." Dragon Boy's eyes widened as he began to understand and Hunter continued, "I have to make it back so that I can that tell them a story that will stop them from coming down here. If I don't, then you and Spot might get discovered."

The implications of Hunter's reasoning settled over both of the boys. Hunter could not stay. The fact that he was still alive meant that they knew something strange was going on. It was only a matter of time before they came to search out the problem. Cutting off his hand might not stop them from investigating. He barely knew the other boy, and he was extremely jealous. Being free and flying around on his own pet dragon sounded amazing to Hunter, but he couldn't endanger his new friend. He knew that the people of Actaeon were clever. He knew that there was a reason they hadn't killed him yet. His only choice was to return.

"How can I get out of here?" Hunter asked.

"Spot and I could fly you out." Dragon boy offered.

Hunter thought for a moment. "I don't think so. If they are tracking me, then they might catch us both as we fly out. Even if they don't catch us, they will see my altitude change way too drastically in a short amount of time, and they will track me as I travel far too quickly along a route that is impossible to cover on foot. For my story to be believable, I need to walk out."

Dragon Boy whistled, "That will be difficult. This whole area is full of dragons. The only way that I can leave the cave safely is on Spot's back." He rubbed his chin thoughtfully. "Your best bet will be to leave at night. Most of the dragons hunt during the day. Some of them are awake at night though. I think they are guarding the other dragons while they sleep. We are pretty close to one end of the canyon." Dragon Boy leaned forward and began to draw in the dirt. With his finger, he sketched a crude map of the area. "If you are quiet and stick to the shadows, you might be able to follow the canyon this way until it ends." He dragged his finger down the simplistic picture of the canyon. "It will take all night and part of the morning, but you should be able walk clear of the dragon's hunting area. When you leave the canyon, you will be three times further from the Raiders camp."

Hunter nodded, "Hopefully, they won't come looking for me right away. I'll leave tonight." He sat back against the cave wall intertwining his fingers behind his head. He couldn't help but feel some small measure of relief. At least he had a plan.

The boys sat in silence for a while until Dragon Boy spoke up. "Hey! Do you want to see the rest of my cave?"

He was excited.

Hunter had begun to relax and was feeling sluggish. He may have slept well that night, but he was also comfortably full of food and recovering from injuries. "Sure," he said through a yawn, "give me the tour."

Hunter had the best day of his slave life. The younger boy's excitement was so infectious that he couldn't help but reciprocate the emotion. He wondered if the kid always acted like this or if he was just excited to have human company. During the tour, Hunter found out that the caves were extensive. Dragon Boy and Spot primarily made use of the first four chambers, which had relatively flat floors. Beyond these first four rooms, though, the network of caves continued on much further. The kitchen turned out to be an expansive cavern with a draft that pulled the smoke from Dragon Boy's fires deeper into the caverns. The library was a large room with many flat surfaces where Dragon Boy had drawn pictures of his adventures. His crude artwork looked like caveman drawings. Hunter watched as Dragon Boy added a scene to the library to show their meeting. They played tic-tac-toe together. They arm-wrestled. Dragon Boy let him play with his hatchets. They were fashioned from short but sturdy sticks and flat sharpened stones. Dragon Boy didn't have much to do in his free time, and so he had perfected the art of creating and sharpening his hatchets. Apparently he frequently broke them while hunting and had to make them over and over again. He always carried two of them and he could throw them with uncanny accuracy.

In the late afternoon, Hunter watched from the mouth of the cave while Dragon Boy and Spot flew back and forth along the canyon. He smiled as he watched the younger boy show off. It looked like so much fun. The dragon was fast. Several times they whipped by the mouth of the cave after coming out of a sharp dive. Spot's wings tucked in close to his body and Dragon Boy ducked his head, laying low against the reptile's neck. He screamed and hooted in pure joy and exhilaration. Hunter pulled out his crystal egg a number of times and stared longingly at the small hazy form of a baby dragon. He was standing in the sunlight. Would it hatch? What would he do if it did? Quietly, he hoped that it would. Watching Dragon Boy and Spot fly together made him want to forget all of his previous reasoning. Maybe, there was a way he could stay. Maybe his thinking was all wrong. He thought hard about the possibility of staying.

He considered the egg in his hand again. Maybe Adam could tell him more about it. How could he even ask Adam? If any of the Raiders knew that he captured an egg, he would have to turn it over. Could he help them understand? To do so, he would have to tell them about Dragon Boy and Spot. He didn't think this would be wise or honest. Doing so would betray the boy's trust. If any of the Leebers discovered him, his life with Spot would be over. Maybe he could just hide the egg? What would he do if it hatched? Could he just keep the egg in the dark all the time to prevent it from hatching? Would the baby dragon eventually die if he did so? Maybe he should just leave the egg with Dragon Boy. He considered these questions long and hard while he watched his two new friends soaring through the canyon.

By the time Spot and Dragon Boy landed, Hunter had made up his mind. Dragon Boy leapt from the back of the great flying reptile. He was grinning from ear to ear. Hunter could see the exhilaration and excitement in the boy's eyes.

"I wish you could try it, but I don't think Spot would let you. You understand, what we got between the two of us is special." He flopped down next to Hunter. "He might eat you if you tried." He said the words slowly as he considered the matter. "Anyway, someday you'll have one of your own." He nudged Hunter on the shoulder. "Won't that be something!"

"Yeah, well . . . about that." Hunter began as he pulled the dragon egg from his pocket. "I don't think I can keep this." He held the little egg out. "You should take this. If I bring it with me, they'll just take it."

Dragon boy looked at the egg and cracked a little smile. "You know, I thought about it. Honestly, I thought about just taking it from you, but... here's the thing. I don't think I want another dragon around here." He cleared his throat theatrically. "You see, I'm a monogamous sort of fella and so is Spot. I think he might get right jealous if I had another dragon skulking around."

Hunter looked at Spot. He had curled up near the far side of the drop-off. The dragon cracked one eye open for a moment and huffed. Did he understand their conversation?

Dragon Boy continued. "And there's another thing." He paused and seemed to consider his words. "I get a good feeling about you. I think that you might just do something important on this dirty planet. I don't know how you're going to do it. You're just a slave like every other human.

By all I can see with my eyes, you'll probably be dead soon, but I can't help but hope for something more." He paused again for a long moment. "Maybe, if I send that egg with you, something good will come of it. Maybe it will help you somehow. I can't handle another dragon out here. It would just hatch into another flying lizard that eats dragon raiders. I think I'm willing to let that little treasure go with you and see what happens. You keep it."

Hunter sighed. After a few more moments of holding his hand out, he curled his fingers around the little egg and tucked it back into his pocket. The two boys sat in silence looking out over the canyon as the light grew slowly and steadily dimmer.

Dragon Boy broke the silence with a question. "What's going on with Earth? I've been here a long time and it's been a while since I've had any news."

Hunter smiled, "So much . . ." He shared everything that he could remember about current news on Earth. All his information was months old, but the other boy was super excited to hear every little bit of news. The two boys laughed and joked like normal kids. Dragon Boy might have been from England, and Hunter was from the United States, but it wasn't hard to share a sense of comradery. They had both been slaves. They shared a hatred for their enemy and even a few things in common.

As their conversation progressed, Hunter talked about his experience with the Dragon Raiders. Dragon Boy wanted to know the names of everyone that Hunter had met. He hoped that maybe some of his old friends were still alive and working with the Raiders. He thought that he might remember Adam, but unfortunately, it seemed that everybody else he had known was now dead. This caused a solemnity to settle over their conversation. Hunter fought back a lump in his throat. Death had become far too much of a reality in too short of a time.

Dragon Boy roughly wiped a tear from one of his eyes and stood. "You've been fine company, Hunter. I'm glad you fell into my little hole, but it's time for you to head out. If you are going to make it clear of the dragon hunting grounds, you are going to need to leave right away."

18 DEAD MAN

Hunter walked determinedly away from the canyon and back toward his life as a slave. Truthfully, he felt better now than he had in a long time. Somehow, the act of choosing to remain a slave made him feel closer to freedom. Slaves didn't have choices. They certainly were not given the option to choose whether to be a slave. Hunter had made this choice. He chose to remain a slave so that he might have the slimmest chance of helping his friends and so that he could protect his new friends Dragon Boy and Spot. In a way, that made him feel not like a slave at all. He had no idea how he was even going to begin to help his friends, but he would find a way. He was sure of it. So, he walked on with his chin up, and a gleam in his eye. He would probably be dead before the end of the week. The thought made him smile.

Despite his newfound bravado, he walked slowly back to the encampment. He needed time to think and though he might have come to terms with his decision to be a slave, it did not mean that he was in any great hurry to get back to life as usual. From a distance, he could see the smoke of campfires rising from a small point in the desert. This, he knew, would be the Raider's encampment. He stopped for a moment, and again he pondered the choice he had made. Perhaps he could still go back and feed his hand to Spot. He knew that he would not, but he could not help but entertain the thought. With a deep sigh of resolution and no small measure of determination, he began to walk again. It made no sense to dwell upon his decision. He would do as he knew he must.

As Hunter closed the distance between himself and the encampment, it seemed more and more apparent that too much smoke rose from the little conglomeration of huts. Idly, Hunter's curiosity began to grow. He could not imagine the cause of so much smoke. He continued to walk and about two and a half hours passed before he crested the last low rise outside of the Raider's encampment. As he did so, he was met with a confusing sight. Nearly all the huts were gone. They had been burned to the ground. Only a few smoldering shells remained. Hunter could see from where he stood the prostrate bodies of many men strewn about the camp. He began to worry for his Raider friends. He walked quickly backwards over the rise and dropped to the ground hiding from the view of anyone that might be alive in the camp. Cautiously he crept back to the top of the rise until he could see down on the burnt little huts. For nearly an hour he lay still and inspected the camp from his vantage point on the rise. He searched for any movement that might indicate somebody was still alive. He saw nothing.

When Hunter felt like it was as safe as it could be, he rose and began to walk toward the camp. As he approached, he could see that the dead bodies consisted of just two slaves whom he didn't recognize. All the other bodies belonged to the Actaeon guards that patrolled their camp. Hunter could see obvious signs of a firefight. Some of the dead guards still had weapons in their hands or lying near their corpses. Scorch marks from the discharge of energy weapons were everywhere. The main guardhouse was completely destroyed. The partial remains of huts showed signs of blaster fire. He stood in the middle of the still burning battle zone and he didn't know what to do. How had this happened? Where were all the humans? Where should he go from here?

Hunter sat down in the shade next to one of the few walls that still stood erect and began to consider his situation. He could take this opportunity to return to the canyon and try to find Dragon Boy, but he would probably get eaten by the other dragons. He could just sit and wait for his alien captors to come looking for him. He still had his tracker and surely somebody would come by if he waited long enough. As he considered the problem, he realized that it didn't matter. With the tracker in his palm, they would inevitably find him and once they did, it would be back to life as a slave. With that consideration in mind, he decided that he would like to try to see April while he still had a small amount of freedom. Perhaps, he could walk across the desert to the small oasis where he believed she would still be working. He thought that the distance between the Raider's encampment and the oasis village couldn't be more than ten to fifteen miles. The worst that could happen would be to have his captors find him wandering the desert before he could successfully find the oasis and sneak in to see April. If he was lucky, maybe he would die of starvation or dehydration before they found him. Death by starvation sounded better than being fed to those dragons in the canyon.

Determinedly, Hunter rose from his place in the shade and began to search the camp. He would need supplies. He felt like he could easily make the walk to the oasis in less than a day, but he was afraid that he might get lost in the attempt. In fact, he was sure that he would get lost. With only a small amount of searching, he found food and water bags that had not been destroyed in the battle. He attempted to take one of the energy weapons from a fallen soldier but found that he couldn't make it work. It probably had safety features to prevent it from functioning for humans. He did however take one of their glowing green knives, which, he knew from experience, would work just as well for him as for his captors.

When Hunter set out across the desert, the sun was beginning to arc downward in the sky. He headed directly toward the horizon remembering that the sunset had been in his eyes when they left the oasis heading toward the Raider's camp. As he walked, he began to calculate time and distance in his head. If the Raider's camp was 15 miles from the oasis, he should be able to cover the distance in less than 5 hours walking at a leisurely pace. He believed that he still had more than six hours remaining in the Actaeon day. He should be able to arrive before dark. His fears of getting lost had been completely unfounded. The direction that he needed to travel was clearly marked by the tracks of many slave carts that had traveled to and from the encampment.

He began to make plans for how he would create an opportunity to talk with April. Once he arrived at the oasis, he would need to appear as though he belonged. He would have to sneak into the little town and blend in. Perhaps he could circle the town and come at it so that the sunset would help to cover his approach. Perhaps he could wait until dark. He could probably figure out where the slaves slept and try to find April after everybody went to sleep. So long as he walked around purposefully, he probably wouldn't be questioned. He would have to sneak about without looking sneaky. He walked onward for hours, plotting and planning his infiltration of the little town. Before his training with the Dragon Raiders, the distance he traveled might have been exhausting. Now though, with water and food, he barely thought about the effort.

Hunter was lost in thought as he crested a sandy rise and the small town came into view. The low buildings, green trees, and blue water stood out starkly against the desert landscape and made it easy to identify. It appeared to Hunter that he would still need to walk for about 30 minutes before arriving at the oasis. He paused, looking at the little town while considering his options. The thought occurred to him that he would probably be a slave again by morning. He shrugged the thought away and steeled himself mentally to execute his plan. He had decided during his walk that the best option would be to try to find April as quickly as possible. The longer he waited, the more likely it would be that his captors would use the tracker in his hand to hunt him down. His plan was very simple. Enter the camp, walk around looking like he was on an important errand and find April. Talk with her for as long as possible and then be taken captive again. It was a terrible plan, but he didn't exactly have a lot of options.

He began to think about what he should say. He would need to say all the most important things quickly. He needed to be encouraging. He needed to help her feel hope.

That would be very difficult, seeing as how he didn't have any great plan that was going to free them. What was there to hope for? Hunter had found hope in simply deciding not to give up. Would that be enough for April? Could he just say, "Don't give up?" That sounded like a slogan to accompany an inspirational picture or a cheesy grin and a slug in the arm.

Hunter's thoughts were cut short by a blue beam of light that shot down from the sky and into the little town in the distance. The beam pulsed steadily, and Hunter could hear a high-pitched whining noise in the distance that was growing increasingly louder. The beam of light completely derailed his train of thought. At first, he stared dumbfounded and confused at the scene but in the back of his mind recognition began to grow. Suddenly, the beam exploded outward forming a blue dome of light that completely encompassed the oasis and as it did realization flooded Hunter's mind. The memories of that night in the park came back to him in vivid detail. The other race of aliens was attacking the oasis village. Hunter watched as three ships descended on the dome. How could this be happening here? What did this mean for him and the other slaves? He remembered the raiders' encampment and realized the camp must have also been attacked. All the guards were left behind. Some of the slaves were killed in the battle but the rest must have been taken. April would be taken. His heart started to race, and he began to panic. He had to stop this. He took off at a dead run.

It felt like a lifetime before he ran up to the edge of the dome. He panted hard and his heart pounded like it was going to explode. Chest heaving, he stood panting and sweating as his eyes swept frantically over the surface of light. Through the wall, he could hear the muffled sounds of battle and watched as shapeless shadows moved swiftly around the dome's interior. Hunter knew all too well what would happen if he passed through the wall. He would be struck by the force of drastically increased gravity that would plaster him to the ground. How could he help? How could he do anything? Then it hit him. He had to step through the wall and allow himself to be captured. April was probably already captured. Even as this thought occurred to him one of the ships broke the surface of the dome and swiftly gained altitude. Hunter knew that the ship was full of slaves. He had to make sure that he was on one of those ships. He took a step forward toward the wall of light.

Even as he took his first step to penetrate the surface of the dome, he was struck hard in the chest and thrown to the ground. At first, he thought that he had been repelled by the dome itself, but then he realized that the body of a stricken alien soldier lay partially on top of him. The man had been propelled from the fighting by an explosion breaking the surface of the wall exactly where Hunter stood. He lay motionless. It was the body of a Cravos soldier. He was about the same size and weight as Hunter. On impulse, Hunter began to strip the man of his helmet and armor. He moved swiftly without thinking. He paused only for a moment to look at the soldier's face. His eyes were open and glassy. They stared lifelessly into the sky. He looked human. He was young. He might have been Hunter's age. His neck was twisted at an unnatural angle. He felt sorry for the dead youth, but he moved on quickly. In a matter of moments Hunter was dressed in the soldier's armor. He left his slave clothing behind and took only the glowing green knife he had scavenged from the Raider's camp and the pouch with his dragon egg which he wore beneath the alien chest plate. He stood and approached the wall of the dome a second time. Pausing, he said a prayer and stepped through the wall. What he found was total chaos.

Explosions reverberated from all directions. The very air around him shook as the discharge from energy weapons screamed by him. Hunter had stepped right into crossfire from the two factions. The moment he entered the dome, he felt the increased gravity begin to pull him down. The armor seemed to come to life slowly. It responded as if it had been damaged by the attack that had killed its previous owner. Nonetheless, it did work. The effects of gravity lessened as the suit came to life and Hunter took off running. The armor amplified his movements and he bounded effortlessly and rapidly toward cover. As he did, his left shoulder was grazed by an energy bolt and he was sent sprawling into an alleyway between two buildings. He scrambled to his feet and plastered himself to the alley wall.

He observed that his shoulder guard had been knocked loose and his arm felt heavy with the effects of the gravity beam. He pushed the armor back into place and the pull of gravity seemed to lessen. Hunter looked around and tried to orient himself. What was he doing? He had only ever seen this town once. He had no idea where he might find April. He decided after a moment that he had to make a run for the Cravos ships. They seemed to be winning this battle and if she weren't dead from crossfire, then she would probably be in one of the remaining ships.

Hunter ran to the end of the alleyway and peered out, looking up and down the street. He spotted the remaining ships easily. They hovered about 50 feet in the air at opposite ends of the town. Soldiers jumped from the ground carrying slaves over their shoulders. They leaped in long, perfect arcs moving in and out of the vessels. He would have to pick one. Without thinking Hunter sped out of the alleyway heading toward the ship that was closest. He darted between buildings, trying to avoid areas where fighting seemed the heaviest. With the suit his movements felt blindingly fast. He could barely control his run, but he sped on recklessly, afraid that April may have already been loaded into one of the ships.

Without heed of what might be around the next corner Hunter turned left and crashed headlong into a group of three Actaeon soldiers. They were hunched together near the end of the alley where they exchanged fire from a protected position. The first soldier was guarding their rear and faced Hunter down with an energy rifle. Hunter's reckless assault caught the soldier off guard. He discharged his weapon, but the blast missed Hunter, passing underneath his left armpit. Hunter had completely forgotten about the knife he carried, but he brought it up reflexively as he barreled into the soldier. The knife drove into the soldier's throat, and then they tumbled into the two remaining Actaeon combatants who had their backs turned. The man closest to the mouth of the alleyway was knocked out into the street. He attempted to scramble back to cover but was almost immediately cut down by opposing fire.

The last soldier and Hunter found themselves tangled together in a mass of arms and legs. The enemy responded immediately with trained fighting techniques. Hunter struck out wildly and ineffectively. The Actaeon soldier grabbed

Hunter's hand and with a quick twisting motion broke his wrist causing him to drop the knife. Hunter screamed out in pain and tried to squirm away, but the soldier twisted his shoulder into Hunter's gut and rolled over. He came up sitting on Hunter's chest and began to punch him repeatedly in the helmet. The first blows were largely absorbed by the armor, but quickly his faceplate began to crack. As the mask failed, Hunter began to feel the effects of the artificially augmented gravity bear down on him. His head began to jar around inside the helmet, and he found it hard to focus or even stay conscious. At last the soldier raised both arms high in the air and prepared to smash down on Hunter's head with a two-handed blow. Hunter looked dazedly up at the alien. He could barely make sense of what was happening, but he was sure that he was about to die.

As his would-be killer bore down to crush Hunter's head, a blinding flash of light exploded into the man's chest, throwing him backwards. In moments, Hunter was being lifted to his feet and he found himself staring through his facemask at a Cravos soldier who looked him up and down and then slapped him on the helmet. He seemed to be saying, "Good job. Now rub some dirt on it and walk it off."

When he looked around, Hunter found himself surrounded by a group of five Cravos soldiers. Three of them had taken up positions guarding access to the alleyway where they released bursts of fire from their weapons. One of them stepped forward and began to work rapidly on Hunter's suit. With tools that Hunter could neither recognize nor even begin to understand, the soldier made repairs and adjustments to his armor. In a matter of moments Hunter began to grow lighter, he felt his damaged shoulder plates grow tight, and the cracks in his visor re-sealed. A speaker in his helmet came to life and a voice came through.

"Can you hear me now?" The voice spoke English. Hunter was dumbfounded and he didn't know how to respond. "I said, can you hear me now?"

"Hurry up." A second voice came across the speaker. "They're about to cut us off." The voice was strained and hurried.

"I told you we should have left him." A third voice sounded.

"Not now, Dean. There'll be plenty of time to say, 'I told you so,' once . . ."

"Once we're all dead." Dean interrupted.

"If it weren't for this soldier, we'd probably all be dead anyway."

"Look boys, we gotta get out of here. My subspace transponder just lit up. A hostile A4 transport unit is on its way. We've got less than 5 minutes before this site gets lit up."

"I . . . I can hear you." Hunter cut in.

"Sweet!" The first voice came in again. "What's your ID block soldier?"

"I . . . umm . . . what . . . my head . . . I don't remember."

"Sid," a voice came in frantically. "The guy probably has a concussion. You can interrogate him later. We have less than 10 seconds to get across this road before we have to fight our way through 20 Actaeon elite guards. Move now!" The voice was practically screaming. One of the soldiers thrust an energy rifle into Hunter's hands, spun him on his heels, pushed him from the mouth of the alley, and suddenly they were all running.

As a team, the group of soldiers moved from one covered position to the next. They operated at breakneck speeds with trained precision. Hunter tried to follow their lead, but he felt clumsy and out of place. In truth, he was just barely keeping up. He was sure that they were going to figure out he was not one of them. Hopefully, they would continue to think that he was just dazed from his fight in the alleyway. In general, they seemed to be making their way toward the same transport vessel that Hunter had been trying to reach.

A voice rang out in Hunter's helmet. "AT 6. This is CAP 2. We have spotted a grouping of assets on your line and we are downloading markers now. Retrieve as many as you can before you bug out. Do you copy?"

"We copy that, CAP 2." Hunter recognized the responding voice as one of the soldiers that surrounded him. The voice continued. "Dean, Miles, did you get the data?"

Two voices responded. "Got it."

"Take point. Manny, you're with me. Sid, handle our clumsy baggage. The guy can barely stay on his feet. He may have saved our butts, but he's gunna get us all killed."

One of the soldiers began to stay closer to Hunter as they moved. He guessed that this must be Sid. The team continued to flow toward their destination, exchanging fire and operating with lightning speed. Hunter managed to get off a few shots as he ran. He was surprised to find out that his rifle worked. He didn't hit anything or anybody and he almost dropped his weapon the first time he fired it, but it made him feel better to know that he was armed. Sometimes they moved through buildings. Other times they moved around buildings.

In a matter of moments, they came upon a group of nearly 20 terrified human slaves and he realized that these must have been the 'assets' that had been described by the voice on the radio. They lay on the ground in various positions and various states of consciousness. Some of them moaned and twitched. Others just lay unmoving. It looked to Hunter like they had gathered together to hide or perhaps they were watching the beam before being pinned to the ground by the gravity dome. The group consisted mainly of women. Baskets of materials, maybe clothing, had been spilled and their contents lay strewn out over the ground.

Three of the soldiers in the small team pulled pistols from their belts. Hunter recognized them instantly. He remembered the one that had been pointed directly at him in Millennium Park. Small pops issued from each pistol. Hunter didn't see anything leave the end of the pistols, but he saw bodies relax as if tranquilized.

The soldier next to Hunter turned and handed him a pistol. "Here, make yourself useful. Grab one, maybe two, if you can."

Each of the three soldiers began to shoulder the bodies that they had tranquilized. The other two soldiers stood guard and prepared to lay down cover fire. Hunter took two steps forward to inspect the human slaves that were sprawled out on the ground. He couldn't believe what was happening. Was he about to help these guys abduct humans? What else could he do? What would they do to him when they figured out he wasn't one of them? Was helping them such a bad thing? Being a slave to the Cravos couldn't be any worse than being a slave on Actaeon 9.

"Hurry up, guys!" A voice sounded in Hunter's helmet. The urgency and suddenness of the words made Hunter jump. "If that A4 gets here before we bug out, this whole operation is going to become very messy."

Hunter scanned the humans that lay in front of him and raised the tranquilizer pistol. He would have to select someone and take them. He would probably be doing them a favor. As he looked around, he spotted her. Her eyes were wide, and she stared directly at him. The shaved head and bruised face had again made her difficult to recognize, but April lay sprawled on the ground amongst the group of slaves. She strained and lifted her head against the increased gravity. Her eyes burned with a fierce intensity that startled Hunter. Of all the changes that he saw in her physical appearance, the sheer force of will reflected in her eyes made her the most difficult to recognize. For a moment,

Hunter questioned his original assessment. Could this be April?

In all the chaos that surrounded them he could not have heard her speak, but he understood perfectly when she mouthed the words, "Take me." Without thinking Hunter flung open his visor and they locked eyes. Recognition, followed by shock and surprise, flashed across her face. For no more than a handful of heartbeats they stared at each other and then she mouthed the words, "What are you doing?"

He responded, "I have a plan. I have to shoot you." She gave him half of a smile and a small nod. He returned her half smile and then slammed his visor back down afraid that his slave brands would give him away. Without hesitation, he raised the pistol, pointed it at April, and pulled the trigger. He felt only a small amount of recoil as the tranquilizer gun discharged and he watched as April's eyes drooped closed almost immediately and her head rolled back onto the ground. He approached quickly, bent down, and scooped her into his arms. With the added strength of the armor, lifting her was virtually effortless. As well, Hunter could feel the gravity dampening technology of his suit affect April as he lifted her.

He turned just as the team of Cravos soldiers was preparing to run again. Three of the team had taken slaves. They each carried two, tossing them over their shoulders. Hunter cradled April in his arms. Her body was limp. Her head rested against his chest armor. They started to run again weaving between buildings and down small side streets. As they drew closer to the transport vessel, Hunter saw other teams of Cravos soldiers that were pulling in to retreat. He noticed that some carried slaves while others laid down cover fire. He was also relieved to observe that return fire from the Actaeon soldiers grew less in this area. Hunter and April were almost home free. Well, home free was a relative term. They were probably just trading slavery to one alien race for slavery to another alien race. At least the Cravos spoke English, Hunter thought sarcastically.

In a matter of moments, Hunter and the team of Cravos soldiers were almost below the transport ship. Without even losing step, members of the team began to leap into the air. Hunter paused to watch them fly in soaring arcs toward the open doors of the ship. The suit he wore had greatly increased his strength and speed, but he wasn't sure that he could make that big of a jump. He wondered if there was a trick to performing the maneuver. Perhaps he should take this opportunity to get away from the group of Cravos but running wouldn't help. Remaining on Actaeon 9 would just ensure his life of slavery.

Suddenly, two of the team members were shot from the sky and sent pinwheeling toward the ground. The two humans that they carried were flung wildly from their arms. All of them fell with alarming acceleration caused by the augmented gravity. They smashed into the ground and into the roofs of buildings, their bodies breaking upon impact.

Hunter tracked the source of the energy blasts across the sky. Less than a hundred yards behind him, an Actaeon ship had entered the dome. Soldiers were leaping from the ship laying down heavy fire against the Cravos. Hunter realized with sudden alarm that he was wearing Cravos Armor. He would have to escape with them or the Actaeon soldiers would kill him. He had no choice. Hunter backed up about 30 feet and he began to run. With April cradled in his arms he prepared to jump. As he did so, an energy blast hit him in the back of his left leg below the knee joint. He was flung out of control and he dropped April. Hunter hit the ground hard and April's body was flung out in front of him. She skidded to a stop, still limp and lifeless.

Hunter's leg was on fire with pain. He rolled onto his back, almost screaming with effort, and looked down the length of his body. All that remained of his leg was a burnt and bloodied stump. He felt panic well up inside him as his mind tried to comprehend the injury, and shock began to overtake his stricken body.

Suddenly, a pair of boots hit the ground next to his head, and in a moment, he was surrounded by Cravos soldiers. One of them knelt next to Hunter, dressing his leg and administering a painkiller. Another snatched April from the ground and bounded into the air. Though he was being jostled around a lot, he strained to twist his head so that he could watch April's arc through the air and onto the ship. 'She is safe. She is safe. She is safe.' The words ran through his head repeatedly and he whispered them into his helmet.

A moment later, Hunter was being lifted by the soldier that had worked on his injuries. The soldier picked him up and took off at a dead run. In an instant they were airborne. Hunter's stomach lurched and he was afraid for a moment that he was going to throw up in his helmet. He looked in the direction that they flew and could see the ship approaching fast. He felt sudden hope and relief flood through him. He was going to make it. April had escaped, and now he would escape as well. Despite the pain, the shock, and the chaos, Hunter smiled. Wherever he was going, it had to be better than this place.

Hunter couldn't see the Actaeon marksman that landed on the roof of a nearby building. Ryson Sud was his name. He was 89 Actaeon years old, which was not old, but also not young by the standards of his people. He was a member of the second generation. This simply meant that he had a chip on his shoulder and something to prove. He had served in the 5th unit of the Aernos drop regiment in the People's Army for 23 years and he was very good at his craft. He was the first of his unit to jump from the drop ship. When he leapt from the vessel, his rifle was already in firing position. He spotted Hunter carrying April as he was about to leap for the safety of the Cravos transport vessel. In less than a second, Ryson identified them as a target and released two blasts from his plasma rifle. He had only enough time to see that he struck Hunter in the leg, before by necessity, he turned his attention toward his landing mark. Approximately 15 feet from the ground, his gravity dampeners automatically engaged, enabling him to hit the flat roof of the low building at speeds that his armor could absorb. He immediately rolled for a partially covered position where he came up in a crouch facing the Cravos vessel.

Ryson was not without pride in his work and he wanted to see the results of the shots he had fired on the fleeing Cravos soldier with the human slave. He quickly scanned the battlefield and found that his target was surrounded by a group of soldiers. He immediately prepared to fire on the group but was forced to duck as a barrage of energy blasts struck the building immediately below his vantage point. Beneath the cover of dust from the blast, Ryson crawled swiftly to a different position and raised his rifle. With tremendous disappointment, he found that the slave was gone, probably taken by a member of the Cravos team, and the injured soldier was about to escape as well. Ryson spotted Hunter as he and his would-be rescuer leapt into the air. This time, he would not have to settle for a wild shot in the leg. He had seconds to track his target as he fired from a stable position. For a marksman of his skill level, seconds were like minutes. He locked onto the leaping Cravos soldier, took time to smile to himself, and then squeezed off a three-round burst from his plasma rifle.

For one moment, Hunter thought he was safe. He believed that he had escaped his situation as a slave to the Actaeon people. He didn't even care that he would probably become a slave to the Cravos. Instantly, that moment was replaced by unspeakable pain. The entire left side of his body exploded. His arm and leg disappeared in a flash of light that burned halfway across the rest of his body. He screamed in agony as the world spun around him. The blasts from the Plasma rifle threw him into an out-of-control trajectory away from the Cravos vessel. He bounced off a building rooftop and his body slammed down into the dirt street, rolling and sliding for nearly 50 feet, before it flopped to a halt at the mouth of an alleyway between two buildings. Hunter was knocked unconscious when he hit the building rooftop. Slamming into the ground cracked his skull, broke his remaining leg and collapsed the one lung that hadn't been destroyed from the plasma blast. Within seconds of sliding to a stop, his heart quit beating. Within minutes all brain activity stopped, and Hunter died.

19 DEAD MAN?

Hunter felt something. How long had it been since he felt something? He felt . . . he felt . . . pain? He remembered something about dying. Was he dead? He was cold, very cold. He thought he remembered an explosion. Was his arm blown off? That can't be right. Why couldn't he think straight? Consciousness felt slippery. It was like trying to hold onto a greased pig. Had he ever tried to hold onto a greased pig? Why would you put grease on a pig? He chuckled. He coughed. His body convulsed into spasms. Now that was definitely pain. His whole body burned. Every inch of him cried out in agony. He lost hold of the greased pig and slipped back into unconsciousness.

It was about six days later before Hunter could feel or think anything again. Slowly, he began to wake. He kept his eyes closed. Where was he? He couldn't think clearly. He couldn't remember anything. It was as if all his memories floated behind an immense dam and he stood downstream watching a trickle of his life meander by. The first thing that floated by was his name. He knew that he was about fifteen years old. He had a family. He was pretty sure that he lived in Mesa, Arizona. He felt calm and very well rested. He was in a bed. The bed was amazingly soft. He felt more comfortable than he had been in . . . how long? It seemed to Hunter that if he opened his eyes, he would find the ceiling fan from his bedroom spinning overhead. He felt way too rested, so that meant his mom should be calling him down for breakfast soon. Right? It must be Saturday. Why else would she let him sleep in? Was he in his bedroom in Arizona or Chicago? Oh yeah, he lived in Chicago now. Didn't he? This bed was way too comfortable to be his bed. His bed was as hard as a rock and Adam would never allow him to sleep in. It was probably time for morning training? Who was Adam? Where did that name come from? If today really was Saturday, then there was a good chance that he had a soccer game. That would be nice. Then again, maybe he was on summer vacation. Summer? She was his friend. How long had it been since he had seen Summer... or Jared... or April? He hadn't seen April since the attack . . . 'The attack,' he repeated in his mind. The dam that held back his memories seemed to crack right down the middle. They came slowly at first but soon the flood of memories broke free and all of his calm was drowned in a chaotic torrent of remembrance and recognition.

His eyes shot open. His breathing grew rapid. His pulse accelerated. He was in a softly lit room. The bed in which he lay was situated almost perfectly in the middle of the room. His eyes darted about trying to make sense of his situation. It looked almost like a medical facility. Countertops circled the room and contained strange electronic devices and laboratory equipment. There was a window on the far wall. It was dark outside, and he could see stars. He couldn't see the wall behind him without sitting up and he didn't want to draw attention to himself. A memory returned and struck him brutally with a sense of dread. He remembered suddenly his last moments of consciousness before . . . before . . . well, before this.

He remembered the battle and the team of Cravos soldiers. He had been shot with an energy weapon. His arm had been blown off below the elbow and the entire left side of his body had been burnt very badly. Slowly he rolled his head back to inspect his left arm and torso. He steeled himself to face his injuries, knowing that at best he would find a mutilated stump where his arm had once hung, and burn wounds covering half his body, but he lifted his arm to stare dumbfounded at a perfect, muscular hand and forearm. He flexed his fingers. An IV-like tube that conveyed a clear fluid had been inserted into his wrist. This was not his arm. It felt like his arm and it moved when he wanted it to, but it was too muscular. He stared at his hand, and he thought he could see an almost metallic shine to the skin. He needed to sit up and inspect himself. He raised his head and then rolled over, lifting himself onto one elbow. From there he sat up and looked down the length of his body.

He was in miraculously good shape. It made him uneasy to look down at his chest and legs. He felt like the body that he inhabited was not his own. He found that he was heavily muscled and probably taller. He could not help but feel a sense of panic. What happened? What had been done to him? He needed to get out of bed. He needed to figure out where he was. He draped one leg over the edge and twisted, sliding up onto his feet. Instantaneously he felt dizzy and nauseous. He took one step and began to stumble. His head swam and his vision blurred. He tried to take another step but slumped and fell to his knees. He managed two more gasping breaths before blacking out, falling to a prone position.

When he awoke again, he was back in bed. This time he did not feel so frantic. His thoughts came more easily, and his body felt rested. His memories did not try to hide from him, neither did they threaten to frantically assail him. He knew who he was, and he began to reason through his circumstances. Somebody had saved him. In fact, somebody had gone to great lengths to heal him and make him feel comfortable. He should be dead. The medical attention he received must have been alien. Nothing else could have fixed the horrific injuries he sustained. It brought to mind the time that Ken had healed his injured hand right before he left Earth.

The lighting in the room was low, and except for the mild hum of electronics, it was relatively quiet. On one hand, he felt secure. On the other hand, his instincts told him that the peace and feelings of security couldn't last much longer, but he didn't really have the desire to try to escape. Whoever his benefactors were, they didn't seem to have any intention of hurting him. Hunter was alive, and somehow he had been pulled from the fighting and brought to this place for healing. He had not been placed in restraints. These were all favorable marks in behalf of whomever it was that had helped them. Once he got over the initial panic of remembering who he was and how his last few moments of consciousness had ended, an incredible and inexplicable calm had settled over him. He knew that if he waited long enough, his questions would be answered. So, he waited.

As he waited, he thought about his family on Earth. He missed his mom and dad and his brothers and sisters. Truly, he had taken them for granted. He had thought that they would always be part of his life. Now they were literally thousands of light years away and they thought that he was dead, killed in a terrorist attack. He thought and worried about his friends. He hoped they were still alive. He worried most of all for April. She could have been killed within moments after their separation. Everything had been so confusing.

He reflected, with amusement, on times when his biggest problem had been getting homework done. He thought about the food on Earth, which made him realize that he was absolutely starving. How long had it been since he had eaten? He suspected that the IV in his arm was being used to feed him. He remembered soccer games and the faces of kids from his classes. He thought about his teachers. He missed and longed for so many things.

After passing many hours thinking too hard about problems that he couldn't fix, he figured out how to raise the bed into a partial sitting position using controls along the left side. It worked very much like any hospital bed on Earth. He looked down the length of his body and took a few moments to consider his physical condition. He observed a number of remarkable changes. Both of his arms were thicker and heavily muscled. His chest was thicker. He came to the conclusion that he was definitely taller. He felt good. In fact, he felt amazing. He worried that if he looked in a mirror, he would find that his face was different.

He no longer had any scars. His hand went to his

forehead and face to find that all his brands had been replaced by smooth skin. He felt strong. His hearing was abnormally keen. His sense of smell was definitely more powerful, and he felt an almost disorienting awareness to his surroundings. He could hear, smell, feel, see, and distinguish so many things at once, that he was almost overwhelmed by the rush of sensory input. What had happened to him? He enjoyed the feelings of strength and health, but he worried that he was not even the same person. His mind conjured numberless disconcerting scenarios to explain his current condition. Presently overwhelming his thoughts was the possibility that advanced alien technology had been used to remove his brain and place it into a different body. It must have been the body of an alien. He certainly didn't feel human anymore. Is this how the people of Actaeon felt all the time? Was he one of them? If so, did that mean that he was free? Would he want to be free, if it meant that he had to become one of them?

With considerable effort, he managed to mostly calm his mind and cease the making of panicked speculations. He could wait a little longer to learn what happened, but he had to fight his imagination, which just kept creating uncomfortable answers to his questions, and making him feel restless and impatient. He thought he had taken all the waiting that he could bear and was about to get out of bed again, when the lights in the room came on and a door directly behind the bed slid open with a hissing sound. Hunter could smell the presence of another Leeber man. He wasn't sure how he recognized it but he was certain that the smell was masculine and alien. He was also aware of the man's individual scent. He had smelled the presence of this scent in the room before the door opened. He also thought, impossibly, that he could feel the man's presence, and it was familiar. Was this person responsible for his rescue? Was he responsible for Hunter's present condition?

Hunter remained still, but he grew tense. His muscles were pulled tight and he was alive with nervous energy. The man stood in the doorway for a long moment before he began to circle carefully around the left side of the bed. Hunter could hear his gentle footfalls on the metal floor. He felt the man's caution in every step. Hunter looked over his shoulder and as the alien came into view, he found himself staring at a familiar face, and he said out loud, "Polka-dot-underwear Ken?"

Ken laughed. "Truly, it warms my heart that you remember me by this name. Are you feeling well?"

Hunter considered and responded slowly, "Never better in my entire life. Is your real name Ken? Where am I? How am I alive?"

"No," Ken answered, "my real name is not Ken, but I do not want you to know my real name, so Ken will do for now. This," he gestured with wide arms, "is where I am hiding out. It is kind of like my home . . . for a time. In truth, it shall be a relatively short amount of time. As for how you are alive . . . that is a more complicated question to answer."

"Why don't you want me to know your real name?"

"Because I am hiding, and if you ever get captured, I do not want you to be able to give my name to my enemies. Trust me when I say that this is better for both you and I."

"Who are you hiding from?"

"I hide from the same people that you run from."

"And who is that?"

"My people."

"Your people?"

"Yes, the people of Actaeon."

Hunter was stunned. "You are one of them?"

"Yes, I am one of them."

Anger began to boil in Hunter. He was looking at the enemy. Somehow, he had thought that this man was on his side. "This is your fault . . ." he began but didn't know how to continue.

Ken held up a hand to stop Hunter, "Yes, this is my fault, but not in the way that you think."

He tried to continue, but Hunter interrupted. "What do you mean, 'Not in the way I think?' You have enslaved me. My friends might all be dead. I have lost everything and everyone I love. You were there when we were taken. You pretended, in some strange way, to want to help me." Hunter was shaking. He didn't know what else to say. His fists were clenched and his knuckles whitened.

Ken held up his hand again. "Please, let me explain. You

may still hate me when I am done. Perhaps you will hate me even more, but you should hear and understand all that I would tell you."

Hunter did not respond but stared intensely at Ken, barely able to control his boiling rage.

Ken stared back evenly for a moment, then he sighed and sat on the edge of Hunter's bed. "This is not easy to explain, and we have so little time." He seemed to gather his thoughts and with a deep breath he began. "A couple hundred years ago, my people were a race much like humans. I do not know how this occurred, but our DNA was remarkably similar to yours. We have existed literally millions of light years from Earth, yet by some means that I doubt we will ever be able to discover, we share a common and ancient heritage. I think that it might have even been possible for us to interbreed. The only real physical difference was that the people of Actaeon were shorter and stockier as a result of the increased gravity on Actaeon 9."

Hunter had begun to calm down. Ken's story had drawn him in. He looked at the large Leeber man skeptically. "Are you kidding? What changed?"

Ken's eyes grew unfocused, "I changed . . . I changed everything." He stared seemingly at nothing for a long moment. "Our people were about 400 years ahead of yours in the development of advanced technologies. Four hundred years ago, we were at a point very close to where Earth is now. This is when I developed my first Nano-biotic serum for immortality. I was old. I was close to dying. My wife had passed on nearly twenty years earlier. We had no children, and so I dedicated myself to my work.

When I completed the serum, I used it on myself. It worked. I was restored to my youth. My first revision of the serum had limited results compared to later versions. It altered my body's ability to repair damaged cells. It also increased intelligence and rejuvenated internal biological functions. I still looked like everyone else, and so I decided to disappear into Actaeon society."

He paused again. Memories seemed to pass before his eyes, and he continued. "At times, I have deeply regretted my early ambitions, but I have come to believe that somebody else would have eventually made the same discovery and perhaps they would have handled it even worse than I did." He sighed heavily, "I lived amongst my people as an immortal for almost a hundred years before I made myself known. I spent many long years considering how I would share my work. I had almost determined that I would never tell another living soul, but then many of our scientists began to experiment with extending life. Each of them approached the problem from a different angle. Some of the experimentation was harmless, but . . . some of it was . . . horrific. I realized that it was the natural evolution of science to aspire to extend life. I myself, had sought for this same goal and in a moment of altruistic fervor, I decided to give my discovery to everybody. By the time I decided to share my work, I had greatly improved upon the serum. Muscle density would be increased, height and stature augmented drastically. Intelligence, memory, comprehension, all brain function would improve drastically. I believed that the heightened intelligence that came with the change would also lead to wisdom. I thought that a society of brilliant people would also be a society filled with kindness, but I was wrong. Intelligence does not eliminate selfishness, greed, gluttony or addictions. In many ways, the change that was wrought in my people made these things worse. We have become very clever at hiding our shortcomings beneath a heavy façade of superiority. This allows us to fully explore our capacities for greed and gluttony without the hindrance of good conscience." Ken offered a bitter chuckle before continuing.

"Over time, I and other scientists greatly improved the technology and eventually developed a serum that offered much more than just immortality. The serum contains Nano-bots that replace much of the functionality of our normal bodies. Blood cell populations are augmented by Nano-biotic cells that work much more efficiently. Muscular composition is improved. DNA is modified. Brain cells and neural pathways are changed to function more efficiently. All of the basic senses are heightened. Bones are strengthened. Height is increased. We released the final version of our serum about two-hundred-fifty years ago and our whole race was changed."

"Is that what you did to me?" Hunter asked.

Ken turned to look him in the eyes. "It was the only way to save you, but yes . . . and no. Hunter, you are the first of your kind. The previous version of my Nano-biotic serum would have only worked on my own people. Human DNA, though very similar, contains minor differences for which the previous serum did not account. It probably would have killed you. I have altered this revision to work on any race. It reads the DNA of its host, extrapolates an improved or ideal version of their DNA and then starts to make changes. Beyond changes to their DNA though, much of the host's mechanical systems are made robotic at a microscopic level. Just like with us, your immune system is augmented by Nano-bots. Bones and joints are reinforced. Most of the functions of blood cells are replaced. Neural connections are strengthened, increasing intelligence, comprehension, and memory. Reflexes are heightened. Oxygen storage in the lungs is optimized. Muscle strength is increased. Healing is quickened. Everything about the body is improved. You might even say perfected. In fact, all of these functions are improved more powerfully in you than in my own people. The serum that I gave you contains many upgrades from my original work. You will find that you have slightly faster reflexes than the people of Actaeon 9. You have a capacity for greater intelligence, memory, and nearly perfect recall. You are stronger. You have programmable memory. If you think carefully, you will find that I have already made changes to your memory." Ken gave him a knowing look.

Hunter began to search his thoughts and realized quickly that he possessed knowledge that should have been impossible. "I speak your language," he said, even as he was startled by the realization.

Ken smiled, "Yes you do. In fact, you've switched back and forth between languages a few times without noticing. I am particularly proud of how well that mind library took. Your grammar is perfect, though you speak with something of an Eastern Continental accent. You are going to sound slightly too educated for your age."

Hunter's initial anger had completely disappeared. "That's incredible. Can you teach me to fight? What else did you put in my head?"

"Honestly, Hunter, not much. You will find that you

know a little bit about the geography and recorded history of our planet. You now have enough knowledge about mathematics to do well in a first-year college calculus class from Earth. It is a very time-consuming process to build mind libraries. So far, the Actaeon Language Library is the only comprehensive system that I've developed, and I don't think that I am going to have time to build large libraries anytime soon. I will however, try to build you a more extensive library of common knowledge."

"Don't the people of Actaeon have information that you could give me? What did you call them? Mind libraries?"

"No, Hunter. The people of Actaeon do not have the ability to assimilate mind libraries. This is one of many upgraded features which you possess, and they do not." With this statement, Ken became very serious. "Hunter, the abilities that my serum has given you are extremely valuable. Improved physical and mental capacity are our most coveted commodity on Actaeon 9. Possession of these commodities is proof, to some of our people, that we are like Gods. To have more of this than others is to be more God-like. Some of them would kill to get what you have, and they would kill to prevent anyone else from possessing what they cannot. What I have done to you is a threat to our whole society. Many in our government have asserted that humans cannot be changed biologically to become like us. They have convinced most of our society that humans are only a few steps up from animals."

"Couldn't you just give everyone an upgrade? Then everybody would be the same."

"No, Hunter, I cannot. It isn't possible, and I would not

even if I could." With a pitiable smile he said, "Remember, I tried upgrading my entire species once, thinking to create worldwide equanimity. It did not work out so well. I told you earlier that my serum would work on any race of people. That's not entirely true. I should have said that it would work with any naturally occurring species of mammal. If you gave the Nano-biotic serum to a dog, it would turn that dog into the best version of itself and the same is true of almost any species of mammal. The race of Actaeon though, is no longer natural. Every member of our race has an advanced Nano-biotic system integrated into their body. Introduction of my new serum would probably result in the inevitable death of the host. The two systems would war against each other. They are fueled by energy from the host and it is unlikely that anybody could survive the constant expenditure of energy that would occur as the two systems battled each other for control of the body."

They sat in silence as Hunter considered all that he was being told. Ken waited patiently. He seemed to know that Hunter would have more questions. "Right after I arrived on Actaeon 9, I saw a lady with pure black eyes. Was she some sort of . . . alien? I mean, you are all aliens, but was she a . . . you know . . . an alien's alien?"

"Ah . . ." Ken smiled. "You know . . . on this planet, you are the alien." He chuckled and continued. "The people of Actaeon are very funny, Hunter. Immortality, heightened perception, increased strength, unlimited health, all of these things are not enough for some of them. As I said earlier, it is a sign of great status amongst many of our race to gain physical advantages over others. It is seen almost as a type of evolution. The eyes on the lady that you saw were probably implants. They gave her the ability to see a broader color spectrum, night vision, thermal vision, along with a selection of other abilities that can be purchased by those who are rich enough."

"What are the Cravos? I heard them speak English. Are they human?"

"In all honesty, I am not completely certain. I believe that they may be members of our own people who broke away shortly after I made my discoveries known. They do not live on Actaeon 9, though I honestly do not know where they live. They began attacks against our planet almost 75 years ago. They kidnap humans and use them to create armies that fight against Actaeon 9. I suspect that they use rigorous mental reconditioning to get the humans to fight. Technologically, they are not as advanced as the people of Actaeon, but they are very tenacious and good at hiding. They execute surprise attacks and then they run. The world government has been struggling in vain to hunt them down for nearly fifty years."

Hunter thought of April, "A friend of mine was taken in the raid that killed me. Where did she go? Will she be okay?"

"I don't know. I don't know how they treat the slaves they take. As I said, they are extremely good at hiding. Our government probably knows much more than I do. My resources are limited. I spend most of my efforts on hiding myself."

"Why do you have to hide?"

"Well, I am considered our world's most dangerous

criminal. When I realized what we were becoming, I spoke out against our government and way of life. I gathered some supporters and we... did things," he sighed. "Things didn't go the way we planned. Many of us were killed. Some were imprisoned. I escaped, more by luck than by any skill of my own."

"What did you do?"

"I am not going to tell you that."

"Why not?"

"Because, I don't like talking about it."

Hunter studied Ken's face and thought better about pushing him for answers. He changed the line of questions. "Why do your people take slaves?"

"Isn't it obvious?" Ken asked. "When everyone on your planet is an artist, scientist, soldier, politician, or engineer, who is left to sweep your streets, wash your clothes, cook your food, or operate your waste treatment facilities? The people of Actaeon take slaves, Hunter, because they consider themselves above the menial tasks associated with everyday life. They consider themselves too busy to bother with simple mundane chores."

"Have you made anyone else like me?"

"You are the only one so far."

Hunter considered his situation, and as he did, he couldn't help but feel an overwhelming sense of frustration.

He came at Ken with a sudden rush of questions. "Why did you do this to me? Why did you choose me? What am I supposed to do now? I feel like you've been following me from the moment you saw me. Can I go back to Earth? Can you get me off this planet? I want my life back."

Ken sat forward and stared hard at Hunter. There was sympathy and regret in his eyes. Hunter returned his stare and waited for answers.

"I can't get you back to Earth," he began slowly. "As I said, I am a criminal here. My movements between Actaeon 9 and other planets are orchestrated at great cost and great risk. Trying to sneak you off Actaeon 9 would likely end with both of us being captured. Besides that, taking you back to Earth could lead to an even greater problem. Hunter, your very existence is a challenge to all that our people believe. Religion has been all but lost on this planet. We worship ourselves. Many of our people, many of our leaders consider humans to be little more than animals. If they found out that a human could be turned into something that was even greater than the people of Actaeon, they would stop at nothing to cover it up. They consider us to be the superior race in the universe. A growing number feel that we should rule all other races. They think that humans are not qualified to manage their world and their resources. They are lobbying to take Earth and enslave all of its population. If these parties in the government garner enough support, then this could become a reality in the very near future. They will lock down your planet and not allow any movement on or off Earth until they have tagged and cataloged every last human. On Earth, your uniquely enhanced biology would stand out like a shining beacon to the Actaeon probes that might someday monitor your planet. You would be found for sure, and when they found you, they would dissect you like a Benastian Hookworm and nobody would ever see you again. Once they were done with you, they would know that I am still actively working, and they would renew their efforts to find and kill me. Hunter, we have to hide you."

Ken paused, seeming to consider the problem for a moment. Hunter took the opportunity to interject. "If I can't go home, is there a way that I can get a message to my parents to let them know that I am alive?"

Ken didn't answer immediately. He seemed to consider his response very carefully. "I follow politics closely. I have some contacts inside the United States government, and I believe that they will soon have to reveal the existence of the treaty and of the people of Actaeon to the public. However, while your government continues to try to maintain this hopeless anonymity, I can't pass information to your parents. Nobody on Earth knows that I am anything but human. That being said, I promise that if your government goes public with information about the people of Actaeon, I will find a way to contact your parents, and let them know that you are alive."

Ken continued, "Now, for your other questions, I will do my best to answer. Yes, I have been following you since we first met. However, you are not the only human that I have been watching closely, you are just the first to present me with the opportunity to steal your almost dead body out of the Actaeon slave monitoring system. You might remember that I helped you while you were still in the Detainment Center on Earth. Healing the scrapes on your hand gave me the opportunity to introduce a specialized nanobot into your system that would aid you with healing. It is mostly undetectable, but it helped you to heal from your beatings, and it is probably the only reason that you were still salvageable when I found your body."

Hunter nodded remembering moments when his injuries had healed faster than should have been possible. He touched his ribs unconsciously. He was pretty sure that those had been broken when he woke in the cart with Boris and John.

"Hunter," Ken continued. "What I am about to tell you is very important. It is a truth that has taken me hundreds of years to learn and it is the reason why I have been tracking you. It is the reason why I saved you and it is the reason for all that I am going to ask you to do. I told you earlier that I once thought my people would be wise if they were intelligent. It turns out that wisdom is much more complicated. Wisdom, I believe, comes from a combination of traits that cannot be created or imitated. It is kindness and bravery. Intelligence and logic are important parts of wisdom. It comes from self-mastery and determination. It is found in the ability to make decisions that extend beyond a person's own immediate interests. It is greatly inhibited by selfishness, addiction, greed, and fear. Hunter, I do not believe that I will ever be able to create wisdom. I do believe, however, that I can measure it. I have technology at my disposal that allows me to rapidly measure and map brain waves. I was scanning everybody I could that day at the hospital. Basically, I chose to follow you that day because my scans let me know that you are highly likely," Ken smiled, "to not be an idiot."

"Well, it is comforting to know that I have been officially diagnosed as "Not-An-Idiot"," Hunter remarked, returning Ken's smile, "but what am I supposed to do now? Even if I am "wise" as you say, I am just one person and this planet is huge. All of my friends are human slaves and I don't even know where any of them are. My only ally is, and I don't mean any offence by this, Ken, a criminal-alien-reject. I am very glad to be alive and I am pretty excited to be an immortal with superpowers but what are you trying to accomplish? I don't see how any of this can end well."

"Hunter, you should not feel like you have to be wise. Just know that I believe you have the capacity for great wisdom. I do not know how all of this is going to play out. I can see many possibilities, and I am very good at making plans, but I am not omniscient. I am continuously searching for opportunities to make right all that I have made wrong. Today that means that I saved a boy's life that was worth saving and I gave him powerful abilities because I believed he can learn to use them responsibly. Beyond what I have done to you, though, I will only say that I have great hopes to undo much of all that I have done wrong. I want to free your people, and I want to change the hearts of my own people. I will also admit that I have plans to use you, though I don't know exactly how yet."

"I don't know if I trust you," Hunter looked Ken directly in the eyes.

"Hunter, you now have the ability to sense my brain waves. Quiet your thoughts and listen carefully to what I am about to tell you. I honestly want to help you and your friends. I want to save the whole human race and I want to help my own people. I will always do what I think is right."

They stared at each other for several moments and then Hunter nodded. "I believe you. I don't know how, but I can feel that you are being honest." Hunter marveled at the sensation and understanding which he possessed.

Ken interrupted his thoughts, "What I need you to do first, Hunter, is very simple. I need you to learn all that you can about the people of Actaeon. Eventually, I need you to learn to love them."

Hunter started, "Ken, I don't believe that is possible. I hate them. I hate every one of them. At times, I just want all of them dead."

"Hunter, I am one of 'them.' Do you want me dead?"

"No . . . I might have said differently when we began this conversation but . . . you are not like the others."

"There are many of us that are not terrible. We are an entire race of people and we are made up of many different cultures. So far, you have only been exposed to soldiers and slave owners. I know that it is hard, but please trust me when I say that many of my people are good."

Hunter put his head into his hands and sighed softly as he rubbed his eyes, "So, what do I need to do?"

Ken put his hand on Hunter's shoulder. "It's easy. I need you to go to school." Hunter looked up and Ken smirked just a little, "I just need you to be a normal alien teenager." He accentuated the word 'alien.'

Hunter's jaw dropped open. "What?"

"I've used some of my remaining resources to create an identity for you within Actaeon society and I need you to lead a . . . normal life for a while. Trust me when I say that creating a false identity in this super high-tech society is no easy accomplishment. The good news is, though, that if you do successfully create a false identity, it is not likely to ever be challenged. It is a crime that is considered completely impossible. The key . . ."

"Look," Hunter interrupted, "I have friends that need me." He was becoming angry again and his voice began to get louder. "They are enslaved. They are being abused. Some of them may even be dead already. My family on Earth thinks that I was blown to pieces in a terrorist attack and you want me to go to alien high school? I can't believe you are even saying this. This is the stupidest thing that I have ever heard. You just said that if I were discovered, they would dissect me and then come looking for you. Shouldn't we just hide or something? If I try to mingle with your people, I'll get caught for sure."

Ken held up his hand to stop Hunter's tirade. "I have to leave soon. The government of Actaeon is always searching for me. The only thing more dangerous for me than sneaking on and off this planet, is staying here for any substantial amount of time. In fact, my next window for escape is two days from now. It has taken far too much time to bring you back to life. If I do not escape in two days, it his highly likely that I will be found and then I assure you that you will be found also."

Ken's expression softened and Hunter could see honest sorrow behind his eyes. He continued. "Hunter, I am sorry, but there is no place in this universe where you can be truly safe. In my honest opinion, the best place that I can think to hide you is right here. I have created your biological signals to mimic our own almost perfectly. You will pass all but the most scrupulous of medical examinations. I know that this will not be easy. In a way, you will probably find this harder than life as a slave."

"Why can't I look for my friends?" Hunter interrupted. "I don't want to waste time."

Ken answered with sensitivity. "Hunter, where would you go? How would you search? Where would you sleep at night? What would you eat? Our society doesn't have vagabonds. You would stand out like a sore thumb and you would be discovered. You are young. You look young. It is common for youth in our society to be sent away to schools. You would blend in well in a boarding school. It will buy us time, and it will give you a chance to learn. Learning, Hunter, is the key to your survival, and though it may not feel like it, it is the key to saving your friends."

With considerable force of will, Hunter calmed himself and considered the man's logic. He had no resources and no knowledge of this world. From his perspective as a slave, he had seen very little of their society. Had Ken not helped him, he would already be dead. He didn't even know how much he didn't know. He hated to admit it, but what Ken said made sense. Hunter was both ignorant and helpless. He bowed his head and tears began to fill the corners of his eyes. Ken squeezed his shoulder, "I truly am sorry. It should not be this way. You do not deserve this.

Your friends do not deserve this. Your whole race does not deserve this. I wish that I could give you all that you ask for, but the most that I can offer you is a slim chance to find redemption, and that slim chance comes with the price of patience."

Hunter sat for a few moments and then raised his head slowly, "Thank you for saving my life. Thank you for fighting against your own people to help us. I am afraid for my friends and it is hard to think straight." He rubbed his eyes with the palms of his hands and paused for a long while, thinking. When he spoke again, it was with a sigh of resolution, "What is it like? You know, school. What can I expect?"

Ken shifted his weight. "Well . . . it has been a very long time since I attended school." A smile touched the corner of his lips. "I would tell you that I have forgotten many things, but in truth, I have a cyber-enhanced, perfect memory of my whole life. That being said, things on this world were very different when I was young. I cannot speak from firsthand experience, but I can tell you that schools on our planet are not at all like the schools you have on Earth. After age ten, almost everybody sends their children away for schooling. Physically and mentally, our people mature very quickly, so we start advanced education at an early age and we spend a very long time in school compared to Earth. Children receive general education until they reach their seventh mark, which usually happens between the ages of 12 and 16. At this point, youth begin to specialize in one of the art forms. The arts include science, craft, and war. They focus on the general study of their art for about five years. Each artform is broken into thousands of sub-studies. After five years of study within one of the three art forms, a sub-study is chosen. Students focus intensely on their sub-study for fifteen years before leaving school to seek an apprenticeship. Our methods of schooling are very different . . . more hands on . . . more intensive. There are many schools run by different groups. Each may have their own system of pedagogy. There is not much else that I can tell you. You are going to have to see for yourself."

Hunter nodded and sat silently for a time. It was so difficult to take in all that Ken had told him. His emotions tried to prevent him from recognizing the sensibility of Ken's proposal, but Hunter knew that he was right. When he spoke, his voice was grim and determined, "I will go to your schools and I will learn everything that I can. Please understand though, that I am going so I can learn how to free my friends and get home. I will never be able to love this planet, and I will only stay here for as long as I have to." Even as Hunter spoke the words, he knew that he was wrong. He would never be able to go home as he was. He also knew that hating all the people of Actaeon 9 was wrong. Ken seemed to recognize the look on Hunter's face, and so he continued quickly. "What else can you tell me about my abilities? We only have two days, and I have to learn everything that you can teach me."

ABOUT THE AUTHOR

Jeromy has always been passionate about storytelling and impressed by the influence it has on people and the decisions they make in life. He believes that some of the most brilliant writers of our time are creating works of science fiction and fantasy. He loves engaging with the projects he works on, diving headfirst into the research, investigation, and production of stories that he feels are creative and engaging. He is a curious and proactive author, interested in expanding the foundations of modern fiction. He strives to create a unique premise for each of his stories. He wants readers to feel like they are hearing a story for the first time with unpredictable elements, characters, and plot movements.

Jeromy married the love of his life nearly 20 years ago. They have 7 children and live on a farm in Florence, Arizona. On his free time, he plays with his kids, rides a dirt bike, plays soccer and works on their property. By day he is an automation and controls engineer. By night he is an aspiring author.